Praise for *Once Burned*

'There is plenty here to adore . . . Karly has the wonderful ability to balance the intense landscape and memorable characters with an alluring plotline . . . engaging the reader with suspense and love. 4.5–5 stars.' —Happy Valley Books Read

'. . . an enduring story of the courage and resilience shown by so many.' —Mic Loves Books

Praise for *Take Me Home*

'Full of romance, humour and a touch of the supernatural, this is another engaging tale by the reliable Karly Lane.' —*Canberra Weekly Magazine*

'Karly Lane is back with another beautiful, cosy story that will sweep you away on a journey.' —Noveltea Corner

'Such a fun read . . . Karly has smashed the contemporary fiction genre with *Take Me Home*.' —Beauty and Lace

'*Take Me Home* is a delight to read. I loved the change of scenery while still enjoying Karly Lane's wonderful, familiar storytelling.' —Book'd Out

Praise for *Something Like This*

'Another unmissable rural romance story of pain, loss, suffering and the power of love . . . Karly Lane is firmly on my must-read list.' —Beauty and Lace

'A great book from an author I love . . . Karly Lane never fails me.' —Noveltea Corner

'There is more to this narrative than rural romance; this is a multi-faceted exploration of loss, grief, families, second chances and courage . . . I loved this!' —Reading, Writing and Riesling

'An engaging story, set at a gentle pace, told with genuine warmth for her characters and setting, *Something Like This* is a lovely and eminently satisfying read.' —Book'd Out

'Engaging, genuine, with a storyline we can all relate to . . . Karly Lane has the wonderful ability to bring the many facets of everyday existence to life. Another fantastic story.' —Blue Wolf Reviews

Praise for *Fool Me Once*

'I adore Karly Lane's books—they always signal a wonderful time curled up on the couch with a cup of tea . . . Lane writes compelling characters and relationship realities, and I'm all here for it.' —Noveltea Corner

'With its appealing characters, easy pace and happy ending, I found *Fool Me Once* to be another engaging and satisfying rural romance novel.' —Book'd Out

'*Fool Me Once* is a guaranteed perfect light read . . . Karly Lane has woven a delicious tale of lust, love, betrayal, consequences and chasing dreams, which as time passes often need to be reconsidered.' —Blue Wolf Reviews

'Karly Lane's affinity for the land shines through in her stories . . . *Fool Me Once* is a feel-good story not to be missed.' —The Burgeoning Bookshelf

Praise for *Return to Stringybark Creek*

'Captivating, entertaining and most enjoyable, this return visit with the Callahans encourages the understanding that sometimes there

are, even from the darkest of times, huge positives to be discovered.'
—Blue Wolf Reviews

'Lane has added additional depth to this story that highlights the plight of Australian farmers and farming communities who are under strain ... I'm grateful for the calm and considered way Lane has approached the topic. The Callahans have become a favourite book family of mine ... they define family and friendship and it's been a real pleasure to read their stories.' —Noveltea Corner

'Karly Lane creates likeable, warm characters as she twists and turns her story ... an entertaining read with an intriguing love story set against the challenges of farming and its stresses.'
—*The Weekly Times*

Karly Lane lives on the mid north coast of New South Wales. Proud mum to four children and wife of one very patient mechanic, she is lucky enough to spend her day doing the two things she loves most—being a mum and writing stories set in beautiful rural Australia.

ALSO BY KARLY LANE

North Star
Morgan's Law
Bridie's Choice
Poppy's Dilemma
Gemma's Bluff
Tallowood Bound
Second Chance Town
Third Time Lucky
If Wishes Were Horses
Six Ways to Sunday
Someone Like You
The Wrong Callahan
Mr Right Now
Return to Stringybark Creek
Fool Me Once
Something Like This
Take Me Home
Once Burnt, Twice Shy

KARLY LANE
A Stone's Throw Away

ALLEN&UNWIN
SYDNEY·MELBOURNE·AUCKLAND·LONDON

This is a work of fiction. Names, characters, places and incidents are products of the author's imagination or are used fictitiously. Any resemblance to actual events, locales or persons, living or dead, is entirely coincidental.

First published in 2022

Copyright © Karly Lane 2022

All rights reserved. No part of this book may be reproduced or transmitted in any form or by any means, electronic or mechanical, including photocopying, recording or by any information storage and retrieval system, without prior permission in writing from the publisher. The Australian *Copyright Act 1968* (the Act) allows a maximum of one chapter or 10 per cent of this book, whichever is the greater, to be photocopied by any educational institution for its educational purposes provided that the educational institution (or body that administers it) has given a remuneration notice to the Copyright Agency (Australia) under the Act.

Allen & Unwin
83 Alexander Street
Crows Nest NSW 2065
Australia
Phone: (61 2) 8425 0100
Email: info@allenandunwin.com
Web: www.allenandunwin.com

 A catalogue record for this book is available from the National Library of Australia

ISBN 978 1 76087 851 1

Set in 10/12 pt Simoncini Garamond Std by Bookhouse, Sydney
Printed in Australia by McPherson's Printing Group

10 9 8 7 6 5 4 3 2 1

 The paper in this book is FSC® certified. FSC® promotes environmentally responsible, socially beneficial and economically viable management of the world's forests.

*For Rourke,
who helped brainstorm the idea that gave me the final
scene but was really the start of the whole story.
I can't wait to see what your next chapter brings,
love, Mum*

One

Phillipa Davenport drove past the rustic-looking bullnosed verandah shopfronts and wondered if maybe she'd just travelled through some kind of time warp.

In the centre of the tree-lined main street was the usual epitaph to the town's war dead that always made her pause and shake her head at the sheer number of young lives ended so wastefully, and at the other end of a narrow, grassed area stood a statue of a man on horseback. Pip had no idea who he was, but her curiosity was piqued and she made a mental note to find out.

Quaint was the word that jumped to mind as she made her way into Midgiburra, and even for a city-hardened journo the town was rather charming, although not the kind of place she would have chosen for a holiday.

It wasn't exactly a holiday—more a case of forced relaxation away from the city grind. 'Bloody Ted,' she muttered. She was still a little annoyed at her boss—and long-time friend—Ted Malone for the part he played in her current situation. While she hadn't exactly been fired, he'd made it clear she was *not* actively working for him for the next three months either. 'We'll call it long-service leave,' Ted had said, leaving no room for reply.

While most people chose when and how they spent their long-service leave—doing something fun like an overseas trip or doing house renovations—Pip was forced into hers to stave off what her mother bluntly termed a 'mental breakdown'.

In fairness, Pip *had* just finished the hardest assignment she'd ever undertaken, one that had come with significant personal danger and unrelenting stress but had put her at the top of her field in investigative journalism. She'd pretty much sacrificed the past four years of her life investigating political corruption and uncovering a high-profile MP with connections to the underworld and crime syndicates. Pip's exposé had led to an Independent Commission Against Corruption investigation into Allen (Lenny) Knight, who had recently been convicted and sentenced to prison.

A series of death threats—which weren't exactly unusual in her line of work—had been followed up by a number of frightening stalking incidents and then finally, the night she was attacked in her home.

After that, for so many months she hadn't left her house. She couldn't take public transport for a long time; the thought of sitting so close to strangers filled her with anxiety. She was wary of everyone and everything. Eventually, with a lot of help from her best friend, Lexi, who was always there encouraging her, taking her out, gently yet firmly making her integrate back into daily life, Pip managed to overcome the worst of her fear, but it was never the same. The unease was always there lurking under the surface, exhausting her, stopping her from enjoying life.

Pip hastily brushed the thought away. Just one day without thinking about the past would be nice.

The police hadn't been able to tie the attack to Lenny Knight, something Pip still couldn't completely make peace with. But in the end there was some consolation in knowing he was now behind bars where he belonged. That was close to a year ago. Although her physical wounds from that night had healed, the after-effects still lingered.

Pip shook off the heaviness that always tried to creep up on her whenever she thought about it and focused instead on the new beginning that stretched out before her.

Midgiburra's main street wasn't long, but to Pip it looked to have all the basics. She passed a small supermarket, a chemist and a bakery, noting they all included the name Maguire in the signage. There was also a newsagent and a butcher, and then further along, a feed store, petrol station and a pub. She drove past these as she followed the directions her uncle had given her to Rosevale, the place she would housesit for the next three months.

She'd never been down here before, hadn't seen her uncle Nev since a family wedding seven years ago. But when her mother had teamed up with Ted after the attack, the call had gone out to family far and wide, and Uncle Nev had come up with the goods. He and his motorhome were taking a trip around Australia and his house would sit empty. Her mother had wasted no time in pointing out that the peace and quiet of country life would be the perfect place for Pip to recuperate and start writing her book.

That was her other dilemma—the book deal she'd recently signed, her no holds barred telling of the Lenny Knight case.

It should have been a celebration, but instead it was proving to be just another thing weighing her down. Where once she'd thrived on deadlines, now the idea sent her into a panic. All of a sudden, her drive seemed to have driven off without her, and she'd been struggling to put together a coherent sentence for weeks. Her passion for the job had evaporated, and the thought terrified her. She'd always loved writing, it was all she'd ever wanted to do, but lately she just couldn't find the motivation.

She ignored the little know-it-all voice in her head that reminded her that the therapist—booked by human resources—had mentioned concentration loss as a symptom for something or other; she hadn't really been listening. On reflection, maybe she *should* have tried to focus a little more, although at the time she hadn't been in the most receptive of moods, having been forced to attend the session as part of her mental wellbeing and general we-want-to-make-sure-you're-not-having-a-breakdown strategy. Pip had declined the extra visits the therapist had recommended.

'A break's all you need,' Ted had told her a few days ago when she'd stopped into the office to collect some of her belongings. She hoped he was right—she was so desperate that she was willing to give anything a try. She hadn't even

A Stone's Throw Away

put up much of a fight when her mother had called to tell her about Uncle Nev's house being available. She just packed her bags and set her GPS. And here she was, in country Victoria with no idea where she was going—much like her navigation system, if the endless circle it kept trying to lead her around was any indication.

She pulled over to the side of the road and scrolled through her messages to locate the directions Uncle Nev had sent her.

> Take the Old Ferry Road for about five k's then turn right onto Clay Target Road. When you come to an old green tank, turn into the next driveway with a wonky gate. The track splits a few metres down the road, take the left and keep going straight until you reach the cattle grid and the house will be on your right.

Clear. As. Mud.

She left the instructions on the screen and put the phone on the passenger seat, ready to grab if she suddenly got lost. She found Ferry Road and assumed it was the old one—there was no sign that mentioned a young version—then went straight past the green tank. Uncle Nev had neglected to mention it was lying on its side in a paddock of overgrown grass. But after a quick U-turn, Pip spotted the wonky gate and managed to follow the rest of the instructions without further mishap.

Her Audi was probably not the best-suited vehicle to drive the dirt track full of potholes large enough to lose a small child in, but she picked her way carefully along it and breathed a sigh of relief as a house came into sight.

She was pleasantly surprised by the small cottage she pulled up in front of. It was the quintessential Australian farmhouse: square, with a wraparound verandah and a bullnosed iron roof.

The house was surrounded by a fenced yard, and off to one side stood two large tin sheds that looked fairly new. Her uncle was an avid traveller, so she assumed one of the sheds usually housed his motorhome while the other contained the workshop in which he designed wrought-iron work and timber signs. After Aunty Effie died a few years back, Nev had sold up and moved from Queensland to Victoria to escape the heat, and what started as a hobby soon grew into a small but successful business.

It seemed, though, that the heat had followed Uncle Nev. The area had been in drought for the past eighteen months, one of the worst in recent history, and Nev had headed down to Tasmania to get away from it.

Pip climbed out of her car. The heat outside was a brutal shock after the arctic breeze from the car's aircon. She stretched her arms above her head and turned to survey her surroundings, noting the gentle sounds of the bushland around her.

She crossed to the gate, framed by a pergola with some kind of climbing plant woven over the top, though bare of leaves or anything green, and walked through. A squeak sounded as the rusty gate protested opening and then groaned again as she shut it behind her.

Beside the front door of the house was a timber sign with *Rosevale* engraved in the timber.

A Stone's Throw Away

The key was supposed to be inside an old metal dairy can, and Pip eyed the collection of milk cans in all shapes and sizes arranged along the front of the verandah despondently. She gingerly tipped a few of the larger rusty-looking cans on their side, but there was no key. Pip worked her way along the row until she ran out of big cans, then turned to eye off the smaller versions scattered on a table and shelving beneath two front windows. A spider ran out of the first one, making Pip grimace and jump back. She poked at the next one a little more cautiously before finally hearing a promising rattle. The key that came out was not your run-of-the-mill house key—this one was a long, old-fashioned bronze skeleton key. An antique, just like the old house it belonged to.

She opened the screen door and fitted the clumsy-looking key into the lock and gave it a twist, happy when she heard a click and pushed the old wooden door open.

A long hallway led straight through the centre of the house to a back door, and Pip walked in, peeping through doorways. Two rooms, one clearly used as an office and the other a spare bedroom, were on one side, and opposite these was a lounge room that opened up into a kitchen. Two more doors on the far side of the house led to the master bedroom and a bathroom.

The house retained many of its original fixtures, with elaborate decorative mouldings and wide timber flooring throughout. She was pleasantly surprised to find a fairly modern bathroom, complete with claw-footed bathtub, and the bedroom with a double bed in its centre was bright and cheery with white walls and lace curtains over a wide window.

She flicked the nearby light switch and breathed a sigh of relief that the power was on before heading outside to bring in her suitcase and bags. As promised, there was long-life milk in the pantry and bread in the freezer, so for at least tonight she'd be fine—tomorrow she would venture into town for groceries.

Pip took her phone out and called her mother to let her know she'd arrived safely, and gave her a rundown of the house.

'Are you sure you'll be okay out there all on your own?' her mother asked.

'I'll be fine.'

'Because your father and I could come out and stay,' she said.

'The whole point of coming out here was so I could write. There's not much chance of that if you two come out here,' Pip pointed out. 'We'd be poking about old second-hand shops and doing morning teas in cafes.' Pip had been slowly making her way through the house checking the windows were locked as she talked. It was a ritual she had performed ever since her attack, and by the time she'd finished she was feeling more settled.

'It would be fun, though,' her mum mused.

'It wouldn't get this book written.'

'No, I suppose you're right,' she sighed.

'I'll be fine. I'm already feeling more relaxed,' Pip said, hoping she sounded convincing. She couldn't actually remember the last time she felt relaxed—anywhere.

'We're just a phone call away. And did Neville leave you his neighbours' phone numbers like he said he would?' she asked.

Pip smiled at her mother's concern. Even at thirty-five it was nice to still have your mum to fuss and worry—to a point.

'Yes, Mum. I'll call them if I need any help with anything, I promise.'

They said goodbye and Pip plugged in her phone to recharge.

She loved her parents—they'd always been there, cheering her on and celebrating her achievements, even though they worried about her working in a field of journalism that could, at times, be extremely volatile. She also knew they were trying to step back and give her the freedom she was desperate to regain, which was hard considering they were the ones who'd picked up the pieces when she'd been at her most vulnerable. Still, she was a grown woman and she needed to get back on her own two feet, and if that meant she had to get used to being out here alone for a while so she could write her book, then that's what she'd do.

But first things first: she needed a coffee and something to eat. After searching the pantry, she located a packet of Scotch Finger biscuits and a tin of instant coffee. She put the kettle on, vowing she would set up her coffee machine first thing tomorrow.

Taking her mug and the packet of biscuits out through the screen door that led off the kitchen, Pip realised that the verandah wrapped around the side of the house and joined the front. There was no railing here, instead a small hedge grew along the edge of a narrow garden, bordering the timber floor and giving uninterrupted views out across the property. A pair of long gumboots sat neatly against the wall, and an oilskin coat hung on a hook near the back door. Pip settled herself at a small round table and put her feet up on the opposite chair as she took in the open paddocks before her. This was kind of nice, she thought, trying not to wrinkle her nose at the cheap, bitter coffee and long-life milk taste as she took a sip from her mug. 'This'll be fine,' she told herself firmly. Tomorrow she would start writing.

A woman sat on a blanket in a small clearing under a huge old gum tree. Her face was partially hidden under a wide-brimmed sunhat. The vintage blue and white wraparound dress she wore was tucked around her legs, which were crossed at the ankles, and a pair of chunky slip-on shoes with a wide heel graced her feet. Everything about the woman looked out of place—as though she were in the wrong time. Pip moved closer, drawn to her. The air was heavy—the ground looked dry and parched. There was no sound. Not even the trees rustled. Everything was completely still.

The woman on the blanket was bent over, writing. The pen in her hand raced across the paper, and Pip followed the graceful movement of her hand as it glided across the page. Who was this woman and why was she out here alone? Pip looked around but didn't recognise where she was. A tall gum tree, its massive trunk smooth and grey, towered over them, casting a shadow across the blanket on the ground.

'Hello?' Pip ventured finally, breaking the silence, and the woman looked up—

A Stone's Throw Away

Pip's eyes opened and she turned to look at the bedside clock. Three-fifteen. God, it was so hot. She kicked the sheets off. The fan whirling overhead did nothing but circulate the warm air around the stuffy room. She glanced at the window behind the pulled curtain but dismissed the idea of opening it. She would never sleep knowing there was an unlocked window. She'd rather swelter than risk throwing caution to the wind like that—besides, it didn't seem any cooler outside.

At some point, though, she dozed, eventually lulled back to sleep by the constant thrum of the fan.

Two

As Pip drove out the next morning, deciding her instant-coffee bravado of the previous day was a one-off thing, she noticed a dam down the hill in the middle of a paddock.

She'd never given much thought to dams, but she could see that this one was quite large—almost a lake. An empty lake. Well, almost empty; there was still water in the very centre, but not much. It was surrounded by a ring of tall trees with peeling bark and drooping leaves, and it looked more like a rubbish dump than a waterhole, with a scattering of metal objects, old drums and containers lying on the cracked, dry earth exposed to the sun and heat.

She was glad there were no livestock to take care of—the few she'd seen on her drive out here yesterday had looked hot and skinny. The vista before her as the driveway wound its way down the slight rise was brown as far as the eye could see. The shades varied, but the colour was the same. The huge gum trees looked tired and washed out—it reminded her of an old painting her nanna used to have hanging on the wall, a bush scene with early settlers setting up camp.

Momentarily her thoughts went to the strange dream she had last night, though she only vaguely recalled fragments. She'd been trying to remember it ever since she got up, without much success. She didn't often dream, which made this an interesting occurrence.

She retraced the route she'd taken the day before and soon found herself back in relative civilisation, the big, shady trees of the main street offering a welcome respite from the dry landscape surrounding the little town.

Inside the grocery store, she fought the urge to strip off and allow the cool air to wash over her as she collected a red plastic basket and strolled the aisles. There weren't many, so she took her time, drawing out the blessed coolness.

She'd written a list—the only writing she'd done so far—but left it on the kitchen bench. She gave up trying to remember what was on it after a few moments and instead started tossing in whatever caught her eye. It was perhaps irresponsible, but food shopping had never been her forte. Her meals were usually taken at her desk—she rarely had time for breakfast and she was always home too late to bother cooking dinner just for herself so would normally pick up takeaway. Having not noticed any big-name takeaway chains since she arrived—nor for the last few hundred kilometres of her drive—she guessed that would rule out her dinner options for a while. It looked like she was going to have to get the hang of cooking if she didn't want to starve.

On the few occasions she did cook these days, she always thought of Bruno. They had moved in together and played happy couples for a while, and Pip had even given cooking a go back then. She'd been young, and at the time it seemed like a good idea. She'd thought she'd been in love, or as close to it as she'd ever been. But the fire eventually burned out. Bruno was a fellow journo who also travelled for work, and all too soon that burning flame she'd mistaken for love had turned into nothing more than two roommates who occasionally had sex if they were in the same place at the same time.

The following decade had left her completely underwhelmed by her experience of romance. When she'd had time to date, she found the men she went out with—usually journalists or in a related field—would rather talk about themselves and their accomplishments than anything else. She didn't have the time or the energy to widen her dating prospects, so she tended to throw herself into work instead, and she didn't feel as though she had missed out on anything.

She had friends who were married with children, and while she loved playing favourite aunty to a number of nieces and nephews, she had no desire to grow one of her own. She could barely manage to keep a house plant alive.

She continued down the supermarket aisle, grabbing things from the shelf and depositing them into her basket. Rounding the end, she slammed into something solid and painful.

'Ow,' Pip said, as the basket hit her shin.

'Sorry, are you okay?'

Pip glanced up at the deep voice and blinked uncertainly at the man in a dark blue uniform standing in front of her. 'I'm fine. I should have been looking where I was going.'

As she straightened, her gaze fell on the bulky gun belt he wore around his waist, and despite knowing this was a police officer, a tiny ripple of unease raced through her.

'No, I was in a hurry,' he said, then crouched down to pick up a bag of chips that had fallen out of her basket.

She took in his short, dirty-blond hair and blue-grey eyes; more dove grey, she decided on reflection, with soft blue highlights, cool yet calming, almost the same shade she'd chosen to paint her lounge room. He had a wide forehead and a slightly crooked nose with a bump across the ridge that looked like it had probably been broken. His lower jaw was covered in a short beard, blond but with a few flecks of copper. As he straightened back up to his full height she realised he was tall, or maybe it was just the uniform that made him *seem* taller.

'Thanks,' she said, clearing her throat as she caught him looking at the rest of her junk food–laden selections.

'Having a party?' he asked, lifting an eyebrow slightly.

'Shopping on an empty stomach.'

'Ah, right,' he nodded in understanding. 'The way I tend to shop, too.'

She looked down at his basket: it held a bag of dog food and two large bottles of milk. 'Yeah, I can see you've gone totally wild.'

As he chuckled deeply, she wondered how long it had been since she'd heard someone do something as simple as laugh.

The news industry was serious business most of the time, and the people she'd been hanging around for the past few years in particular had little to laugh about—most were criminals she'd interviewed in jail or informants with too much to lose to waste time laughing.

'Today I'm on a mission. I brought a list,' he said, waving a piece of paper.

'Show off,' she muttered but felt a smile tug at her lips.

'Are you here visiting family?' he asked, adjusting the basket in front of him.

She was momentarily distracted by his forearms, which bunched at the movement. 'Sorry?'

He smiled easily at her. 'It's a pretty small town and I haven't seen you around before. Do you have family here?'

'Oh. My uncle lives here. I'm housesitting for him. Neville Worsley.'

'I know Nev. Does some pretty amazing stuff with wrought iron.'

'Yes, he does.'

'He mentioned he was going away. I've been driving past a few times a week to keep an eye on the house. How long are you staying for?'

'He's away another three months, so probably that long. I'll see how I go.'

'You don't think you'll last three months?' he asked jovially.

'I don't think I've ever left the city for more than a week at a time.'

'You'll *probably* be okay,' he said with amused sympathy.

'We'll see,' she said, smiling despite herself. What was going on here? How was this complete stranger making her feel . . . happy and . . . oh God . . . *chatty*?

'Well, welcome to Midgiburra. I'm Erik Nielsen.' He moved the basket under one arm, which was even more distracting than the forearm move, and Pip had to snap herself out of whatever giddy schoolgirl nonsense she'd found herself in to shake his hand.

'Phillipa. Pip,' she added quickly.

He smiled and gave her a nod. 'If you have any problems, let me know,' he said, before releasing her hand from his warm grip.

'Shall do. Nice to meet you.'

Pip forced herself not to turn and watch him walk away, but as she reached the end of the aisle she caught a final glimpse of him as he finished at the checkout and waved farewell to the operator.

'How odd,' she mused quietly. She had no idea why she'd had such a strange reaction to Erik Nielsen, but by the time she'd reached the house, she had convinced herself it was most likely low blood sugar levels from lack of food, or maybe she just needed caffeine. Nothing a strong cup of decent coffee and a home-cooked bacon and egg roll couldn't set right, she decided as she unpacked her groceries. As soon as she had something in her stomach she'd be ready to start work. After all, that was the whole purpose of her coming out here.

Pip dropped her hands from her hips and let out a frustrated bellow. This writer's block was doing her head in. This never happened to her. Ever. She thrived on deadlines. Thrived! At least, she always had in the past. But today she was struggling to stay focused on one task at a time. It was getting past a joke. She eyed the phone and weighed up the wisdom of her next move.

With a resigned groan, she grabbed her phone from the table and called her best friend.

'Well, well, well,' Lexi said on the other end of the line. 'I was wondering when you'd call.'

'I called you a week ago,' Pip said.

'To tell me you were going off the grid and not to worry. Oh, and thanks for the invite.'

'I'm here to write—it's not a holiday,' Pip said calmly.

'Whatever. Anyway, enough of that—I'm glad you're back. Let's go out for drinks tonight?'

'I'm not back,' Pip said. 'I'm still trying to write.'

'I'm hearing something I haven't heard before,' Lexi mused. 'Okay, spill. What's going on?' Lexi had always, since the day they met at university, had an annoying habit of being able to read Pip—apparently even over the phone. Pip couldn't recall a monumental event in her life since that hadn't involved Lexi—usually as the instigator in some kind of alcohol-fuelled disaster.

'That's kind of the problem. I have no idea. I've been trying to write ever since I got here and . . . nothing,' she said helplessly.

'Nothing?'

'Nope. I have written a total of one page in the last week.'

The line went quiet, and Pip pulled the phone away from her ear to check the call hadn't been disconnected. 'Lexi?'

'I think you've put yourself under a bit too much pressure. It really hasn't been that long since . . . everything. Maybe just relax. Try not to force it.'

'I can't relax anymore! I've done all the damn relaxing I can possibly do. I just need to write.'

'Yes, it sounds like you're completely zen, my friend,' Lexi muttered.

'I just don't understand it. It's like I've forgotten how to write.'

'You haven't. It's just your brain telling you it needs time to recover. Pip, don't understate the significance of the trauma you went through. It was a big deal.'

'I'm completely fine,' Pip brushed off.

'And that's why you're stuck. Until you actually face the fact you were almost killed, you're not going to be able to move forward.'

Pip went to shake her head and deny it, but Lexi cut in briskly. 'And don't brush this off. I know exactly what you're doing.'

A best friend could be both a blessing and a curse. When someone knows you so well, it's almost impossible to get away with things you'd get away with talking to a stranger.

'How could I *not* have faced it? I was there!'

'You haven't talked about it, dealt with how it made you feel, what it did to you . . . the emotional side of it, Pip. You need to talk to someone about how you're feeling so you can let all that pent-up stuff out.'

'You know all that touchy-feely stuff isn't my thing.'

'There's no touchy stuff. But the feely stuff is what I think you need to deal with.'

'I just want to write this bloody book.'

'I may not be an expert, but it's possible that the subject of your book is most likely the reason you've got a mental block happening.'

'Which makes no sense. Writing this book was supposed to free me from it all. It was going to be all cathartic and shit.'

'You know, your way with words is truly poetic,' Lexi said.

'Well, it's true. That was the main reason I agreed to the book deal. It was supposed to be easy. I was looking forward to it, but now . . . I just don't know what the hell's happening. I sit down to write and my mind literally goes blank. There's just nothing there. I'm really starting to panic, Lex. I'm not sure I can do this.'

'Of course you can. You just need to work out how to release all that blockage.'

'Why do I feel as though there's going to be some kind of metaphor here about a plunger and a sink?'

'Laugh all you want, but I know you, and I know how you think. You bury your head instead of facing things when they get too emotional. Maybe when it's your career that's at stake you'll finally realise you can't ignore it.'

Pip wished she *could* laugh it off, but as much as she hated to admit it, she knew her friend was more than likely right. There *was* something stopping her. It was more of a feeling that hung over her as she sat in front of the screen. Each time she tried to sort out her thoughts she saw the man in the ski mask standing there in the middle of her room.

Pip shook away the creepy sensation that washed over her once more and realised with a sinking heart that ignoring it wasn't making it go away. 'I'll think about it. Maybe I can see if they'll do a phone consultation or something.'

'Well, I guess that's a step in the right direction. You could always just come back here and see someone in person,' Lexi reminded her.

'I don't have time to waste travelling back and forth—this book needs to be finished . . . or started, even, would be good,' she added.

'Okay,' Lexi conceded. 'Let me know how you go.'

The two friends said goodbye and Pip hung up feeling . . . not exactly better but maybe a tad more hopeful. The idea of spilling her guts to a counsellor who would ask her all kinds of intrusive questions didn't hold much appeal, but if it managed to budge some of this blockage and let her writing mojo flow again . . . Pip pulled out one of her notebooks and opened to a blank page. She would go to a counsellor as a last resort. All she needed to do was concentrate.

She slid the key into the lock and pushed open the front door. Kicking off her heels and dropping her handbag on the hallway table, she gave a small sigh of relief at the instant pleasure of soft carpet under aching feet. She reached out and switched on the light, but nothing happened. Damn it. All afternoon she'd been

looking forward to a long, hot soak in her bathtub and a night binging the last few episodes of Peaky Blinders. *A blackout was going to ruin all her plans. Digging in her bag, she pulled out her phone and turned on the torch to make her way through her dark apartment to locate the candles she kept in the sideboard. As she walked across the open room, something moved. She turned, and her breath caught in her chest and a scream froze in her throat as the dark figure lurched towards her—*

Pip sat up in bed, a scream echoing in the room. She felt the cold chill of the sweat that made her T-shirt cling to her uncomfortably, and ran a shaky hand through her hair, moving the damp tendrils off her forehead. Dropping her head into her hands, she waited for her breathing to settle and her heart to slow to its normal rate before steadying herself enough to climb out of bed. She headed to the kitchen, and her hand shook slightly as she filled a glass from the tap and took a sip. She hated the nightmares more than anything. They always felt so real. Her hand went to her neck, and she timidly pressed her fingers to the skin expecting to feel tenderness. *It was just a nightmare*, she told herself firmly.

It was stupid to keep thinking it would ever happen again. After all, Lenny Knight was behind bars. It was over. And yet, the police had never found the man Knight had paid to attack her. She pushed that thought away. It didn't matter. Lenny had lost and was locked away, and whoever he paid had only been doing a job and would be long gone by now. The thought made sense logically, but Pip suspected that not knowing the attacker's identity was behind the lingering nightmares. As long as she continued to have the nightmares and gave into the fear, it felt like Lenny Knight was still winning. Fear blended with anger, always.

She hated it—this constant reminder she carried with her. When she'd heard of his arrest, and then through the trial that followed, she'd been relieved that it was all, finally, going to end, and she could put the last year behind her. But it hadn't ended. With each shadow she jumped at, each noise that made her heart pound, he won all over again. Which is why she was determined to ignore the fear and the constant unease she lived with. If she ignored it, then she was the one in control, not him. But even locked away where he couldn't hurt anyone anymore, the man still managed to haunt her.

Three

Friends in Low Places: The Fall of Australia's Favourite Bent Front Bencher
by Phillipa Davenport

Pip stared at the title page on her screen and gave a frustrated sigh. A total of fourteen pages from two days of writing.

She pushed back the chair from the kitchen table irritably and walked outside onto the back verandah. *What the hell is wrong with me?* she wondered forlornly as she took in the view before her. She had peace and quiet, nothing but paddocks and bush for as far as the eye could see. How much more bloody peaceful did it have to get before she could relax and write?

This wasn't like her. She was a seasoned journo! She pumped out articles even on her worst days.

With a final, irritated growl, she stepped off the verandah and kept walking. This was bullshit, sitting around hoping for inspiration. She needed to *do* something. She needed a distraction.

The dry grass crackled and crunched beneath her feet as she picked her way through the paddock filled with long, dead-looking stalks before she suddenly—and nervously—remembered about snakes, but with a quick glance over her shoulder at the house she realised she was already some distance away. Snakes were either attracted to or repelled by vibration, she recalled, but the specifics escaped her, so she took a chance and loudly stomped the rest of the way across.

When she reached the gate on the other side, she noted with relief that the ground was clearer. It was rocky, though, with a lot more dirt as it gently sloped down towards the dam.

As she reached the nearest bank, she surveyed its vast outline, standing with her hands on her hips and wiping away the beads of sweat dotting her forehead. It was either ridiculously hot or she was a lot more out of shape than she'd thought. The dam wasn't a neat circular hole designed to catch water like the ones she'd seen from the car during her trip—this one was more of a figure eight with one end rounder than the other. In the middle was a small island, its banks eroded over time. The exposed roots of a large tree with a dangerous lean seemed to be the only thing holding the little piece of land together.

It was deep. Where she stood at the edge was maybe only six feet or so from the bare dirt, but further in it sloped down and she estimated it to be three times deeper at least. She walked around the edges, marvelling again at its size. Maybe it wasn't manmade, she thought, studying it critically. Maybe it was a billabong, part of a river, before it changed course a long time ago. She could imagine what a beautiful spot this would be to relax by when it held water. The trees surrounding it, which partially hid it from the rest of the property, would normally be shady and green, she suspected. At the moment they looked faded and the leaves drooped listlessly. Everything around here just looked . . . hot.

There was a strange stillness about this place, she thought, tilting her head back to take in the barely moving leaves on the tall trees that surrounded the waterhole. Maybe it was just the heat sapping whatever energy anything had left and sucking it out of the atmosphere.

Something nagged at her as she stood there—like trying to remember someone's name, on the tip of her tongue but just frustratingly out of reach. It was an odd sensation and she pushed it aside to think about later.

She squinted across to look at the rubbish that was now exposed as the water level had evaporated. Drums and old car parts were some of the more recognisable things she could see. Surely that couldn't be good for the environment? She toyed with the idea of climbing down to poke about to see what else was down there but had visions of getting stuck and having to remain there until someone eventually came out looking for her.

Someone like Erik, perhaps, when he came out to check on the place for Uncle Nev. The idea that he could just happen to drive past unexpectedly sent a brief flutter of excitement through her. But then, she realised with a disappointed sigh, that was before she told him she was out here housesitting, leaving little need for a drive-by.

Still, it was a shame such a beautiful place was littered with so much crap. Uncle Nev popped into her mind and she had an idea. Maybe if she got someone in to clear out the dam and stack all the junk in a pile somewhere, Uncle Nev could sort through it when he got home and maybe use some of it. What he didn't use he could sell for scrap. And in the process, his water feature would be clean and junk-free like it hadn't been for quite a number of, well . . . decades, by the look of it.

Again she felt the weird urge to jump down into the empty waterhole and . . . do what? She wasn't exactly sure. There was nothing particularly interesting that caught her eye about all the junk, it was mostly rusted-out old tin. There was a very antique-looking washing machine, twisted and bent and half buried in the muddy remains of the dam floor and yet . . . Pip shook her head to clear away the strange brain fog that had hovered about and turned away.

She went back to the house with the first bit of determination she'd felt in a while. It was just a shame it wasn't directed at her book.

The woman sat on a blanket in a small clearing under a huge old gum tree, her blonde hair pulled back from her face and large bouncy curls pinned at the nape of her neck. Her head was bowed over the small notebook on her lap as she wrote.

There was something familiar about her, Pip thought. Like she'd seen her before, but she wasn't sure where, or why she was even out here.

Pip saw the woman wipe a tear from her eye, but she didn't look up from her scribbling, and Pip wondered what she was writing about that made her so sad. Pip could feel the woman's sadness radiating from where she sat on the blanket—so much loss and pain. Was that what she was writing about? Pip took a tentative step closer. Her foot stepped on a branch and the loud noise broke the bubble of silence they'd been trapped in moments before, and the woman's head snapped up in alarm—

Pip turned her head and groaned at the red numbers on the bedside clock before pulling out the pillow from under her head and covering her face with it. All she wanted was just one good night's sleep. Was that really too much to ask?

The next morning, Pip stepped outside and breathed in the bushy smell of eucalypt and a sweet native floral smell from the flowers high up in some of the gum trees she could see. She was discovering a whole new side to herself since coming out here. Exercise was something she usually avoided like the plague. She owned a multitude of T-shirts and coffee cups friends and family had bought her over the years that would attest to the fact. One T-shirt said: *Run? I thought you said Rum!* And another: *If my body is ever found on a jogging trail, know that I was probably murdered elsewhere and dumped*

there. However, lately she'd taken to going for a walk each day to clear her head, and she was finding that she looked forward to them.

She wasn't much of an early riser usually, but she'd discovered by accident that coffee on the front verandah just after the sun came up provided the most gorgeous of views, with the glowing red and gold rays of morning light filtering through the long, wispy grass out in the paddock. It was a reprieve of sorts to breathe in the fresh, clean morning air before the sun continued its rise and went on to scorch everything below.

This morning she bypassed the dam and headed along a well-worn, narrow cattle track, which remained despite no cattle being on the property since Uncle Nev bought it. She felt something like a small rock digging into the underside of her foot and stopped, tapping her heel on the ground to try to dislodge it. She felt it move and the discomfort stopped as she continued on.

Her T-shirt stuck to her chest and she pulled it away from her skin irritably. Loud insects zoomed past her, buzzing loudly, while the odd fly followed her, dive-bombing her face and dodging her flapping hands. The track beneath her feet was washed-out in places and eroded in others as it wound its way through the paddock and the bush surrounding the property. It was only wide enough for a person to walk on single file, and Pip smiled as she imagined what a herd of cattle following each other in a long procession from the waterhole must have looked like.

She stopped near a large gum tree and leaned against its massive trunk as she took off her shoe and knocked it against the palm of her hand to dislodge the annoying pebble. It was quiet here, sheltered by the bush that bordered the dam. Native grasses grew in clumps, not pasture like the rest of the property in the cleared paddocks behind her. The trees here were tall and their massive canopies stretched high into the sky, creating a cathedral above the clearing below. This was a nice spot, she thought. A feeling of peace settled within her.

As she replaced her shoe and straightened, she experienced the most incredible sense of déjà vu. For a moment she felt disorientated, and she frowned, wondering if she might have a touch of heat stroke. As she pushed away from the tree, she turned and felt the ground tilt slightly.

This place . . .

She took a few steps back and stared up at the huge tree she'd been resting against before her gaze fell to the ground below it. All it was missing was a blanket on the ground, she thought numbly. For the past few days she'd been trying to remember the dreams that had woken her in the early hours of the morning. Now she remembered. The woman with the notebook.

This spot looked exactly like the one from Pip's dream.

She shook her head, more to dislodge the thought than in denial. It had to be some weird coincidence. She sent a nervous glance around the clearing, half expecting a woman to come walking out of the surrounding bush any moment carrying a blanket and a notebook, but then she dismissed the ridiculous notion. Maybe this afternoon she would have a nap and catch up on some of that sleep she'd been missing. She clearly needed it.

Two days later, Pip was drawn to the front window as a rumbling sound caught her attention, and she watched as a semitrailer with an excavator on the back crawled up the driveway. She finished washing up the breakfast dishes, and by the time she went outside, a short, round man who looked to be in his late sixties jumped from the truck cabin and called out a hello, followed by a tall, willowy younger man, maybe in his early twenties, who looked like he was trying, unsuccessfully, to grow his first moustache.

'Hi. I was worried you might not get up the driveway,' she said as the driver began undoing clamps and hooks and a variety of other gadgets that secured the huge excavator to the back of the truck.

'Nah, piece of cake. This is one of the easier places to get to. Bob,' he said extending a slightly dirty-looking hand. 'And this is my offsider for the day, Danny. You must be Pip.'

'Yep,' she said, shaking his hand quickly and then nodding towards the younger man who was leaning against the truck with his hands in his back pockets. 'I thought I'd do something constructive while I was here and oversee the dam clean-out for my uncle.'

They all turned to look, following the tree line down the paddock to the dam.

'Yeah, we get a few of these every time we have a drought.'

'I can't actually believe people throw stuff in their dam.'

'Usually you'll find it's from earlier—before they brought out all these rules and regulations,' he informed her. 'Bloody greenies,' he added, dragging out the word like it tasted bad.

'Yeah, well, I'm sure we all miss the days of metal and poisons leaking into the waterways,' she muttered, but Bob didn't seem to hear. 'Will you be able to get down to it?' she asked, eyeing the large excavator doubtfully. It had a considerable distance to cover to reach the dam from where the truck was parked.

'Yeah. No worries. Only good thing about having no rain—less chance of getting bogged,' he said cheerfully.

She had to admire his silver-lining attitude.

'So, you just want me to drag it all out and put it in a pile?' he said.

'Yes, thanks.'

'Where do you want the pile?'

Pip looked around and shaded her eyes against the early sun. 'Maybe on the other side, out of the way and out of sight.'

'Righto, we'll get stuck into it, then.'

She gave them a nod and left them to it, deciding that maybe this would be the day she could settle in and get some writing done. She was feeling positive. Today was going to be a good day.

Four

Pip glared as the cursor on the blank screen blinked at her, taunting her to type something, anything.

A loud clunk, followed by a bone-jarring bang, sounded once more as another barrel or engine or old tractor part was dropped onto the steadily growing pile of scrap out in the paddock.

Pip plugged in her USB and searched for the file she needed, her gaze once more falling on the one titled 'Guardian' followed by a string of seemingly random numbers and letters. This was the only file on the drive she hadn't been able to open. It was encrypted, and not with your average find-a-tutorial-video-and-open-it-yourself kind of encryption. This one was high tech, and after exhausting her skill she had sent it to the computer geek she'd worked with a few times over the years with a brief to do whatever he needed to in order to open the file.

He called himself The Warlock, due to his magic touch when it came to doing all the illegal things people weren't supposed to do with computers. Pip humoured him because despite the fact the guy was clearly delusional and had a questionable police record, he hadn't failed her yet.

The hard drive had been given to her by Tony Vesco, her number-one source in the Lenny Knight investigation. Tony was an insider who gave key evidence in the trial—then suddenly went missing. A shiver ran through Pip despite the heat of the day. She'd spent countless hours interviewing Tony in a number of shady places, probing him about Lenny's connections to the underworld. It had taken a long time to gain his trust, but she'd persevered, knowing that Tony was the only man still alive who had the kind of intel on Lenny Knight that could put him away. Tony may have been a criminal himself but he didn't condone the lengths Lenny Knight had been willing to go to in order to make his money. It never ceased to amaze Pip that even in the murky depths of the criminal world, there were still some boundaries that just didn't get crossed—and once Lenny had overstepped those boundaries, he'd gone too far.

She'd taken precautions in order to protect Tony's identity, always mindful that if she revealed her source, even to the police, his life would instantly be in danger; the responsibility weighed heavily on her shoulders. In the end, however, it had all been for nothing when police arrested Tony on an unrelated matter and offered him a plea bargain in exchange for his testimony in court. It was after the trial that Tony had secretly managed to send her the USB and told her about the file. He hadn't revealed its contents to the police and he didn't say what was on it—only that it was important. That was the last contact she'd had with him.

Standing here surrounded by the beauty of the bush, it was easy to forget the dark and dangerous world she'd lived with one foot inside of for the better part of four years. People went missing all the time—and if they did turn up, it was rarely alive.

Once the book was done, Pip was getting out of the game. She was tired of the greed and violence that went hand in hand with power, and despite the fact she believed passionately that corruption needed to be exposed, she knew she'd done her part and it was time to step away and hand over the reins to someone else.

Her thoughts returned to the hard drive. She really needed it, but contacting The Warlock wasn't as easy as picking up the phone and calling him. Due to his hyper paranoid state of mind, contact was made by a series of forwarded messages, and the rule was that once he agreed to do the job, you waited for him to call. The only reason she put up with his over-the-top secret-agent drama was because he was the best at what he did.

It wasn't like she didn't have plenty of material she could start with. But she thought about that file often, wondering what it hid. She had a lot riding on whatever was in there. It was her pièce de résistance, the secret information that would shoot this book to instant bestseller rank before it was even released. At least that's what her publisher reckoned. She did try to warn them that the file might not contain anything exciting—but her rather substantial advance was banking on it being something juicy.

But first, she needed to get the bloody manuscript written. Pip gritted her teeth and closed her eyes, breathing out slowly. She could do this. *Just focus.*

Thank goodness for peace and quiet, she thought, then stopped, looking up from the kitchen table with a small frown. It *was* quiet. Too quiet. She glanced at her watch, but it seemed a bit early for lunch. Surely they hadn't already finished? She chewed her bottom lip a little as she eyed the computer screen. She was finally on a roll, but she couldn't shake the feeling something might be wrong. With a frustrated huff, she got up from the table and headed out the back door.

She spotted the large, now blessedly silent excavator at the edge of the bank and saw that both men were down in the dam.

'Is everything okay?' Pip called out, making both men jump slightly as they spun around to face her.

'Scared the living bejesus outta me, missus,' Bob said, splaying a hand across his chest.

'It's Ms,' she corrected, picking her way down closer to the edge.

'What?' Bob called back.

'Doesn't matter,' she yelled, then waited until she got closer and tried again. 'What's going on?'

'We gotta stop work,' Bob said, taking off his floppy hat and wiping a hand across his bald head.

'Why?' she asked cautiously. Was this some kind of workers' strike? Had she been supposed to supply them with tea and cakes or something?

'Copper said to.'

'Excuse me?' Pip blinked.

'We had to call in the cops, and they said to stop work immediately until they get here.'

Pips eyes narrowed in confusion. 'Why would you call the police?'

''Cause of the body.'

'The body?' Pip wasn't sure she was even hearing this right. '*What* body?'

'The one we just found in there,' Bob said, pointing at the rusted remains of an old ute that looked like it had been dragged from decades' worth of mud in the centre of the dam.

'A body!' *What the actual hell?*

'Well, what's left of it. There's a skull in there.'

Pip stared at the two men. They had to be kidding. Just then, the roar of an engine alerted them to a vehicle approaching, and Pip turned to find a police four-wheel drive bouncing its way across the paddock. The man she'd met a few days earlier climbed out and put his hat on before heading down the bank towards the two men. 'Bob. Danny,' he said before turning to look up at her. 'Phillipa, wasn't it?' he said with a nod.

'Pip,' she corrected quickly, moving to climb down to join them.

'Actually, just stay up there a minute, Pip,' Erik cautioned and turned back to the other two. 'Have either of you touched anything?'

Bob pointed at the vehicle and the excavator and explained how they'd uncovered the ute and been attaching chains to it in order to drag it out when they'd noticed the skull in the cabin.

'Righto. Well, you'll both need to move out of here, follow the same path you walked in on. We're going to have to preserve the crime scene.'

'Crime scene?' Bob said. 'Cripes—who would have thought, hey?'

'I've got to tape the area off and wait until Homicide get out here. You'll need to give them a statement about how you found it—where you moved it from, that kind of thing—before you go.'

'Yeah, righto. No problem,' Bob said, looking a little concerned now that it seemed to be all very official.

Pip studied the vehicle, critically. It was old, that much was obvious, caked in mud and sludge from where it had been buried, partially submerged for who knew how long. From her vantage point she could see a few holes rusted through the driver's side and another along the back panel. It was impossible to tell what colour the ute had once been, now sporting various shades of rust and brown beneath the mud. The shape and design seemed distinctly old, but Pip was no car expert and had no idea what model and type it was. But she could find out.

Pip slid her phone from her back pocket and discreetly snapped a few photos.

The journo in her wanted details. What was a vintage car doing in a dam? How long had it been there? Who was inside it? She itched to get down there and have a look in the cabin. She'd given up worrying about morbid curiosity years ago. It was part of her job. She'd been a homicide reporter for a few years and knew her way around a crime scene—at least, the part from *behind* the taped-off area. She'd forged a friendly working relationship with a number of detectives and been kept in the loop with most investigations back then.

That was until she'd broken the story on a few heavy-handed cops, leading to an internal investigation into their actions. After that she'd been deemed a troublemaker and shunned. It hadn't mattered that she'd only gone after a few bad cops, not the entire police force; her days of the inside scoop were over. It still annoyed her. Those cops *were* bad. There'd been a multitude of complaints and accusations, none of which had resulted in any kind of disciplinary action; victims were ignored or coerced into silence. It was her job to expose unlawful and unethical behaviour and make sure people were held accountable for their actions. However, by doing so, she'd made a name for herself among the local constabulary, and that was that.

Pip knew that journalists sometimes got a bad rap for doing their job—and there were journos who gave everyone in the profession a bad name—but she was fair. Pip was meticulous in her research and always fact-checked before putting pen to paper, but when she saw something that wasn't right, she went after it with everything she had. She couldn't stand injustice or corruption and wasn't afraid to call someone out who was doing the wrong thing.

Over the years, Pip had developed a sixth sense for sniffing out a lie or a cover-up, and she prided herself on doing her part to ensure bad people were brought to justice. Like Lenny Knight, she thought absently. An image of his face twisted and reddened in outrage as they dragged him from the courtroom flashed through her mind.

A second police vehicle pulled up and a female officer got out, carrying a large tackle box as she scrambled down the bank to join Erik. Her brown hair was pulled back in a tight, no-nonsense bun and her serious face made it difficult to pin an age on her, but Pip decided she couldn't be more than early twenties.

Bob and Danny stood close by, Bob scratching his chin as he watched the proceedings with interest while Danny stood hugging his elbows, looking on nervously. 'You don't think they reckon we had anything to do with it, do you, Bob?' he asked, as he watched the officers wrap crime-scene tape around trees to secure the old ute inside.

Pip slid a curious glance sideways at the young man.

'What? Nah. Course not. Why would they?' Bob said gruffly, eyeing his young companion warily.

'It's just that I can't have any trouble—not with my parole and stuff. I'm not allowed to be around anything illegal.'

'Well, did you put that body in the dam?' Bob demanded bluntly.

'No.'

'Then you'll be apples, won't ya. Look, I promised your mother I'd keep you out of trouble and that's what I'll do,'

Bob said with a confident swagger. 'Besides, that skull was old. Probably been there years.'

'How long do you reckon, Bob?' Pip asked, her curiosity piqued.

'Easy twenty years. Clean as, it was.'

She wasn't sure what made Bob some kind of expert on remains, but he had a kind of confidence that suggested he knew what he was talking about. Regardless, the fact that there was nothing left on the bone did suggest that this was not a recent event. She'd seen enough bodies—in both murder investigations and, sadly, undiscovered elderly—to know that up until a certain point, a skull would still be somewhat gruesome, with tissue remaining attached, and this clearly wasn't the case with the discovery in the ute.

'Hey!' Bob said, moving forward as the young female constable began wrapping the tape around Bob's excavator. 'What's going on? I can't have this thing tied up in some investigation. I got jobs booked tomorrow.'

Pip saw Erik hold a hand up in a reassuring gesture.

'It's just a precaution until the forensic guys get here and take a look. I'm sure it won't be held up too long, but we need to secure the whole site until they've had a chance to check everything out.'

Bob frowned and continued to glare at the officer but took a reluctant step away as she went about her business taping off the scene.

Pip felt bad for the poor bloke. If it wasn't for her hiring him for the job, he wouldn't be tangled up in all this mess.

'How about we head back to the house and I make us a cuppa?' she suggested, and watched as Bob sent one final glance towards his machine before giving a brief nod. 'Yeah. Righto. I guess I could do with one.'

She waited for the two men to walk ahead of her before turning and catching Erik's eye as he sent her a nod of thanks. Neither of them looked away, and Pip felt that little spark of interest instantly flare back to life inside her. The constable called out to him and the moment was gone as he turned away.

As she walked back to the house absently listening to Bob complaining, her thoughts were once more back with the crime scene. There was no harm in poking about a little bit to see if she could find any info on the car.

Once she'd settled the two men outside on the verandah, Pip sent a photo of the wreck to a contact to see if he could work out the make and model, which might help give some kind of timeline. When the kettle boiled, she placed the cups on a tray and put the last of the Scotch Fingers on a plate before taking it all out to the verandah.

As she sat, her phone beeped in her pocket, and she surreptitiously took it out, eyeing the message with surprise.

> Hi gorgeous. Looks like a Ford coupe utility 1934 model from the angle you've sent. Send me a couple more from front on and I can confirm.

Pip thought for a moment and then quickly dashed off a reply.

A Stone's Throw Away

> How positive are you on the make and model?

> From the shape of the cab, wheel arches and tray, I'd say 99 percent positive. It's in pretty shit condition though. Hey, you still owe me a beer from last time.

> Thanks for the info. Take a raincheck on the beer. I'm out of town for a couple of months.

> Sometimes I think you only keep me around for my good looks and car knowledge. Ha.

> Good looks are questionable, but your car knowledge is second to none. Thanks again for your help.

> Anytime. Let me know if you need any more help.

Pip tucked her phone back into her pocket and sent a distracted smile across at Bob, who was still busy grumbling about the jobs he was yet to get to.

'Have you always lived in the area, Bob?' Pip asked.

'Nah, the missus and I moved up from Adelaide a few years back. She wanted a tree change,' he said with a slow drawl.

'So any idea on who the mystery skull belongs to? Any local legends about missing people?'

Bob scratched the stubble on his chin thoughtfully. 'Not that I can think of. Could be some kind of drifter, I s'pose.'

'Wonder how they ended up in the dam?' Danny mused.

That was a good question, Pip thought, her gaze moving back across in the direction of the waterhole. There wasn't any kind of road or track leading to it; it was in the middle of nowhere.

'I remember at school there were lots of stories about places around here that are cursed. Maybe this is one of them,' Danny said.

'Bloody typical. Had the excavator a week and now it's stuck out here with flaming police tape all over it. Place *has* to be bloody cursed.'

A curse did not sound conducive to solving Pip's problem of writer's block.

She really hoped there wasn't one here, though—she needed all the good luck she could find, not bad. Yet, the waterhole *did* feel different. She wouldn't say it felt particularly *cursed*, but when she was down there it did feel as if she were somehow stepping into a bubble. It was peaceful . . . except for the excavator and the police combing the area.

So much for getting any writing done today.

Five

'Bet you didn't count on this much excitement during your stay.'

Pip looked up to see Erik walking across to where she was standing at the edge of the dam.

'I certainly did not,' she agreed. 'So were forensics willing to estimate an age on the bones?'

He sent her a sideways glance before turning to face her fully. 'That's not a typical first question a bystander would normally ask.'

'What's a typical bystander question?' she asked, kinking an eyebrow, unperturbed by his wary tone.

'Who do you think it is? Was there really a body in there? That kind of thing.'

'So who do you think it is?' she asked, tilting her head slightly as she studied him.

'We're only in the early stages of the investigation,' he said, and there was a twitch of a smile on his lips as he looked back over at where the two officers in protective clothing worked.

'Standard responses, I see.'

'If I'd known you were a reporter I wouldn't have been so quick to welcome you to town.'

'Ouch,' she said, but she wasn't surprised by his response. Police tended to adopt an instant closed-mouth policy once they learned they were talking to a journalist, but she was impressed that he'd made the deduction so quickly. 'If it makes you feel any better, I'm currently not working. I'm here on a break.'

'Yeah, right. A journo on holidays. You lot can't help but stick your noses in everything,' he pointed out wryly.

'Hey,' she said, taking a step back and holding her hands up, 'I was just here minding my own business—you guys turned up on *my* doorstep.'

'So you won't be covering this, then?' he asked doubtfully.

'Nope.'

'Not even freelance? A big case like the discovery of human bones in a dam and you're not going to write it up?'

'So they *are* human, then?' she said, nodding, then smiled slyly at his narrowed stare. 'Calm down—I told you, I'm on a break.'

'Constable Jenner said you told her in your statement you'd hired Bob to clean out the dam?'

'Yeah. After seeing all the accumulated rubbish that's been sitting here for so long, I thought it would be a good idea to clean it out while it was empty.'

'Your uncle's wife—I believe she died some years ago?'

Pip frowned a little at the question. 'Yes.'

'So *before* he moved here?'

'Yes. A year or so, I guess—before he left Queensland. Why?'

'Just checking out lines of enquiry.'

'So forensics think the skull is female?'

'I didn't say that.'

'Right,' she continued thoughtfully, 'female deceased. They haven't given you an estimated age of the bones?'

'They can't tell that out here. That would be a lab job,' he told her pointedly, but he seemed to be enjoying this unexpected banter they were engaged in.

'The vehicle's a Ford coupe utility 1934 model, if that helps narrow down a timeframe,' she said, holding his suspicious gaze with an innocent look of her own.

'Don't tell me you're a car expert now too?'

'Nope—but I have a contact who is, and he reckons that's the make and model.' She smiled as he gave an exasperated shake of his head. 'Who owned the property before Uncle Nev?' Pip asked, her gaze falling back on the two people huddled over something on the far side of the vehicle.

'I don't know. That was before my time out here.'

'I'm pretty sure Uncle Nev's only had the place five or six years, so since about 2015? That's where I'd start looking.'

'Okay, thanks, detective,' he added with a touch of sarcasm. 'I didn't catch your surname the other day.'

'Davenport,' she supplied.

'Phillipa Davenport,' he mused, turning her name over on his tongue pensively before his eyes narrowed. 'That's why I felt like I knew you from somewhere,' he said, his gaze locking onto her. 'You busted the big case on Lenny Knight.'

Pip glanced at him briefly before returning her gaze to the forensic officers. 'Yeah, that's me.'

He let out a low whistle. 'No wonder you're taking a break.' His voice switched from interest to something a little more serious. 'You probably should have mentioned this to me the other day.'

'Mentioned what?' She frowned as she took in the stern-police-officer face he was now presenting.

'The case you've been working on. You've just helped put away a high-ranking political figure, one with underworld connections.'

'So? It's over and done with.'

'You're not at all concerned about any fallout from that?' he asked doubtfully.

'It was months ago. Lenny Knight has more to worry about at the moment than a reporter who wrote a story on him.'

His silence made her fidget a little under his scrutiny, which annoyed her more than his questioning. She *wasn't* worried about her safety. 'I'm assuming you'll let me know when forensics are finished with the dam? I'd like to continue getting it cleaned up.'

'I'll let you know . . . but I wouldn't count on being able to do much for a few more days yet.'

She turned to walk back to the house. Just one mention of that name had ruined her whole mood. Each step she took felt heavier than the one before. 'Damn it,' she muttered. She'd thought she'd shaken off the uneasiness that had settled on her following the sentencing. Of course there'd been a time when she'd been worried Lenny Knight would want some kind of retribution, but when nothing happened, she'd managed to push the thought away—for the most part, at least.

When she reached the house, she shut the door behind her and locked it, looking around the room and making sure all the windows were shut before sinking down onto a chair and opening her laptop. She needed to focus on something else. Work. That's what had always got her through before.

'Hey, Mum,' Pip said when her mother's voice came on the phone.

'Darling! How are you?'

'I'm good. I, ah . . . just wanted to give you a heads-up.'

'About what?' Instantly her mother's voice was wary.

'Nothing bad—well, nothing that involves me. It seems Uncle Neville's dam has become a crime scene.'

'A *what*?'

'There was an old car in the bottom of the dam. It's been there a long time,' she added quickly. 'Anyway, they've found human remains inside it.'

'Oh my goodness,' her mother breathed on the end of the line.

'I just wanted to let you know in case there was anything on the news.'

'Does Neville know?'

'I've tried calling but he's probably out of reception. I think the police are trying to get in contact with him.'

'He's not in any trouble, is he?'

'No, not at all,' Pip said quickly. 'They think the bones are quite old. They've been there a long time.'

'What a terrible thing to find . . . are you all right?'

'I'm fine, Mum. It's just been a little bit noisy with all the people coming and going around the place.'

'Darling, I know this is something you feel you need to do . . . but you don't have to do it alone.'

Pip gave a weary sigh as she sank down on a chair. 'I kind of do—that's the whole point. I need to start doing things on my own. I'm sick of living like I'm the one in prison, locked behind doors all the time. I want my life back.'

'I know, sweetheart,' her mother said gently, 'but it takes time. It's not something that's going to disappear overnight.'

It had been almost a year since she'd been attacked. She'd eventually recovered from the physical injuries, but it was the other things that had been taken from her that night that had yet to completely heal.

Pip had taken her independence for granted. In all the years she'd lived alone and worked in the city, she had never felt unsafe, never felt afraid. And then, suddenly, she was. She was scared of everything.

The trial, and all the media surrounding it, almost six months after the attack hadn't helped her anxiety, but ultimately it had been the thing that had forced her to face her fears. There was no way she was going to let a piece of scum like Lenny Knight see how much damage he'd caused.

The fact she was still alive to testify seemed to annoy him no end, and she took great pleasure in seeing his usual smirk disappear the day she took the stand. Facing Lenny Knight in court and giving her testimony had been liberating. She'd noticed a turning point after that—there had been a moment of clarity and then closure of a sort. She had felt a little of her old self return, and with it some of her old fire. Yet still those remaining wisps of fear lurked in the back of her mind, like bothersome cobwebs that loitered in corners—almost invisible until the light caught them and revealed their annoying presence.

She could picture her mother's eyes crinkling slightly in sympathy, and she missed the warm hug she would have received if her mum were there in person before remembering this was the whole point of coming out here—so she could stand on her own two feet.

'How's the writing going?' her mum asked.

'Slowly, but I'm getting there.' She hoped it sounded convincing.

She listened to her mum fill her in on the rest of the family's news and her father's latest run-in with the neighbour with whom he'd had an ongoing feud for years. It was nice to have her mind taken off everything else for a short while. Once all the news had been exhausted, they said goodbye and Pip promised to keep her parents up to date about the mysterious bones in the dam.

Pip put the phone on the table and listened to the sound of the bush outside. In particular, the bird songs. She'd never really taken time to listen to birds before, but she was discovering she could differentiate the kinds of calls being made after watching them from the verandah over the past few days. She didn't know what most of them were, making up her own names for them, like twittery, nervous little blue and black birds. Loud, bossy grey and white ones. Annoying, squawky green ones, and some that she had never been able to actually see but could hear them singing from somewhere high in the trees. She did, however, rather like the magpies who chortled loudly first thing in the morning and hung around the verandah waiting for crumbs from her plate. Two of them had been getting very brave and were now happy to sit on the edge of a plant pot nearby.

Pip had always been wary of magpies—the only experience she'd had with them was being swooped by a particularly nasty one as a kid on her walk to and from school during spring. She hated that stupid magpie. But these were different. They watched her with curious, beady eyes, but they didn't seem interested in swooping. She suspected her uncle probably fed them now and again, since they were happy to hang around the verandah.

Who knew something as simple as taking time to listen to birds could prove so relaxing? Maybe once she returned to the city, she would make time to stop and listen to them more often. God, when she left this place, she'd practically be Sir David-bloody-Attenborough.

Six

While she cooked dinner, Pip switched on the TV in the kitchen.

It had been a hive of activity at the property all day, but she managed to stay away and mind her own business. After all, this had nothing to do with her. She was working on her book, not investigating a story about a possibly murdered woman. It could have just been a car accident, she knew. In fact, that was the most likely explanation. And yet, a pesky thought nagged at the back of her mind: it was an odd place for an accident. There was no major road nearby, so the driver must have travelled across rough paddocks. And surely, judging by the vintage of the vehicle, speed wouldn't be a factor. So, how *did* the car end up in the dam?

With a frustrated huff, she pushed the thought away. The police would work out what had happened—that was their job. Not hers.

When the next story came on, she turned the volume up as a shot of the now familiar front gates at the driveway came on the screen, showing footage of an assortment of police vehicles as they drove away.

'There was a brief press conference outside the property where the discovery was made, and reporter Glen Effrick was there to cover it,' she heard.

'Yesterday, a local contractor doing some work on the Midgiburra property stumbled upon what he described as a number of bones inside some scrap metal he'd been clearing from the bottom of a dam.'

The picture switched to a pre-recorded interview with Bob, dressed, surprisingly, in a set of new-looking work clothes, complete with a shirt that said 'Bob's Earthmoving Services—When you want to feel the earth move, we can move it for you'.

'Yeah, we got a terrible shock when we discovered it,' he said, leaning against his truck. 'There we were, just minding our own business, and suddenly there's a human skull rolling around on the floor of some old car. Don't mind telling you, it rattled me a bit.'

The camera switched back to the straight-faced reporter. 'Late today the forensic team finished collecting evidence on site where the body was discovered. Earlier we heard from Sergeant Erik Nielsen of Midgiburra police, who spoke about the crime-scene investigation,' the young reporter told the camera earnestly.

The shot went to a picture of Erik looking every inch the formidable police officer as he stood in front of a small group of people holding recording devices and cameras.

'Police were alerted to the discovery of bones in a dam that was being cleaned out by workers. Forensic officers were called in and have been collecting evidence from the scene and an investigation is currently underway headed by detectives from Coopers Creek. At this stage we have no further information to share.'

'Do you have any leads about who the bones belong to?' a reporter called from the back of the group, and Pip gave a small humourless guffaw as she thought back to the usual questions Erik had mentioned people would always ask.

'The investigation is still in its very early stages,' Erik answered, like the seasoned professional he was.

'As if he's going to give you a name even if he had one,' Pip scoffed.

'Do you have any suspects at this stage?' another reporter asked.

Pip shook her head slowly. Clearly this wasn't a hot story if they were sending out all the junior reporters to cover it. She itched to head down there with her notepad and ask a couple of questions herself, but of course she couldn't do that, and not just because she had her own deadlines hanging over her head. The news report ended and moved on to another story about the opening of a new koala sanctuary.

'Not my monkey, not my circus,' she said as she switched off the TV.

Pip looked out towards the clearing beyond the dam. She hadn't been back there since a couple days before things had got a little hectic, but the weird connection of that space with her dreams of the woman played through her mind again now as she headed out. This morning she took a new path and angled across the paddock at the front of the house and down a gentle slope, where she followed the fence line to see where it led.

It was peaceful walking under the canopy of gum trees high above. Speckled sunshine filtered down through the leaves, and birds flitted to and fro, going about their daily life among the smooth white branches that stretched overhead. Now and again Pip would hear rustling from the sides of the track and pray she wouldn't encounter a snake or one of those prehistoric-looking goannas—she was fairly sure under those circumstances she would consider running, but she really hoped she wouldn't have to. It was far too hot.

As she rounded a bend, the bush began to thin out and she heard the sound of an engine nearby. The bush had opened up into a wide strip of cleared paddock on both sides of the fence and she realised it must be some kind of fire break. Fires had been burning across the country thanks to the drought supplying the perfect conditions for bushfires to take hold. She hadn't heard of any around these parts yet, thankfully, but she cast a nervous glance at the thick bushland that surrounded her uncle's property. She was no expert, but this looked like a prime place for a bushfire to run riot.

The sound she'd heard earlier grew louder, and Pip looked over as an old red tractor appeared on the other side of the fence. The driver seemed just as surprised to find someone out here as she did, judging by his hesitant wave just before he rolled to a stop and turned off the engine.

'G'day,' the man said, eyeing her curiously. 'You must be Nev's niece.' He had a wide neck and sandy-coloured hair, and she placed him somewhere in his late sixties.

Pip felt her eyebrows raise in surprise. 'I'm Pip,' she said a little cautiously. 'How did you know?'

'The missus got a call from Nev the other day and said we might see someone over here—so we didn't shoot any intruders,' he added, then gave a wry twist of his lips that she thought must pass as a smile. 'Just kidding . . . we'd at least ask who you were before we did any shooting. I'm Pete.'

'Well, it's a good thing Uncle Nev called to let you know, then,' she said, smiling vaguely and now kind of regretting her decision to walk so far away from the house.

'Bit of excitement going on over at your place, I hear,' he said in the kind of laidback drawl that Pip associated with a lot of country-born-and-bred people. She enjoyed the deliberate downplaying of things and the tendency not to panic or overreact, as well as their direct, no-nonsense way of making conversation.

'Yes. Not what I was expecting when I decided to do something useful around the place.'

'I bet old Nev was thrilled with the news.'

She'd been dreading that conversation and hadn't been able to contact her uncle before the police had; they had already filled him in on everything by the time he'd called her back.

'I'm so sorry about all this, Uncle Nev,' she'd said. 'I just thought getting the dam cleaned out might be a good idea. I should have asked you first.'

'Well, we'd have never known what was down there if you hadn't. So, I guess it's a good thing—only wish I'd been home while it was all happening so you weren't having to deal with it alone.'

'No, don't feel bad. It's fine. There's really nothing anyone can do.'

And there wasn't. Until the police had some kind of idea what they were dealing with, everything was up in the air.

'They wanted to know if I recognised the vehicle,' Nev had said. 'But I've never seen it before. Had no idea it was even in there. Who knew? Kind of wish I had—I think I'd like to have had it for a project, rebuild it and get it going again . . . but of course, without the body and everything . . . I guess that would have thrown a spanner in the works a bit.'

'It's certainly a bit of a mystery.'

Pip had promised to keep in touch if she heard any more news, but so far she'd heard nothing.

'He took it better than I thought he would,' Pip replied now to Pete.

'Me missus, Anne, she's been on about getting you over for a cuppa. Why don't you pop round today?' Pete said, pushing his hat further back on his head as he waited for her reply.

'Sure. That would be great,' she smiled, trying not to think about the fact she should be writing. The lure of conversation and a legitimate excuse to get out of the house proved too strong.

'Good-o. Well, we'll see you in a bit, then.'

'Ah, what time?' Pip asked as he reached to turn on the tractor once more.

'Smoko's usually about ten,' he said.

'Okay. I'll see you then.'

The tractor drowned out any further conversation, so she simply waved and turned around to head back to the house.

Inside, she sent her computer a grimace in apology as she walked past to get changed and tidy up after breakfast. She would sit down and write this afternoon—all afternoon.

Seven

Pip pulled up in front of a two-storey brick house at the end of a long driveway. She found the idea of driving to her next-door neighbour's house a novelty; where she came from, neighbours were usually only a few feet away. Not that she'd really met any of hers. She always nodded to the couple in the next-door apartment if they happened to bump into each other in the underground carpark, and she occasionally recognised the tall, Mr Bean-like man in the supermarket from her apartment block, but she hadn't ever introduced herself, nor did she know their names.

As she got out of the car she heard yapping coming from inside, and a small bundle of white fluffy fur exploded from the front door as it opened and a woman in a floral sundress stepped out.

'Winston! Come here,' the woman called, but the white fluff ball continued to run towards Pip, jumping up on her

A Stone's Throw Away

leg as it yapped and wagged its tail in a frenzy of excitement. 'Sorry, love,' the woman called out as she hurried down the path towards her. 'Winston, get down!'

'It's okay,' Pip called out, and dragged the animal, still holding onto her jeans-clad leg, as she walked towards the woman.

'You must be Pip. Nice to meet you. I'm Anne,' she said, hurriedly tucking her short grey hair behind her ear before bending down to gather the small dog into her arms. 'Pete said he bumped into you this morning. Come inside, I just put the jug on.'

'I hope I'm not interrupting anything,' Pip said as they walked inside. On the walls of the hallway and then through to the lounge room were framed photos of children. Some were clearly Anne and Pete's children, dressed in late seventies attire, with toothless grins, while others seemed a lot more recent—perhaps grandchildren.

'Not at all. I've been meaning to drop in and say hello, but then everything happened and I didn't want to just show up on your doorstep while all the police were over there. How terrible. Such a shock.'

Pip took a seat at the table as Anne went across to a high kitchen bench and brought over a plate of biscuits, setting them down on the table.

'Yes. Not something you expect,' Pip said, only imagining how much gossip would be circulating around the small town. 'How long have you and Pete been here?'

'This was Pete's family farm, so he's been here all his life, and his parents inherited it from his grandfather before that.'

'So a long time,' Pip nodded. It always amazed her when she heard of people who'd lived in the same house for so long. Her parents had bought a number of different houses as she'd grown up. With each promotion or job change they'd moved to be closer to her father's work. She herself had moved several times over the past few years until she'd bought her apartment, but still, she'd never really had an attachment with any one particular house growing up.

'Yes. I'm not considered a local, though,' Anne laughed, then paused to ask how Pip had her coffee before continuing, 'I've only been here about thirty years or so.'

Pip smiled. She'd heard Uncle Nev say it was almost country law: to be considered a local, you had to have at least several generations behind you.

'Anne, do you know who owned Uncle Nev's place before he bought it?'

Anne nodded as she carried the coffees over, placing a cup in front of Pip before taking a seat across from her. 'It was the Bigsby place.'

'Old Bert lived there for years,' Pete said, walking in from the rear of the house. He wiped his hands on a tea towel before tossing it on the bench.

'Your tea's there,' Anne informed him and he picked up a cup before joining them at the table.

Pete's face had the weathered look of a man who had worked long hours outside for most of his life—the creases around his eyes were deep, and his hand that held the cup looked tough and calloused with dirt beneath his fingernails.

'What was Bert like?' Pip asked, popping the last bit of her biscuit in her mouth. Anne certainly could bake.

'Cranky old bastard,' Pete said before being reprimanded lightly by his wife.

'He just had a very hard life,' Anne said. 'I used to cook for him towards the end—take him over some meals, that kind of thing. He was a nice enough old fella, just lonely.'

'He was a bit of an odd one,' Pete said, reaching for a biscuit.

'Odd? How?' Pip asked, following Pete's lead and taking another herself.

'The war messed him up,' Pete said. 'I remember my dad telling me stories about him. Old Bert had been a POW before he came home, and he was never the same.'

Instantly Pip felt something shift inside her. She had a soft spot for war veterans. It had all started when, as a young journo, she had been assigned to interview a group of former World War Two prisoners of war in the lead-up to Anzac Day. The stories they'd told were horrific, and it was clear that the effect their time in the POW camp had on their lives afterwards had been devastating. They'd been old men when she'd interviewed them back then, but she suspected their experiences had helped to age them even more.

She'd gone on to write a number of stories that featured World War Two, in particular the battles and campaigns fought in the Pacific theatre due to its close proximity to Australia. Previous wars Australia had been involved in had always been fought in far-off places most Australians had never even heard of, but by the latter half of World War Two, the fight had come alarmingly close to home—far closer than many people realised.

But the story that still haunted her to this day was that of a woman who as a child had been evacuated with her mother from Rabaul to Sydney in 1942, just weeks before the Japanese invasion.

The evacuated women and children left behind fathers, husbands and brothers who were never heard from again. Pip had gone to New Guinea to try to find some answers for the heartbroken families, and what she unearthed was horrifying. The woman's family had been captured on their plantation by the Japanese army. They, along with other neighbouring Australian families including women and children, and many Papuan locals, were executed by the Japanese, accused of spying. Among them, a boy of just eleven.

'The locals around here call him Butcher Bigsby,' Pete added, cutting into her thoughts.

'Did he own a butcher shop?' Pip asked, pushing away her memories as she sipped her coffee.

'Nah. That's how they found the bloke he murdered.'

Pip choked on her coffee, coughing uncontrollably before gratefully accepting the handful of tissues Anne passed across to her. 'Murdered?'

'He was cleared of that,' Anne cut in briskly. 'It was a such a shame about everything that happened,' Anne said, slowly shaking her head.

'What happened?' Pip asked.

'His wife left him not long after he came back from the war,' Anne began.

'Or tried to leave him . . . she didn't get very far,' Pete added with a knowing look at his wife.

Pip's glance switched between them.

'The body in the dam,' Pete said, taking another biscuit. 'That'll be Molly Bigsby.'

Pip felt the biscuit she just swallowed get stuck in her throat.

'It may not be,' Anne admonished before sending Pip a concerned look. 'The story went that she ran away. Bert never heard from her again.'

'That's part of the story,' Pete scoffed. 'Tell her the rest.'

Pip looked at Anne expectantly, resisting the urge to yell, *Someone tell me already!*

'The fella Molly was having a fling with,' Pete jumped in, clearly unable to handle the suspense as well, 'was found murdered out on Clay Target Road—just up the way a bit. Found him stabbed to death in his car. There was a witness that saw Molly and Vernon Clements together in his car, and Bert's car parked nearby earlier in the night. When the police got there they didn't find any sign of her, or Bert and his car, but they did find blood all over the passenger side of Vernon's vehicle that they reckon belonged to Molly.'

'So . . .' Pip said slowly, trying to piece together the story, 'did they charge Bert with the murder?'

'Nup,' Pete said, sitting back in his chair. 'Bert had an alibi for the night. He was down in some Melbourne returned-vets psych ward.'

'It wasn't a psych ward—it was a hospital. He'd been trying to save his marriage. Molly had been begging him to get some help, and when he realised she might leave him, he booked himself into that place in Melbourne,' Anne said, looking a little teary. 'He once said it was the best thing he'd ever done and the worst.'

'What did he mean by that?'

'Apparently, whatever happened down there turned things around for him—he said he felt like it had helped but that in the end it hadn't mattered because Molly still packed up and left him.'

'But you think that's Molly in the dam?' Pip asked Pete.

Pete shrugged his shoulders. 'Who else would it be? The woman goes missing—no one ever hears from her again . . . I'm no Sherlock Holmes, but it seems a pretty logical conclusion to me.'

'You think Bert killed her and dumped her body?'

'Absolutely not,' Anne said adamantly.

'Anne's always been a sucker for a sob story—too kind a heart she has,' Pete said with a weary yet tolerant smile.

'Bert would never have hurt his wife. He still loved her after all that time. I would have known if he were a murderer. Your father never believed the gossip either,' Anne said pointedly to her husband.

'Yeah, but my old man had a soft spot for Bert. And anyone who could stand up to a Maguire in this town deserves a bit of respect.'

'What do you mean?'

'There wasn't much love lost between Bert and the Maguires when he got back to town after his time in the POW camp. They cashed in on land during and after the war, buying up places when husbands and sons were killed and families couldn't keep up mortgages. Didn't sit well with a lot of people, especially Bert. They hounded him to buy that old place of his, but he wouldn't budge.'

'I had noticed the Maguire name around town,' Pip mused.

'You can hardly miss it,' Pete grunted.

'Well, Midgiburra is somewhat famous because of them,' Anne chimed in, but when Pip blinked at her blankly, her smile slipped a little. 'Edward Maguire,' she prompted pointedly. 'The politician. You didn't learn about him in school?' she asked with a confused frown.

'Ah, no, can't say I did.'

She saw Anne swap an exasperated glance with her husband across the table before turning her attention back to Pip. 'Edward Maguire was born and raised right here in Midgiburra and went on to become the Victorian premier. He only missed out by a whisker on becoming the prime minister before he died.'

It was clear locals took this claim to fame very seriously indeed.

'That was a long time ago. There's not as many Maguires as there used to be. Over the years, kids packed up and left and the oldies died off. The old animosity around town isn't there like it was back then.'

'Do you think Molly's death could be linked to someone else? Maybe this Maguire thing?'

'Nah, I doubt it,' Pete said. 'I don't think things ever got that heated. Nah, this was something else. His wife was having an affair—it was common knowledge,' he said, leaning back in his chair.

'You think he killed her,' Pip said, more a statement than a question.

'Happened before my time, but I believe that a jealous man is capable of pretty much anything. And Bert was also more than a little unstable. Who knows?'

'You lived next door to him for all those years . . . If you thought he was a murderer, how did you trust him?'

Pete scratched his nose and folded his arms across his barrel-like chest. 'He kept to himself, never caused a problem—at least not with us. There was the odd time he chased kids away from his place with a rifle, but that was only because they liked to hang around and throw rocks at his roof and whatnot back in the day. I mean, it's not like he was a serial killer—it was a crime of passion,' he said matter-of-factly, as though it made complete sense.

'Anyway, I still don't think it's Molly,' Anne said, getting up. 'Anyone else like another coffee?' she asked, but both Pip and Pete shook their heads as Anne crossed to the kitchen.

'Well, I think I'd sleep better if it is, otherwise there's a real murderer out there somewhere,' Pete added.

As opposed to a murderer who had a justifiable reason for killing his wife and her lover, Pip thought sarcastically.

'I guess if it does turn out to be her, there won't be any answers, seeing as everyone involved is gone,' Pip mused.

'Oh no,' Anne said, sounding surprised, as she came back to take her seat. 'Bert's still alive. He's in a nursing home.'

What the hell? Suddenly Pip's interest in the whole conversation perked up. 'He's still *alive?*'

'He's a tough old bastard,' Pete said with a touch of reluctant admiration. 'He had a stroke a few years back and had to be put in full-time care.'

'That's when your uncle bought the place,' Anne said, then gave a sad smile. 'Poor old Bert—he hasn't been able to speak a word since his stroke. I try to visit him now and again, probably not as much as I should, though . . . He's got no one else.'

Pip's mind started to spin as the bits and pieces of information she'd just heard began to slide into place and she started to write the story. *No!* she told herself firmly. This wasn't her story. She wasn't on assignment. She had a book to write. She was not going to get mixed up in some tragic—yet really, *really* interesting—love-triangle tale. She really wasn't.

Eight

Pip walked into the bakery and breathed in the delicious aroma of freshly baked pies and pastry and could almost *feel* the calories moving to her thighs. Today's trip had been a reward for finally making some progress with her writing.

Her gaze ran over the glass display cabinet as she waited for the two women at the counter to finish talking, and her ears pricked up at the mention of Rosevale.

'Had to be him. I always knew he was a weird old bugger,' the customer was saying as she packed the white paper bag with her purchases into her carry bag.

'Fancy the nerve of him—dumping her right there on his property. All this time telling people she'd run off and really she'd been in that dam,' the woman serving said with a disgusted tsk.

'I wonder if they'll be able to charge him?'

'I wouldn't think so—I heard he's practically a vegetable. He'd have to be nearly a hundred if he was a day. Nah, he'll get away with it, the old bastard.'

'They need to pull the plug on his life support,' the customer said, shaking her head as she turned away from the counter.

Pip had been standing there quietly as the two women talked, taking in their words and their reactions. It was clear people had very strong opinions of this man, and the level of animosity seemed to be growing steadily about town as news of the discovered bones spread.

The customer gave her a brief glance before opening the door and heading outside and Pip smiled at the woman behind the counter.

'What can I get you?'

'I'll have a vanilla slice, thanks,' she said and watched the woman bustle about with a pair of tongs as she selected a large square pastry with white icing and slid it into a white paper bag.

'I'm sorry to have overheard you just now, but were you and the other lady just talking about Bert Bigsby?'

'Butcher Bigsby,' the woman corrected stiffly. 'Yeah. Killed his wife and her lover years ago. They've just found her in the bottom of a dam on his property.'

Pip winced a little at the directness of the woman's stare. 'What was he like? Bert . . . before he ended up in the nursing home?'

'I don't know . . . bit of a loner. Always wore a hat and a green trench coat—left over from his army days. Never spoke much. Only came into town when he needed supplies till he couldn't do it for himself anymore. You new around here?' the woman asked, leaning one arm back on the bench behind the counter, waiting as Pip tapped her card.

'I'm just here visiting.'

She could feel the unasked question hanging in the air as to whom she might be visiting, but Pip sent the woman a bright smile as her payment was accepted and reached for her purchase. The last thing she wanted to do was draw attention to herself by announcing where she was staying.

As she stepped outside into bright daylight, she slipped her sunglasses from her head back down onto her face and looked up and down the wide main street. There wasn't much traffic to speak of in Midgiburra. The highway didn't go through this way and it wasn't in a direct path to anywhere bigger, so it was a fairly peaceful town. Cars were parked either side of the street, which made the place look busy, but there weren't many people walking around. Admittedly, it was too bloody hot to hang around outside, and Pip assumed most people would do their catching up with friends and neighbours inside one of the air-conditioned shops.

She'd done her grocery shopping, and the back of her car was loaded up; it looked like she was planning to feed a family of ten. Sitting in the driver's seat, she took out her vanilla slice and bit into it, savouring the gooey goodness of the custard filling. The pastry wasn't too thick and the top was perfectly melt-in-your-mouth flaky. God, she loved a good vanilla slice. It might be worth a trip into town every so often to get one . . .

As she sat and finished her slice, she caught sight of a dark sedan pulling into the police station driveway and saw a man in a white business shirt and navy trousers climb out before reaching for his suit jacket from the back seat and shrugging it on. The white of his shirt was stark against his dark skin, and he had detective written all over him. She figured he must be here for the investigation and she couldn't help but watch him closely.

Things had been fairly quiet on the dam front, with just the occasional police car on site. Pip knew that most of the forensic material had been already collected and taken away for testing, but there was still a team poking about in search of anything else interesting that might relate to the case.

Experience told her the police should have the results back on the bone dating by now, and it wouldn't be difficult to sex the bones if they'd recovered a significant amount of the skeletal remains—which she was assuming they would have since it was contained inside a vehicle underwater and had little chance to have been disturbed by animals as a body left in the bush would have. There was, however, frustratingly little information coming from the police in the media to date, and despite her best attempts to completely wipe it from her mind, she found herself searching for updates now and again when she took a break from the writing that was now thankfully forthcoming.

She had been going through the boxes of information bought along from her office relating to the Knight case. Some of it she'd found interesting—a lot of it only bought back bad memories, but it did serve to refuel her anger at the man she'd finally been able to expose as the greedy, corrupt person he really was.

It was scary just how good he'd been at hiding his real self from the majority of the world. On the outside he seemed like the perfect family man—the charismatic member of a political party whose reputation was that of a champion for the underdog and all-round good guy—when the truth was he'd been doing deals behind his party's back and taking money for favours in securing government contracts for underground criminal syndicates. He was also involved in a run of murders—contract-style hits on prominent union members—as well as bribing a number of government officials.

Lenny Knight's sentencing had been a long time coming. It had taken Pip years to unravel his paperwork trail and find solid evidence to tie him to the crimes he'd been instrumental in planning, but she'd done it. It hadn't come without a price, though, and she had years of frustration and hitting brick walls to prove it.

This man in his navy suit couldn't have looked more out of place in this town if he'd been eight foot tall and dressed like a green alien. This was predominantly an Anglo farming community where the general uniform was flannelette and denim. She watched as he disappeared inside the old brick building. Opening her door, she shook off the crumbs from her T-shirt before latching her seatbelt and starting the engine. Whatever was going on in there, it was nothing to do with her. She had bigger fish to fry.

Pip was on her way back from her morning walk when she decided to circle up around the dam. At this time of the day, everything was quiet—except for the birds. They were never quiet. The magpies and their cheerful little chortles, and the kookaburras with their uproarious laughter; the rest she couldn't identify, but they could be extremely noisy when they were all squabbling over whatever the hell birds argued about.

The dried-up dam was still marked out in a grid pattern where the forensics team had conducted a search, and there was an empty space where the old rusted-out car had once sat in its muddy grave.

'G'day,' a voice called out, and Pip yelped, taking a quick step backwards, her heart pounding in her chest. 'Sorry. I didn't mean to startle you.'

Pip located the owner and realised it was the man she'd seen walking into the police station the day before. He was standing a short distance away, hidden perhaps by the trees as she'd walked up. She looked around for a car but didn't see one nearby.

'I'm Detective Jarrett,' he said as he made his way across and stopped a short distance away from her. 'Chris Jarrett,' he said in a low, calm tone, offering a friendly smile. 'Are you okay?'

'You just surprised me. I didn't see you.'

'I parked the car out on the road and walked in,' he informed her, flipping through the notepad in his hand. 'Are you Ms Davenport?'

'Yes.'

'I see that you gave a statement to the officers on the scene?'

'There wasn't much to tell. Have they dated the bones yet?' she asked.

'We're still waiting on an official report,' he hedged.

'But you have a rough idea of how old they were?' she prompted.

'I was told you might show an interest in the case,' Detective Jarrett said, shutting his notebook as he eyed her thoughtfully. 'Quite the stroke of luck, an investigative journalist being on hand as a mystery unfolds.'

'Trust me, this is a distraction I *don't* need right now,' she told him with a note of self-deprecating humour.

'You were spot on about the make and model of the vehicle,' he told her.

She bit back a smug grin at the news. 'Were you able to trace it?'

'We've yet to confirm but we believe the car belonged to Herbert Bigsby. The previous owner of this property. There was a report of it missing at the same time he reported his wife missing in nineteen forty-six.'

'And the bones?'

'As I said, we're still waiting for an official report on those.'

Detective Jarrett was a hard one to read. Detectives with Aboriginal heritage weren't a large demographic she'd encountered, especially here. On the outside he seemed easygoing enough, but he had a shrewdness about him that told Pip he wouldn't miss much.

His dark hair, cut in a short, almost military style, matched the suit and tie, but the neatly trimmed stubble beard that went across his jawline and top lip gave him a slightly dangerous look. Although, instead of taking away from the professional clean-cut suit, it only seemed to enhance it. He seemed to take his personal appearance and his job extremely seriously, but they were at odds with his laidback personality and disarming grin.

'If the bones come back as Molly Bigsby, are you going to open a new case?'

'For someone who claims not to have any interest in it, you seem pretty interested,' the detective said almost lazily.

'I'm curious, not interested.' Something about the way he held her gaze, probing hers gently, made her momentarily forget what she was about to say. She straightened her shoulders a little and swallowed nervously. He really was good looking.

'Well, it's an old case,' he said eventually. 'There's only one individual still alive who was of any interest to the police at the time—and he had an alibi,' he said, leaning his back against a nearby tree.

She followed the movement, noticing his solid build beneath the suit, and moved on quickly. 'Bert Bigsby,' she said, nodding. 'Maybe you should release a statement saying that, to put an end to all the gossip going about in town.'

'Most people around here seem to have their minds made up about the whole thing,' he agreed. 'I don't think a statement will change that.'

'No, but it might finally, officially, clear a man of any wrongdoing.'

'From what I hear it won't make any difference—the old guy can't talk and is pretty much on his last legs, and there's no known relatives,' he said simply. 'But we're still investigating it until we can work out the most logical way it all played out.'

'So you'd be basing it on circumstantial evidence, then?'

'That's pretty much all we have to go on after all this time.'

'Any idea which way you think it will pan out?'

'Are you on the record with this?' he asked, cocking an eyebrow. She made the mistake of holding his sleepy-eyed look, his brown eyes seemingly tugging her towards him, and felt a shot of red hot desire slice through her unexpectedly. What was wrong with her? It was like her libido was suddenly homing in on every eligible male within a hundred kilometre radius.

'Of course not,' she said briskly. 'I'm just curious.'

'Well, between you and me,' he said thoughtfully, 'it's a pretty interesting case. You've got an eyewitness placing the husband's vehicle at the scene of a murder that happened on a road leading to this property only a few kilometres away, but the husband had an alibi, which after reviewing the initial statement taken, actually has a few gaps in it. Then there's the husband's mental state to take into account—after the war, there were statements given from locals who had run-ins with him when he came back. And of course, the infamous affair between his wife and Vernon Clements and that man's subsequent murder. And now the remains of a woman found on Herbert Bigsby's property in his vehicle.'

'You said his alibi had holes?' she prodded, searching his dark gaze warily. She knew he probably wouldn't elaborate, but it was worth a try.

His eyes lowered slightly, the action setting off another weird tsunami inside her. 'Oh, for goodness sake,' she muttered, then froze, realising she'd said it out loud.

'Sorry?'

'Nothing,' she dismissed abruptly. 'The gaps in the alibi?' she prodded, now impatient as she fought off the heat she felt rising up her neck.

'I can't go into too much detail at the moment, but there's a possibility the husband may have had time to get back here at the time of the murder. We have to follow up a few details—made more difficult than usual due to it being over eighty years ago when roads and travel times were a lot different,' he added.

'It sounds to me like you're leaning towards the general consensus in town that suggests Bert was involved in his wife's murder?' She wasn't sure why she was feeling suddenly defensive on Bert's behalf. She'd started out playing devil's advocate, but after talking with Pete and Anne the other day, suddenly Bert had become a person—not just a name.

'I didn't say that,' he said calmly, tilting his head a fraction as he took in her defensive stance. 'But clearly you don't agree?'

She wasn't even *supposed* to have an opinion—she'd just accidentally got caught up in the whole story. 'I was just—'

'Curious,' he supplied for her, with a small grin.

'Exactly.'

'Well, I'll admit I've got a case load that's getting out of control back on my desk in Coopers Creek, so an almost eighty-year-old cold case isn't something I really have a great deal of time to prioritise.'

'That's comforting,' she muttered, her hands going to her hips as she eyed him with a frown.

'However,' he went on pointedly, and with maybe even a little amusement behind his dark eyes, 'I will be going over all the evidence we've located on scene and considering all possible leads.'

'Including linking the unsolved murder of Vernon Clements?' she asked.

'Now you sound like a journalist,' he nodded knowingly.

Her eyes narrowed a little as she held his gaze determinedly, refusing to let him off the hook by avoiding her question. There was something incredibly sexy about this exchange they'd become embroiled in. As annoyed as she was by his lurking amusement beneath some of his answers, she also found it a little refreshing.

Her exchanges with Erik had had that teasing kind of feel at times too, but looking back, there was always the realisation that she was talking to a cop, first and foremost.

She didn't get that with the detective.

'Yes, I'll be also looking into the unsolved murder of Vernon Clements,' he said and gave an amused groan. 'I wasn't expecting to have to handle the media out here this morning.'

'You're not. I'm simply . . .' She paused as he waited for her usual comment and replaced it with a slightly haughty, 'looking out for the public's interest. I think locals have waited too long to get to the bottom of all this. Now it's the police department's opportunity to show taxpayers how clever you all are and solve it. Once and for all.'

'I can see why grown men shake in their boots when you ask for a one-on-one interview,' he said, pushing away from the tree.

'Only if they have something to hide, detective,' she said, turning away from him to retrace her steps back home.

She heard his soft chuckle as she left and wondered at the small bubble of interest inside her at the deep timbre of his voice. What was happening to her? She'd been in the back of beyond a handful of days and she'd had more chance encounters with men here than she'd had in the city in the better part of the past decade.

Maybe she should try looking up a few of her possible contenders for a date when she got back to the city—the ones she'd previously knocked back because she was too focused on her career to bother shaving her legs and getting dressed up to go out with.

'You're not getting any younger,' she heard her mother's voice echoing.

Whenever she was stupid enough to dwell too long on things like her age, she'd usually feel the beginnings of heart palpations and do what every sensible, well-adjusted person did—completely erase the thought from her mind and bury her head back in the sand. But perhaps it *was* time to consider her mother's advice, that she should think about making time in her schedule to find someone she might consider worthwhile enough to try having a relationship with.

She flinched slightly at the word relationship. It sounded so . . . permanent. Actually, it wasn't even the permanent thing she had an issue with—it was more the whole rearranging-her-entire-life-to-fit-someone-else-into-it thing.

She liked not having anyone to answer to. It took an incredible amount of discipline not to let out a snort or roll her eyes when her friends talked about 'when my husband finds out how much I spent on that pair of shoes', or before they could commit to a catch-up, they'd 'just have to check with the hubby that they didn't have plans for that day first'.

Seriously? If that was what marriage ultimately came to—checking in to get permission to do something for yourself or feeling guilty about buying a pair of bloody shoes—then they could keep all the other *good* stuff they raved about. The babies and the company and the partnership, oh, and the soul-mate thing . . .

How ridiculous. With a gazillion people on the planet, to believe you have one person you were destined to be with forever seemed a little limiting. Not to mention how convenient it was that most people claimed to have found them without having to leave *the state* to bump into them. If you only had *one* soul mate, how come they were always so close by? You rarely heard of anyone travelling to Kenya to find them, or Greenland—oh no, they bumped into their soul mate at a hen's night in a pub in Surry Hills.

Pip sighed as she reached the house. She didn't know the exact moment she'd became so jaded about love. It seemed to have happened gradually with each story she uncovered. There wasn't a lot of romance attached to dealing with corruption and the underbelly of society. It wasn't that she didn't believe in love—she'd just never experienced the Hollywood version of it, and she doubted it was as magical as filmmakers wanted everyone to believe it was.

The detective's smile popped back into her mind and she instantly found herself comparing it with Erik's. It was like comparing chalk and cheese—the laid-back, sleepy-eyed gaze and lingering amusement that seemed to hover just under the surface in contrast with Erik's open, confident frankness. Two men so very different and yet both had managed to stir something inside her.

Pip gave a frustrated huff as she reached a decision. As soon as she got back from this writing retreat she would find someone suitable and arrange a date. Surely after spending a couple of hours in painful politeness she would return to her senses and remember why men were a distraction she could do without and go back to living for her work.

Nine

A few days later, Pip's forced isolation came to an end when she realised she was running out of toilet paper and other vital supplies, and she headed back into town. Heaven forbid if toilet paper ever went out of stock—what would the world come to?

As the sliding door of the supermarket opened, the cold air from inside hit her in the face, momentarily catching her off guard. The small blissful sound that escaped made her pause to savour the sensation. She really needed to work on Uncle Nev about installing an air conditioner at the house.

As she perused the shelves, she overheard a number of conversations. At the end of the aisle a pair of older women were chatting about an upcoming flower show they were entering, and Pip gave a small smile as she stepped around them, only to have to squeeze past another two women blocking the aisle, this pair in their early thirties with children in their trolleys, discussing something juicy that had happened during playgroup last week.

Pip had never considered grocery shopping as a social event before. It was a chore—something you ran in to do on your way home from work, getting in and out as quickly as possible. Apparently that wasn't the case here. In fact, no one appeared in any kind of hurry. Even the customers not talking to anyone were contentedly picking up items and strolling along, seemingly with no timetable or other place they needed to be.

Pushing her fuller-than-anticipated trolley to the checkout, she stood quietly behind the customer currently being served and tried not to listen to the conversation going on, which was difficult seeing as there was no way she couldn't. She got a lot from the exchange, though—it was amazing what you could learn about a complete stranger.

For instance, she knew that Beryl was the customer's name and that the cashier was married to Phil, who was the local electrician. Beryl was having trouble with a power point and the cashier was going to call her husband to drop around later today and take a look at it. At this, Pip felt her mouth drop open.

To get an electrician to come and install a security camera had taken about an hour of phone calls, and then she'd had to wait all day for him, only to have him not show up. In Midgiburra, all you had to do was complain about an issue to the local checkout operator and she'd organise the electrician with one phone call home.

'I used to wear that look,' a woman behind Pip said in lazy amusement.

Pip turned, feeling caught out, but managed a relieved smile when the woman only laughed.

'I can spot a city slicker from a mile off—purely because that used to be me when I first moved here. I'm Rebecca Adams,' she said, introducing herself.

'Pip,' she said, managing to mask her surprise at the unexpected exchange, 'Davenport.'

'Have you just moved here?'

'Ah, no. Not really. I'm just housesitting at my uncle's while he's away.'

'Oh, well that explains it, then.'

'Sorry?'

'The sideswiped look. It takes a bit of getting used to—small-town life.'

'Oh. Yes, it seems to.'

'Where are you from?'

'Sydney,' Pip said, finally able to start unloading her trolley as room appeared on the conveyor belt.

'Me too—a long time ago.'

Pip eyed the woman. She didn't look old enough to be able to say anything was 'a long time ago', but on closer inspection she wasn't as young as Pip had first assumed, placing her in her thirties. Her blonde hair was pulled back in a neat ponytail that curled at the end, and she wore a brown and turquoise knee-length dress with short tan boots.

'I grew up on the northern beaches, but my family moved to Brisbane when I started high school,' she explained.

'How did you end up here?'

'Love,' she sighed with a wistful shrug.

Oh no. One of them, Pip thought sadly. Just when she thought she'd met someone likeminded out here.

'I met my husband out on a stag night in Brisbane in a bar I was working at.'

Of course she did. Soul mates.

'We moved to Victoria and I started uni, then realised he was a tosser after he cheated on me barely six months into the marriage, by which time I'd decided I liked the idea of teaching more than I liked being married to a jerk. So, I divorced him and finished my degree, then eventually got transferred out here, where I've been for the last eight years.'

Maybe not so much one of them after all.

'So what do you do with yourself all day out here, Pip? I'd imagine Midgiburra is a lot quieter than what you're used to.'

'I'm actually working while I'm here . . . well, supposed to be,' she added.

'Oh? What kind of work do you do?'

'I'm a journalist . . . but I'm writing a book at the moment.'

Rebecca's eyes lit up. 'A journalist! How exciting.'

'Sometimes,' Pip agreed, 'but usually it's just a lot of waiting around and making phone calls,' she said honestly.

'The kids would love to meet you,' Rebecca said, and Pip could see the woman's mind racing as she clapped her hands together. 'Oh my God, this is amazing timing. I teach high school, and at the moment the kids are doing a term on communication. Would you maybe consider coming in and giving them a talk about journalism?'

Pip blinked uncertainly.

'I'm sorry. I know, I'm always rushing into stuff—this was probably the last thing you thought you'd be confronted with when you ducked into the store to buy groceries today.'

Pip managed a nervous laugh. This woman was like a small cyclone. 'Kind of.'

'Have you got time for a quick cuppa at the cafe next door? I'd really love to go over what I'm doing in class and give you a better idea of how a visit from you would help these kids enormously.'

'Well, I do have a bit of work to get back to,' Pip started, but she felt instantly bad when she saw the other woman's face fall slightly. 'But I guess I could spare a few minutes to have a coffee.' It wasn't like the book was actually flowing out of her right now, anyway.

Ten

The cafe was squeezed between the supermarket and the stock agent's office and looked deceptively small until Pip walked inside and realised it opened up into a spacious courtyard at the back. Tables with umbrellas provided a shady retreat, and the cobblestoned floor and rock wall that surrounded the area added an old-world charm. Baskets of brightly coloured flowers hung from the wall, and a small water fountain with a half-naked woman tipping an urn of water trickled merrily in the corner.

'I didn't even know this place was here,' Pip said, looking around wide-eyed.

'It's a hidden gem, mostly known only to locals,' Rebecca grinned.

They'd ordered at the counter on the way in from a young girl with jet black hair and a nose piercing. Pip had noted the way the girl's polite but cool expression lit up the moment she spotted Rebecca. 'Hi, miss. Do you want your usual?'

'I take it the waitress was a former student of yours?' Pip asked now as they settled into their seats.

'Yeah. She was a bit of a handful at school but one of our success stories.'

'How so?'

'She was missing a lot of school, making some bad choices,' Rebecca said, her eyes going back towards the counter inside. 'We managed to get her a traineeship here in hospitality and it's turned her life around. She wanted to leave town and head to the city—most kids from out here do, there's limited job opportunities in town—but so many drop out of school and head off without any kind of skills. We convinced Kaycee to finish school with a traineeship so she'd have something to put on her résumé when she moved away. At least this way she'll have a better chance of finding a job with some experience behind her. She's doing really well.'

The quiet pride on the young girl's face when she delivered their coffee and Rebecca commented on how great it looked made Pip smile.

'You obviously love your job,' she commented as she took a sip of the coffee.

'I really do,' Rebecca smiled across at her. 'Of course, there's some days they like to test you, but I think all they're really looking for is some direction and maybe a little bit of discipline. I don't put up with any crap in my classes and I make that clear from day one. Once they realise you're serious and you won't take disrespect, things settle down. It works both ways, though—once I show them that I also respect them, they get it.'

'I think schools everywhere could use a lot more teachers like you.'

'Teaching's got to be something you're passionate about. I mean, let's face it—if you're not teaching because you love it, it shows and kids pick up on it. If you present the subject with enthusiasm and make it fun and exciting, that's way more interesting than someone standing at the front of the class reading from a textbook with zero care factor.' She shrugged. 'It's not rocket science.'

Pip smile. 'I can't argue there.'

'I have to make a confession,' Rebecca said, lowering her eyes briefly and fiddling with her paper napkin. 'While you were packing your car, I googled you.'

Pip couldn't help the surprised chuckle that escaped following the woman's admission. She honestly looked contrite.

'You're *Phillipa* Davenport,' Rebecca announced, finally looking up, almost warily.

'Yep.'

'I swear, I had no idea that's who you were when I sideswiped you with that invitation. I just thought maybe you worked for a regional newspaper or something . . . not the *Daily* freakin' *Metro*.'

'Well, it's really just a *bigger* regional newspaper,' Pip said, trying to downplay the woman's astonishment.

'I feel like an idiot. You're probably used to lecturing at universities and appearing at literary festivals . . . oh my God,' she gasped, sounding horrified as yet another thing occurred to her. 'You probably also get paid to do them, and here I am asking you to come along and talk to a bunch of country kids about being a newspaper reporter,' she groaned and shook her head. 'People are always telling me to think before I speak, and you'd think by now I'd have got it.'

'Don't be silly. It's fine. Of course I'll come and visit, if you think the kids would be interested.'

'They'll be over the moon. They've never met a celebrity before.'

Pip laughed at that. 'Oh no, I'm not a celebrity—seriously.'

'Please,' Rebecca flipped a hand impatiently. 'You're an investigative reporter who's worked on some of the biggest stories in recent times and ended up on our news at night. When would kids from Midgiburra ever have another chance to meet someone like you?'

Pip moved in her seat a little. 'Well, I'm happy to come in to try to entice some fresh blood into journalism.'

'Sometimes it's just showing these kids that there's a bigger world outside of Midgiburra, and it's theirs for the taking if they just open their minds to new things. If I can give them new experiences, spark some curiosity, that's often all it takes to set them along a new path and a really exciting future.'

'I admire your enthusiasm and dedication. And you're right. I had an English teacher, Miss Grace, who took the time to encourage me when I was at school, and I think it played a big part in my decision to go into journalism.'

'Don't you just love fate,' Rebecca grinned, picking up her mug and cradling it in both hands.

'Or coincidence?' Pip shot back.

'You don't believe in fate?'

'Not really. I think opportunities come along and you either take them or you don't.'

'So fate didn't put you in that checkout line at the same time as me today?'

Pip smiled. 'The fact I was running out of toilet paper and coffee put me in that line. I don't think fate would lower itself to something so mundane.'

Rebecca made a small singsong sound as she shrugged. 'Sounds like fate to me.'

Pip wasn't going to argue; if Rebecca wanted to believe in fate and destiny mumbo-jumbo, that was fine—each to their own. But as far as Pip was concerned, fate was right up there with the whole soul-mate thing. You made your own luck and choices in this world, and the consequences of those choices determined your so-called *fate*. Sugar-coating life didn't make it any easier in the long run.

'Tell me what you're making of Midgiburra's big news,' Rebecca went on brightly. 'Have you been covering it for the *Daily Metro*?'

'No,' Pip answered, putting her coffee cup back down on the table, 'I'm writing a book. That's what I came out here for—to find a nice, quiet place to write.'

'And then a murder scene throws the whole town into mayhem. So much for quiet.'

'That's not even the half of it,' Pip said. 'The bones they found are on my uncle's land. And I was the one who decided on cleaning out the dam.'

'Oh no! So you're to blame for ruining all your own peace and quiet!'

'Exactly.' Pip gave a smile laced with self-reproach.

'But that must be stirring the creative juices, surely? As an investigator?'

'I'm trying really hard not to get involved.'

'But why?' Rebecca asked, her eyes widening. 'This would be a fascinating story—whatever the outcome.'

'I'm under a bit of pressure to write this book. I really don't need that kind of distraction right now.'

'I can understand that,' the other woman nodded thoughtfully. 'But writing must be an exciting venture?'

Pip nodded. 'It is. It's just . . . bringing up a lot of things from the past and proving a bit more difficult than I anticipated.'

'I remember hearing about your attack,' Rebecca said, her voice softening. 'That must have been awful.'

Pip lowered her gaze to her cup and traced the handle idly with her finger. 'It took a while to get over.'

'I can imagine. Be kind to yourself,' she said, and a moment of silence settled between them. 'It's understandable that you'd be having trouble trying to focus, but you have to allow yourself to heal in your own time. You can't force it. I'm here if you ever want to talk,' she added.

Pip felt an unexpected sting behind her eyes and blinked quickly, managing a brief smile. 'Thank you.'

Rebecca's bright smile returned as she sat back in her chair and finished her coffee.

'So, you said you've been here eight years?' Pip said, trying to lighten the mood a little. 'Why here?'

'My parents keep asking me the same thing,' she said with a grin, then she looked around a little wistfully. 'I don't know. At first I liked the idea of a smaller school and somewhere out of the way to start a new life. I'd done a lot of my prac in bigger schools and decided that really wasn't for me. Then I just fell in love with the town, the people, the fact that in a smaller school I get to know each kid as an individual. I can't really picture working anywhere else.'

Pip tried to imagine living somewhere like here and was surprised when she actually considered it momentarily. Maybe in an ideal world, she thought absently. She had grown to enjoy the quiet mornings on the back verandah and the freedom of unobstructed views for miles around, but she wasn't sure she was cut out for rural life on a full-time basis.

When Pip glanced at her watch, she got a shock. 'I didn't realise how late it was getting. I should get back.'

'Thank you so much for taking the time to stop for a coffee. It was really great to meet you,' Rebecca said, digging through her handbag to pull out a battered organiser. 'I'll give you some time to think about when you want to do a visit, but I'll just let you know what days might be best to organise something.'

Pip pulled out her phone and noted the dates down, before sending Rebecca through her email and phone details. 'I'm pretty free, so just email me a date and time that suits you.'

'I'll take a look at the schedule and let you know.'

She still didn't think it was fate that had placed Rebecca in her path today, but whatever it was, Pip was kind of glad she'd been there.

'Hey,' a deep voice called as Pip walked across the carpark and took the sunglasses from the top of her head. She stopped and turned to find Erik standing beside a car, dressed in a T-shirt and long, loose-fitting shorts, carrying a gym bag over one shoulder.

'Hey,' she said, smiling back. 'I almost didn't recognise you out of uniform.' She quickly adjusted her gaze from the T-shirt that was stretching across his broad chest.

'I do occasionally take it off,' he said with a grin as he tossed the bag into his boot.

Don't go there, don't you dare go there, she warned herself sternly as her mind suddenly threw a heap of inappropriate innuendos about Erik taking off his uniform.

'How you been?'

'Fine,' she said, nodding. 'You?'

'Can't complain,' he said, closing the boot and resting against it casually.

'Any developments on the bones front?' she ventured.

'Not that I'm aware of. They sent it all over to Coopers Creek station.'

Pip couldn't help but notice his demeanour change. It was subtle, but she picked up on the tensing of his jaw and his arms flexing as he stiffened slightly. 'Is that normal procedure?' she asked.

She watched his shoulders lift, the movement stretching the soft fabric of his T-shirt. 'That's where the detectives are based. They've got some new hotshot running the show now.'

A set of dark eyes and a slow, sexy grin instantly came to mind as Pip recalled her recent encounter with the mysterious Detective Jarrett. She quickly pulled herself up. Sexy? When had his smile suddenly turned sexy? She tried to bring back the image of him smiling, to prove she'd been overreacting, but that tiny prickle of awareness was there stronger than ever. Damn it. It was definitely sexy.

'How long have you been out here?' she asked Erik, mostly to distract herself from wayward thoughts about a certain detective.

'Going on three years.'

'Do you like it? I mean, the small-town life and everything?' she added when he seemed surprised by her question.

'Yeah. It's quiet. Pretty cruisy most of the time. Why do you ask?'

'No reason,' she said, offering a smile. 'You just don't seem the quiet-country-town type. Where were posted before here?'

His reaction was less subtle this time as his expression cooled and his eyes narrowed slightly. 'You sound like you're back in reporter mode all of a sudden.'

'No. I was just asking. It's just that you strike me as the kind of person who'd like a little more . . . well,' she hesitated, 'just *more* than this place.'

'Yeah, well, it is what it is,' he said as he lowered his gaze then lifted it once more and that confident, flirty look in his eye was back in place. 'You finding enough to keep you occupied out here?' he asked. 'Must be a bit of an adjustment from the fast pace of Sydney.'

'I'm actually enjoying the quieter pace. And work's keeping me busy.'

'I thought you weren't working out here?' he countered, eyeing her curiously.

'Other work,' she hedged.

'Sounds interesting,' he said, seemingly settling in for a long conversation.

'Not really. I'm writing, just not for the newspaper.' She didn't want to talk about the book. It took up her every waking hour and she simply didn't have the energy to talk about it when she was away from her computer screen. Her phone rang from inside the depths of her handbag and Pip ignored it, smiling apologetically when it stopped and then immediately started ringing again. 'Sorry,' she muttered, opening her bag.

'Sounds like someone really wants to get in touch with you,' he said, easing away from his car. 'I've got to get going anyway.'

'It was nice to see you again.'

'See you around,' he said, holding her gaze briefly before the phone went silent then started ringing once more, making her swear quietly under her breath as she went back to digging through the contents of her bag. She finally brought it out and saw her agent's name on the screen as she swiped the answer icon impatiently.

'Pip, finally.'

'Hi, Jane,' Pip said, biting back her irritation at the agent's usual brashness.

'I've had the publisher on the phone wanting an update. I need something to send them, Phillipa. Tell me you have some chapters ready?'

'I'm getting there,' she answered vaguely.

The phone went silent. 'How many chapters have you written?' Jane demanded.

'It's been a bit slow, but it's going okay now.'

'Pip, I've held these people off for weeks now, promising them something to look at. I cannot hold them off indefinitely. They want to see some results from that rather large advance they paid.'

Pip closed her eyes briefly and fought back a wave of panic. 'I'll have something for you by next week,' she promised, already mentally trying to tally up exactly how many pages she'd need to write to fulfil that promise.

'Next week, then,' she said firmly.

'Okay, no worries. I have to get back to work,' she said, quickly shutting down any further conversation. Not that her agent was ever big on conversation—she wasn't the nurturing kind of agent who doted on the people she represented. She was, however, one of the best and most highly sought after—if Jane Caruso was your agent, you did your job and she took care of your career. End of story. The call did give Pip the motivation to get home and start writing, though. The last thing she needed was a lecture from Jane.

Eleven

Pip glanced at the phone screen and noted the unfamiliar number. 'Phillipa Davenport.'

'Ms Davenport, it's Chris Jarrett.'

'Detective,' she greeted, surprised by the caller's identity but instantly curious.

'I just thought I'd give you a ring to let you know we've got the forensics back on the bones.'

'Oh? And?'

'They appear to be from a female, late twenties, approximately one hundred and sixty centimetres tall.' Pip heard the shuffling of papers before the detective continued. 'The missing person's report Bert Bigsby filed on his wife has Molly Bigsby's height at five feet three inches, which is one hundred and sixty centimetres, and her age at twenty-five years.'

'Well, that seems pretty conclusive,' Pip said slowly.

A Stone's Throw Away

'Listed on the missing person's report were some personal items Mrs Bigsby may have been wearing at the time of her disappearance, which included a gold wedding band and distinctive eighteen-carat yellow-gold, three-stone diamond engagement ring and a small gold locket on a chain. All items have been recovered from the submerged vehicle and identified.' He paused. 'We're confident enough with the evidence at hand to identify the body as that of Mrs Molly Bigsby, formerly of Rosevale, Midgiburra.'

Pip held the phone a little tighter. She wasn't sure how she'd expected to react to the news, but a deep sadness washed over her, unexpectedly.

'Since you were so curious,' he added pointedly, 'I just figured you'd like to know where we're up to. The details are going to be released to the media within the next hour or so.'

'So . . . what now? Do you have a cause of death? Are you still looking at the Clements case?'

'Give me a break,' he said, and Pip heard that slow smile of his through the phone. 'I thought this might tide you over for a bit.'

'Sorry. Thank you. I *have* been wondering, and it was really nice of you to let me know you'd made an ID.'

'Wow, that sounded almost genuine.'

'It was. I *am* grateful,' she said, feeling exasperated. Why did she let this guy push her buttons like that? 'I'm just wondering if you know how she died?'

'Still ongoing,' he told her with a shrug in his tone.

'Have you managed to link the two cases?'

'No comment,' he said lightly.

'Come on, detective,' Pip tried persuasively, 'you said yourself, this is a cold case.'

'It's still an active case at the moment, and until I have anything more concrete, I'm not at liberty to share any of it with the media.'

'But I already told you—I'm not working this story.'

'And yet here you are, pumping me for info like a seasoned journo,' he said, sounding amused.

Pip gave a short, forceful huff. 'Fine. Don't tell me.' Oh God, did she seriously just say that? What was she, a seven-year-old?

'Ms Devonport, are you pouting?'

'Thank you for the update, detective,' she managed to get out through clenched teeth, feeling like an idiot, hearing his soft, deep laugh before she ended the call.

Two days later, Pip had just finished a call with her mother when she heard the front gate protesting as it opened. Her heart began to race and she took a moment to do the slow, steady breathing her doctor had taught her. She'd thought she was getting past all this, but maybe it was only because it was an unexpected visitor.

She forced herself to walk to the front door, peeking through the window before breathing out a long breath and unlocking it.

'Hi, Anne,' she said, hoping her voice didn't sound as shaky as she was feeling on the inside.

'Hello, Pip. I'm sorry for barging in on you like this but, well . . . I was wondering if I could talk to you for a minute?'

The Anne she'd met the other day had seemed relaxed and happy as she'd pottered about her kitchen, but today there was a different feel about her. Pip noticed she was wringing her hands together slightly as she stood on the doorstep, and her smile was strained.

'Of course, come on in,' Pip said, worried that something terrible may have happened but unsure how it might relate to her. She led the way through to the bright sun-filled kitchen and asked if Anne would like a coffee.

'This was always such a lovely room,' Anne said, and this time her smile was softer. 'Bert loved sitting out here, especially in winter.'

'I'm finding it's a nice space to work,' she said, hesitating only briefly as she came over to gather up the assortment of books and paperwork spread out on the table to toss back into the box. 'Sorry about the mess.'

'No, please don't disrupt your workspace for me,' Anne said quickly.

Pip looked around helplessly at the clutter she'd created over the past few days trying to sort her research into piles. 'Maybe we should go outside and sit,' she said awkwardly.

'That sounds perfect,' Anne smiled, looking relieved that Pip had stopped trying to clean up.

As she went across to where her coffee machine took pride of place on the kitchen bench, she noticed Anne darting a curious glance at the contents on the table. Pip tried to decide if she was annoyed or okay with it. On the one hand, there was nothing top secret there and, as far as anyone else knew, it was just a bunch of court documents and legal mumbo-jumbo.

On the other hand, she'd never had to worry about anyone disturbing her work because she lived alone and usually had an office to contain her mess.

'I hope you don't mind,' Anne started cautiously, making Pip glance up a little apprehensively. 'I overheard someone talking about you in town this morning . . . Is it true? Are you really a journalist—the one who broke the story on Lenny Knight?'

Pip concentrated extra hard on stirring the contents of the coffee cup before her to hide her surprise. 'That's me. Although I wasn't aware anyone would know me here.'

'Jan from the bakery said she recognised you from the TV, when all that . . . trouble happened.'

Pip didn't have to ask what trouble she meant—clearly her infamy had preceded her.

'That must have been awful, you poor thing. I'm so glad you're okay now.'

Yeah, nothing to worry about—I only have the occasional panic attack now and again, she thought blandly. 'Shall we go outside?' Pip said, leading the way out the back door and setting the mugs down on the small table on the verandah.

They settled themselves for a few moments in silence before Anne took a sip of her coffee and carefully placed it back down in front of her. 'I came out here to see you because . . . well . . .' She gave a frustrated little sigh. 'I honestly don't know who else can help.'

'Help? With what?'

'Help Bert.'

'Bert Bigsby?'

A Stone's Throw Away

Anne nodded encouragingly.

'How would I be able to help him?'

'You could uncover the story behind Molly's disappearance. I've just come from visiting him, and he was very agitated. The police had been to see him, apparently, and they told him about Molly being found.'

'Anne, I don't really think there's much to uncover. Molly didn't disappear—she died. On Bert's property. What if you're wrong and he might have actually had something to do with it?'

'But he didn't,' Anne said adamantly. 'If you knew him—before, when he was younger—you would have seen how devastated he was. He was a broken man. He loved Molly. He told me, every day he woke up and hoped that would be the day Molly came home. He didn't kill her. He's been living with everyone around him accusing him of this terrible thing—and he's innocent.'

'Look, I know it's hard when you believe someone . . . you *want* to believe them. But you said yourself that the war changed him. Even if he is innocent, I don't know what you think I can do for him. It was seventy-odd years ago. The police are treating it as a cold case. He had an alibi, and they're not going to reopen an investigation when Bert's the only one still alive, and he's in his nineties. They only have circumstantial evidence after all this time. Bert won't be thrown in prison or anything.'

'It's not that,' Anne said, her eyebrows drawn together in distress. 'The town's . . . well, it's just dug everything back up again. People are saying the most terrible things about him, and it just breaks my heart.' Anne touched the corner of her eye quickly before sniffing and clearing her throat. 'He's lived his whole life being called a murderer—can you imagine that? People calling you names and accusing you of killing the one person you loved? All the while knowing you didn't do it and that she was missing.' Anne stopped and shook her head slowly. 'He's led such a lonely, sad life. I just wish his innocence could be *proven* so he could go in peace—*finally*. Instead, all this hate has flared up again.'

'I'm sorry, Anne, but I came here to write a book, and to be honest, I just don't have time to take on something like this at the moment. I mean, I'm not even sure I know what to believe about the whole thing myself.'

'I understand,' Anne said quietly, standing and picking up her cup. 'I just thought you of all people wouldn't be so quick to judge—you always seem so impartial and fair-minded in your stories.'

Pip inwardly rolled her eyes. That one hit a nerve. She *was* impartial, damn it! She'd been going back and forth with the whole Bert thing for days. The fact his missing wife had been found on his property *was* somewhat damning, and the police were being close-mouthed about the whole thing, which made her wonder if maybe they'd discovered something new. Then there was the alibi that they were still looking into. It wasn't exactly clear-cut despite Anne's unwavering certainty of Bert's innocence. Yet Pip found herself *wanting* to believe he was innocent too.

As a reporter, Pip knew she had to weigh up both sides of the story and gather all the evidence. And yes, she was bothered by the fact that the whole town already seemed convinced Bert was a murderer and had convicted him in the court of public opinion without a fair trial. But clearing Bert's name wasn't her job.

She followed Anne inside and towards the front door, then stopped as the woman turned to face her. 'Pete and I helped oversee the sale of this place before it went on the market,' Anne said with a small smile as she glanced around slowly. 'We sold all the furniture and cleaned the place up as per the solicitor's instructions. We were told to donate or throw away anything that wouldn't sell, but I couldn't bear to get rid of a lot of Bert's personal belongings, so I packed them up and stored them at our place in case some long-lost relative turned up one day.' Anne's smile didn't suggest she was hopeful of that happening. She seemed to hesitate briefly. 'If you change your mind, you're welcome to come and look through Bert's belongings. In case there's something in there that might help.' She bit her lip before blurting out, 'If you went to see him, you'd understand.' Pip saw her eyes begin to fill with tears, but she turned and hurried back to her car before Pip could even reply.

Pip watched until the car disappeared and a trail of dust slowly settled in its wake. Anne was clearly upset by the whole thing. Pip understood that, but she still didn't see that there was anything to be gained by looking into the story after all this time. Still, she felt bad for her neighbour. Anne was clearly a very caring woman who'd taken the town oddball under her wing and looked after him for the last thirty or so years. Of course she would want to try to find some kind of justification for it all . . . but Pip wouldn't be the one to do it. She had enough to worry about, writing her own story.

Twelve

Pip glanced around and realised it was getting dark. She'd made slight progress on the book, compiling the notes she wanted to expand on to create a chapter, so she was feeling somewhat positive about the afternoon's work for a change as she went through the daily ritual of closing the curtains and checking the windows were all locked. It was a little later than she normally began to lock up—darkness had already descended. As she looked out through the window she could no longer see the trees along the far boundary fence, and the light from the kitchen spilled out across the lawn casting a dull yellow glow across the dry ground.

An unease settled in the pit of her stomach at the thought of just how secluded the little house was. At home, there were neighbours and streetlights and the constant sound of passing traffic—out here, there was nothing. She didn't mind it through the daylight hours—she liked the quiet—but at night, it was just so *dark*. There wasn't even any moonlight this evening, which made it even blacker. Logically she knew that there was nothing out there in the dark that wasn't out there in the daylight—it was simply hidden. But it was the hidden things that were the problem. Pip pulled the curtains shut and turned away. *You're fine. There's nothing out there that's going to hurt you. You're safe here.* That was the mantra she'd been using since she'd arrived, and it usually worked, but tonight it took a lot longer to restore her calm.

She gave up on getting any more writing done tonight—the last thing she needed was to be consumed with Lenny bloody Knight while she was so jumpy. Her mind briefly went to the make-up bag in the bathroom and the bottle of prescription medication inside, but she forced the thought away. Her doctor had given her the tablets to take if she needed them, but she didn't like the way they made her feel—she liked to be in control and she didn't feel that way when she took them.

Those first few weeks after her attack had gone by in a blur. She'd been in hospital for close to a week and then stayed with her parents until the worst of her injuries had healed. When she thought back to that time, all she really remembered was the utter vulnerability she'd been submerged in. She'd felt as though she was drowning. She never wanted to feel like that again—powerless, weak. She'd been determined to fight back, and she had by facing Lenny Knight in court.

He'd threatened her when she began digging around in the early days, then attempted to bribe her, and when that didn't work, he'd tried to have her killed and she still hadn't backed down. Despite facing him in court, looking him in the eye when she gave her testimony, there wasn't the magical return of her earlier confidence. She was still trying to put back all the pieces he broke.

Pip's eyes shot open, her heart beating hard as she tried to work out what had woken her. A creak of timber boards outside on the verandah sounded, and her body went rigid, her senses instantly tuned in to every tiny sound and movement. For a long moment she waited, listening, then just as she was ready to relax, another creak, louder than the last one, made her sit upright and reach for her phone. Taking it with her, she crouched behind her bedroom door, fingers fumbling as she turned it on, the greenish glow from the screen lighting up the room as she found the keypad and dialled triple zero.

She crept along the hallway as she waited for the call to connect, her heart pounding painfully through her chest.

'Triple zero, what's your emergency?' a female voice came over the line.

'I think someone's outside my house,' she whispered in a low tone.

'Can you see anyone?'

'I haven't looked. But I heard footsteps.'

'Are your doors locked?'

'Yes.'

'Is there anyone else in the house with you?'

'No. It's just me.'

'Okay, I've got your location and I've put in a call to the police. Someone will be out there shortly.'

Pip's eyes darted around the dark room, every shadow making her heart rate increase. Another creak from outside suddenly spurred her into action and she moved swiftly to the light switch and flicked it on, lighting up the outside porch. There was a thud followed by a crash and Pip let out a scream, sinking to the floor and covering her head with her arms as her whole body shook.

She had no idea how long she sat there for, but it was long enough for her body to feel stiff and sore. The sound of an engine approaching and a car door opening and closing made her lift her head and listen intently. Heavy boots echoed on the step outside before a loud knock made her leap to her feet and stare wide-eyed at the front door.

'Pip, it's Erik Nielsen.'

Pip let out a long, shaky breath as she reached for the doorknob, slowly opening it to peep out.

'We got a call for a disturbance. Are you all right?'

'Yes,' she said, having to clear her throat. Her voice sounded hoarse and scratchy. 'I'm sorry to get you out here like this,' she said. Now that she had someone with her, the earlier fear had begun to ebb away, leaving her feeling a little stupid.

'No worries. What happened?'

Daylight had begun to lighten the dark sky and she could just make out the silhouette of trees across the paddock. 'I heard something outside . . . on the verandah.' Pip stopped then pushed the screen door open wider to step outside. One of her uncle's tin milk cans from the shelf under the window lay on its side on the wooden boards. 'When I turned on the light, they ran away and knocked that over,' she said, nodding towards the can.

'They? As in more than one? Did you get a look at them?' he asked, instantly alert and looking around.

'Not exactly,' she said, then gave a small grimace when he looked back at her. 'I didn't actually see anyone, and I don't really know why I said they—it could have just been one. I could just hear someone out on the verandah . . . the boards were squeaking.'

'It's an old house, Pip,' he said, his demeanour seeming to relax slightly. 'They're full of creaks and groans.' He moved across to the fallen can, inspecting the immediate area around it before sitting it upright. 'Could have been a possum nosing about up here,' he said, putting the can back on the shelf.

'Surely a possum wouldn't have been heavy enough to make the boards squeak?'

'You'd be surprised. They can grow pretty big around here. But I'll take a look around and see if I can find anything, just to be sure.'

'Thanks,' Pip said, managing a slight smile as she watched him leave the front verandah and walk around the side of the house. She closed the door and headed to the kitchen to make coffee. As she opened the tin and took out the scoop, she noticed her hands were not quite steady, and she forced herself to calm down. Erik was most likely right. It could have been an animal snooping about that got a fright when the light came on, only . . . She gave a small, frustrated huff. The more she thought about it, the more convinced she was that she'd heard footsteps . . . the human kind, not tiny possum ones.

'Hello?' she heard Erik call as he opened the front door a few moments later.

'In the kitchen,' she called back, taking down two mugs.

'There's no sign of anything out of place around the house. I couldn't find any footprints or damage to any of the windows. Thanks,' he said, accepting the mug she handed him. 'I reckon it was just a possum or maybe a stray cat.'

'Sorry to get you out here at this stupid hour. I feel like an idiot now.' Pip winced and tucked her hair behind her ear.

'Not a problem, all part of the service,' he said, taking a sip of his coffee. 'It's understandable you'd be a bit jumpy.' He held her startled glance before adding, 'After the assault and all.'

Pip eyed him silently as she drank from her mug, concentrating hard on keeping her hand steady. She wasn't sure she liked that he knew about her attack, though it had made the news at the time, mainly due to the high-profile case. 'It's over and done with now.'

'I guess it goes hand in hand with the job? I mean, you guys dig up a lot of dirt on a lot of people—it's bound to come back on you at some point.'

'Occasionally.'

'So why do you do it? I mean, is it worth it? The threats and, in your case, almost getting killed?'

She tried not to flinch at his words but it was hard not to. 'I do it because, like you, I want justice. If someone's doing something wrong or abusing their power, they shouldn't get away with it. And yes, I guess it *is* worth it when you know you've helped uncover something that can lead to that person being put away.'

'But it's not your job. It should be up to the police to investigate,' he pointed out.

Pip shrugged. 'You guys don't have the manpower to investigate every single lead that comes up. That's where we come in. We can put the time in and get answers in ways police often can't.'

'There's usually a reason police can't do anything—it's called the law. I just think sometimes journalists think they're above the rules we have to play by. It's dangerous.'

His high-handed tone irritated her. 'It's a huge investment, timewise, so we don't go after someone if there's not a good reason. You can't tell me that as a police officer you don't come across people you know are guilty but can't do anything, because you just don't have the evidence you need to warrant going after them?'

'Sure. Happens all the time. Only when we do find the evidence—and usually, we *will* eventually,' he added, his tone clipped, 'we don't go splashing it all over the news. It's our job to catch criminals. You guys turn it into a three-ring circus.'

'It's our job to keep the public informed,' she threw back at him. 'It works both ways. The criminals also have the protection of being in the public eye. No one wants to go back to the bad old days when police used to wield their own justice,' she said. 'This way, everything's out in the open.'

'You think all police are corrupt?' he asked stiffly.

'Of course not,' she said, frowning slightly. 'I never said that. I said *in the past*. A lot of things were different back then.'

'I just don't get why you'd want to stir up trouble and risk your safety to do it. Surely the pay's not that good?'

'Nope. I guess it's just who I am,' she said matter-of-factly. 'I don't like watching bullies hurt other people, and it doesn't matter whether that bully happens to be a politician, a plumber or a crooked cop.'

'As long as you get a story out of it,' he added, and there was a decidedly mocking edge to the statement. But before she could respond, he glanced at his watch then placed the empty cup on the bench beside him. 'Thanks for the coffee. I better get moving.'

His abruptness momentarily threw her off balance and she found herself scrambling to catch up. 'I'm sorry I dragged you all the way out here for nothing,' she said, standing up to follow him.

'Just doing my job,' he shot back, still sounding a little annoyed.

'Look, Erik,' she said, waiting until he turned to face her, 'if anything I've said has offended you, I didn't mean it to. My comments weren't directed at *you*,' she said, still confused by his attitude.

For a moment his expression remained aloof before he gave a quick shake of his head. 'No, I'm the one who should be sorry. It's been a long night.'

'Made longer by an early-morning call-out,' she added dryly.

'It's all good. Better to be safe than sorry. I'll see you around.'

Pip walked the policeman out and waved. Closing the front door, she rested her head against it and let out a small groan.

She couldn't go through this again. Not long after she moved back into her apartment after the attack, she'd called the police out on a couple of occasions when she was sure there was someone trying to break in through the night. She'd been too embarrassed to call any of her family or even Lexi; she couldn't, not after they'd all been so worried and thought it had been too early for her to return to her own place alone.

The police had politely suggested installing a state-of-the-art security system, increasing the cameras and locks she'd already had installed before moving back in, which she did, and eventually her panic-calling days ended.

Yet here she was now, calling the police the first time she heard a bump in the night—they'd think she was crazy, and she definitely didn't need to be making a name for herself among the locals as some pathetic city-sider who jumped at possums on her verandah at night.

Maybe she'd look for some of those trail cameras used for checking what kind of animals came past at night. If she set them up on the verandah, at least she could see if there really was a possum problem around the place, or something more . . . well, maybe she just wouldn't think about what else might be out there right now.

'Hey,' Pip said as she answered the phone later that day.

'I hope I'm interrupting a steady flow of words,' Lexi's hopeful tone greeted her.

'I wouldn't quite call it steady,' Pip said.

'Should I call back later? I just had a few minutes before my next meeting.'

'No, it's fine. I was just about to get up and make a coffee anyway.' She'd lost count of how many she'd had already—and none of them seemed to be clearing away the fog of her interrupted sleep and early morning.

'How's country life going?'

'Fine. Once I get used to all the weird noises and would-be criminal possums,' she answered before filling her friend in on her eventful morning.

'I'm glad you called the police,' Lexi said, sounding far more serious than usual.

'I wish I hadn't,' Pip groaned. 'It was so embarrassing. I'm sure he thinks I'm an idiot.'

'Better to be thought an idiot than not call and end up . . . well, you know,' Lexi said awkwardly.

'I suppose.'

'Did you make an appointment with a counsellor?' Lexi asked.

'No, I've been a little sidetracked with police scouring all over the place lately.'

'That was weeks ago. You know you've just been putting it off. And after last night, I think you should seriously think about doing it. Talking to someone might help put your mind to rest.'

'Yeah, maybe.' She pressed the button on the coffee machine and watched the creamy flow of dark liquid fill the cup, breathing in the heady scent of the strong African coffee. 'I was asked to look into the story in connection with the bones they found,' Pip threw in, hoping to distract her friend from pushing her on the counselling issue.

'By whom?'

'Uncle Nev's neighbour. Apparently, she knew the husband of the woman whose remains they found in the dam. He used to own this property. She asked me to look into it.'

'So? Are you going to?'

Pip took a sip of her coffee before answering. 'No.'

'Why not?'

'Because I have a book to write.'

'You always have multiple stories on the go. This one sounds interesting.'

'It is,' she said. 'It has it all: love, drama, a crime of passion, mystery.'

'Then find the time to write it.'

'Time is not on my side at the moment.'

There was a notable silence on the other end of the line and Pip found herself rolling her eyes. Lexi was her best friend and she loved the woman dearly, but she hated when she did this silent-treatment thing. It only drove her mad because her friend knew her so well and could push her buttons without even trying. It was Lexi's way of calling her out on something. 'I don't care what you think—I don't have the time,' Pip said doggedly.

'I didn't say anything,' Lexi said, and Pip heard a smug smile in her tone. 'I certainly didn't point out that if something was important you'd find a way to do it.'

'Nope, you didn't say any of that,' Pip agreed.

'I've got to go. I'll give you a call tonight. Get back to that writing.'

'Talk soon,' Pip said, hoping she didn't sound as unenthusiastic as she felt. As she headed back towards the table, she suddenly made a detour, pushing open the screen door and breathing in the hot, sweet smell of early summer. In the far distance she saw the wavy dance of a mirage, the heat hovering just above the dry, parched earth, making it feel even hotter than it was. The low, desolate cry of a crow sent a prickle of unease across her shoulder blades, and she held her coffee mug a little tighter, drawing in its warmth.

Thirteen

Coopers Creek was a metropolis compared to Midgiburra, but even so, it really wasn't that much bigger. It did, however, boast a small rural hospital as well as a library and some community outreach programs, so for all intents and purposes it was quite the hub.

Pip had ordered some research material, and her city library had agreed to send it through to Coopers Creek. She'd been meaning to drive over this way and check out the next town over from Midgiburra but until now hadn't had the opportunity to do so.

She parked the car once she'd located the library, which was set back from the road in the middle of a well-tended park. Pip took in the green grass and bright flowerbeds and wondered if the rate payers minded that the council was clearly not under the same water restrictions as the rest of the district.

She could see why they tried to keep it so nice—it had to lift the town's spirits. With everything for miles around brown and dead, this was a little oasis of life. If she lived here and had children, she thought suddenly as she stopped to admire a bed of roses, she would bring them down here just so they knew what green grass looked like. With the drought going into its third year, there would be young children who may have never seen anything other than this depressing, dry landscape. It made her sad to think about it.

It was the topic every conversation eventually came around to. *When it rains . . . It's gotta rain soon . . .* Pip wondered at the mental strength it must take these people to wake up each day in the hopes of seeing clouds in the sky—and to keep going through the day when there weren't.

That's another story I could write. The thought popped into her head but quickly left again. She wasn't out here looking for stories.

On her drive back into Midgiburra, her gaze fell on the sign outside a tired old brick building: *Shady Acres Nursing Home.* Her hands momentarily tightened on the steering wheel and, with a muttered curse, she turned into the driveway and found a spot in the carpark at the front. It had been a week since Anne's visit and, until now, Pip hadn't allowed herself to act on it.

'This is stupid,' she said out loud as she stared through the front windscreen at the building before her. 'It's not going to achieve anything.' With a frustrated sigh, she pushed open her door and stepped out then slammed the door shut behind her. She didn't even know *why* she was here. She didn't have to be. No one was making her, and yet deep down she knew she wasn't going to be able to shake Anne's comment about making up her mind without even meeting the man.

Pip hated nursing homes. She remembered a childhood visit to her great-grandmother in a nursing home—the smell of urine and bleach had almost knocked her off her feet. It had been a dark, morbid kind of place. They had at least improved a bit since then, though. These days the rooms were bigger and well-furnished and usually painted nice bright colours to cheer the place up and make it feel more like a home rather than a hospital.

As she walked into the foyer, there was no one around and she was instantly relieved. At least she'd tried, she thought, coming up with a defence in case she needed to use it with Anne.

'Can I help you?' a voice called as she started walking towards the front door, and Pip closed her eyes and mouthed a silent swear word.

'Hi,' she said, turning and putting a friendly smile on her face. 'I was just stopping in to visit someone, but I can come back another day.'

'You're more than welcome to visit today. It's a bit quiet around here at the moment—it's outing day. Who did you want to visit?' asked the young woman dressed in an admin uniform.

'Herbert Bigsby,' Pip said quickly, waiting for some kind of dramatic reaction.

'I'm new here, so I'll just have to check the room number,' the woman said. A few moments later she looked up from the computer behind the desk. 'Room 12B.' She pointed the direction out and Pip thanked her with a quick smile before hurrying down the long carpeted hall.

Outside the room, Pip once more had the urge to turn around and leave, but something kept pushing her on. Feeling as if she were mentally digging in her heels but still skidding forward, she eventually gave up and knocked on the partially opened door.

Inside Pip could hear voices, and when she carefully poked her head around the side of the door, she saw a man in a hospital bed with the sides pulled up and two nursing assistants sitting on the chairs, their backs to the patient, chatting and laughing. As Pip went to excuse herself, the women jumped up and moved the chairs back into position before fussing about the room.

'I'm sorry, I didn't mean to interrupt.'

'Nah, it's all good. Who were you looking for?'

'Ah, Mr Bigsby, actually.'

'What? Really?' The two women looked at her wearing varying expressions of disbelief. 'You a relation?'

'No, not exactly,' she started cautiously, but found something about the women's mannerisms annoying.

'No one ever visits old Butcher here,' the older of the two women said.

Pip frowned and her glare hardened on the woman. 'His name's Bert,' she snapped.

'Been Butcher for as long as I've been alive. That's all anyone's ever called him.'

'I think he deserves a little more respect than that as a patient,' Pip pointed out, eyeing the woman, who had lost her smirk and was now regarding Pip suspiciously.

'You're that reporter,' the woman finally stated. 'Are you doing some kind of story on him or something?'

'I'm just here to visit.'

The other woman gave a small scoff. 'You wrote that piece about corruption or something, didn't you? What are you digging about around here for?'

'I'm not digging around for anything.'

'Well, good luck getting anything out of him,' she said, nodding towards the bed.

'I hope I'm not holding either of you up from doing anything in here?' she asked pointedly.

'Nah,' the first woman stepped in. 'We were just leaving.'

Pip stared after the two women. They were clearly using Bert's room as a quiet place to take a break—most likely an unauthorised one, judging by the guilty response when she'd first walked in—and this idea filled Pip with indignant outrage on Bert's behalf.

She would deal with the women later. Now, though, she found herself alone with Bert, and she knew there was no turning back.

Bert Bigsby was just as she imagined a ninety-eight-year-old man to be. His hair was wispy and white, and his skin, once probably hard and callused like Pete's from working a farm, was now thin and splotchy. He was asleep, his eyes closed and his breathing slightly raspy, and just as Pip was again wondering what had possessed her to stop by, he opened his eyes. She felt like a doe trapped in headlights. She could hardly run now—but would this man appreciate a stranger suddenly appearing in his room? Putting on her best journo persona, she decided that if this was a story to look into, then she'd treat it like one.

'Hello, Mr Bigsby,' she said, taking a step closer to the bed. 'My name's Phillipa Davenport. My uncle bought your farm and I'm currently staying out there.'

His eyes followed her, but there seemed little expression in them and his face remained blank. 'Anne, your next-door neighbour, asked me to stop by. I think she's a bit worried after the police came to see you. I'm very sorry about your wife.'

There was no change in his expression—his mouth remained slightly turned down but his eyes were alive. At the mention of his wife, they seemed to open slightly and grow more alert. Anne had told her that Bert had suffered a stroke, but Pip wasn't sure how she was supposed to communicate. Maybe she wasn't supposed to? Clearly Anne had wanted her to simply *see* Bert, maybe hoping that once she understood how vulnerable the man was it would change her mind about helping to clear Bert's name.

Something changed inside Pip in that instant. She knew what it was like to feel defenceless. Her mind flashed back to the night of her attack and the feeling of despair that had overwhelmed her when she'd opened her mouth to scream but found she couldn't. She also knew what it was like to have the ability to speak taken away. A flash of a hospital bed and doctors talking across her as she frantically clawed at her bandaged throat momentarily made her feel dizzy.

Pip glanced around the room, to distract herself from the memories. There were no photos or knick-knacks, nothing that made this space feel like home. It felt more like a cold hospital room.

'I'm not sure if Anne mentioned I was a journalist?' she explained carefully. 'I guess she thought that maybe I could take a look at the story—at what happened,' she corrected quickly and cursed herself for the slip of the tongue. This was a man's life, not just a story. 'Although I'm just not sure how she thinks I'm going to help,' she said as her voice petered out under Bert's intense gaze. 'Anne believes you had nothing to do with your wife's disappearance, and now that they've found her, found Molly, the police should be able to determine what really happened. I think Anne hopes that we can look into it some more and try to clear your name once and for all.'

At this, Bert seemed to become agitated—his eyes moved from side to side and there was a faint sound in his throat like a muted grunt. Pip could see he was trying to communicate. Gently she placed a hand on his shoulder and his gaze settled on her once more. 'I can imagine how frustrating this must be for you,' she said quietly. It had to be hell: unable to move, unable to speak and make people understand what it was you needed. She could feel the man's frustration burning through his intense gaze, but she had no idea what it was he wanted to tell her.

Tentatively, she suggested blinking—once for yes, twice for no. 'Do you understand, Bert?' For a long moment he continued to stare at her, and Pip felt her hopes begin to fade, then he slowly closed his eyes and opened them again.

It seemed to take considerable effort for him to do it, and she feared this wasn't going to be an effective form of communication for very long. 'Are you worried about the investigation?'

Slowly he closed his eyes once more and opened them. Hope began to flare inside her at this latest discovery, and she dragged a chair across to the bedside.

'I understand that there wasn't a lot to go on about Molly's disappearance before, but now that they've found her, I think there could be some leads the police can follow to work out what happened.' She paused then continued carefully. 'You understand that means they'll uncover the truth . . . whatever that entails.' She could only hope that he understood that if he was connected to any of it, he wouldn't be able to hide. The evidence might be irrefutable rather than just local gossip and innuendo. 'Did you have anything to do with Vernon Clements' death?' she asked calmly.

His eyes closed, and Pip waited. He opened them and closed them a second time, and she slowly let out the breath she'd been holding. No. And just like that, her gut instinct kicked in. She believed him. There was nothing more than a feeling, but it was certain and she had learned long ago she to trust it.

'Bert, do you believe Molly's death was connected to Vernon Clements' murder?'

He closed his eyes slowly.

'Did you put Molly's body in the dam?'

Two slow blinks.

'Anne has some of your belongings in storage—photos and letters,' she said gently. 'Would it be all right if she lent them to me to have a look through?'

His eyes closed once.

'It's going to be all right, Bert. We'll work out what happened to Molly.'

His gaze didn't seem as agitated as before—maybe he still couldn't say everything he wanted to say, but at least he had a way to participate in a conversation. He seemed weary all of a sudden, and Pip imagined it must have taken a tremendous amount of concentration and effort. 'It's okay, Bert. You rest now.'

She waited until he closed his eyes before leaving, feeling strangely guilty, as though she were abandoning him.

As she neared the foyer, she stopped. She wasn't sure how much help she could really be to this investigation, but what she *could* do was stand up and speak for Bert and his rights.

'Hello,' her helpful admin woman said as she looked up and recognised Pip.

'I need to speak to someone about Mr Bigsby.'

'Oh . . . um, well, who do you want to speak with?'

'Does he have a doctor?'

'Our doctors aren't here until rounds later on this afternoon.'

'Then the nursing-home director,' she said, and the woman hesitantly reached for the phone on her desk.

Pip drummed her fingers on the desk as she waited, listening to the timid voice on her end saying 'Yes', 'I understand' and 'Sorry' several times before she replaced the phone and looked up at Pip anxiously. 'Mr Newman will be out shortly,' she said, brushing her fringe out of her eyes.

Just then, a man wearing a grey suit opened a door behind the front desk area and came through, looking somewhat distracted as he smoothed his tie before coming to a stop before her. 'Andrew Newman,' he introduced himself briskly, not hiding how inconvenient he considered this interruption.

'I've just been in visiting Mr Bigsby,' Pip started as the man looked at her expectantly. 'I'm concerned about the lack of respect I just witnessed from two of your staff towards him.'

'Excuse me?' the director said, then tilted his head and frowned. 'I'm sorry, are you a family member?'

'I'm a family friend,' she continued, figuring the small stretch was acceptable under these conditions.

'My staff always treat every resident they attend with the utmost respect.'

Pip's eyes narrowed and she saw the man straighten a little. 'I'd appreciate it if you had a word to your staff about how they address their patients. I'd hate to find there was some kind of prejudice being demonstrated in this facility. If Mr Bigsby's solicitor were to become involved in the matter, it wouldn't garner very favourable publicity.'

The director puffed out his chest and glared at her. 'I have no idea what you're suggesting.'

'I walked into that room and there were two nurses' aides sitting about doing nothing but talking about their weekend, completely ignoring the patient. If you've got people here trained to provide health care to vulnerable patients and are *not*, simply because of who this patient is, then that's a serious concern.'

'I can assure you, Mr Bigsby is treated no different to any other patient here.'

'Really? These women addressed him by a very derogative name.'

'If that's true then I will look into it.'

'I'd appreciate it. Oh, and you will be seeing me around here more often,' she added, pushing away from the front desk. 'I'm a journalist with the *Daily Metro* and I'll be doing a story on Mr Bigsby,' she said, walking away.

As she walked she felt her steps falter a little. What the hell had she just gone and done? She hadn't even decided she was going to write Bert's story until it just slipped out then. But she knew that her fate had been sealed when she heard those women call Bert the Butcher. Her anger only grew the more she thought about how isolated and lonely Bert must feel—trapped inside a body that no longer moved, unable to speak or defend himself, instead forced to lie there and listen to those women laugh and gossip, ignoring their duty of care.

Was it neglect simply because of Bert's reputation? Pip certainly had heard enough around town to recognise genuine unrest about the situation. The disappearance of Molly Bigsby and murder of Vernon Clements may have happened seventy years ago, but it still had the power to incite an uproar. There was clearly a reason Bert had become a recluse—his personal safety.

Whether or not he was guilty, Pip could not abide someone being treated like a neglected animal. She had to get involved.

If she found out Bert had killed his wife as well as Clements then he would be acknowledged as guilty and everyone could go about their business. But if he wasn't responsible for these crimes, it would mean the entire town had made the life of an innocent man pure hell for the past seventy years.

She hesitated as she reached the front door, thinking of Bert. What if today's incident was only the tip of the iceberg? What if Bert was subjected to even worse kinds of neglect or even abuse in here? He was unable to communicate and rarely had visitors, so how would he ask for help? Shaking her head, she turned around and retraced her steps to Bert's room. She knew she wouldn't be able to stop thinking about it if she didn't find out.

She sat down on a hard plastic chair by the side of the bed and waited. Bert's eyes opened shortly after and Pip managed a small smile.

'Bert, do the staff treat you okay here?' she asked quietly and waited as he blinked slowly in acknowledgement. 'It's okay to tell me if they aren't. I can help you.'

Bert only stared at her, and she realised she needed to make things a yes or no answer. 'Do you need me to step in and do something about the staff here?'

Slowly he gave two blinks.

'I heard the way they addressed you and I suspect they don't often show a great deal of respect when they're caring for you. You don't have to put up with that. I can follow this up if you want me to?'

The watery, pale eyes seemed to momentarily stare through her, as though he'd drifted off, before he refocused on her and blinked twice.

Pip paused for a moment before nodding. 'Okay. Go back to sleep,' she said gently. 'I'm sorry I disturbed you.'

A Stone's Throw Away

Pip hadn't seen any signs of neglect or mistreatment, though she got the impression he was simply resigned to living with the disrespect because it simply wasn't worth the hassle of complaining. This annoyed her even more because the people who treated him badly would get away with it. She knew that this really wasn't any of her business—she wasn't family—but who else did Bert have? He was defenceless, unable to move or communicate, and spent his days knowing that pretty much everyone around here hated him. What a terrible way for anyone to live out their last years.

A movement at the doorway made her look over.

'We meet again,' Erik said, his legs braced apart, his arms folded in typical cop fashion. She searched his face for any lingering animosity left over from their last exchange but was relieved to find nothing except a tiny glint of amusement.

'Are you here to speak with Bert about Molly?' she asked. 'He's just gone to sleep.'

'Actually, I'm here to speak with you.'

Pip lifted one eyebrow in surprise.

'Andrew Newman called to report an incident.'

'Did he now?' Pip said, settling back in her chair and crossing her legs.

'He's asked that you be escorted from the premises.'

'He's *what?*' she demanded, getting to her feet. *That little weasel.*

'You can't come in here throwing around threats about patient care and think they'll just let it slide.'

'I simply brought up the fact that his staff were being disrespectful to a resident.'

'I'm not here to get involved with all that—I'm just here to ask you to leave peacefully.'

'Are you serious? You're really kicking me out?'

'Look, for the sake of keeping the peace, I'm simply asking you to wrap up today's visit. Now.' When she continued to glare at him, he gave a small sigh. 'Let's not make this a thing.'

She watched him for a moment. She had to admit, the big policeman had spiked her interest, and there was no denying she found him attractive, but their last few encounters had left her feeling a little irritated. And what was going down right now was only adding to it. Sure, he might only be doing his job, but he hadn't made any secret of the fact that he wasn't a fan of journalists. She couldn't help but wonder if he was getting just a little too much enjoyment out of the situation. She knew that unless she wanted to cause a scene, she had no other option but to admit defeat. 'Fine,' she said gritting her teeth.

Erik stepped aside to indicate she should walk ahead of him, and Pip narrowed her eyes.

'If I don't go, what are you going to do—handcuff me?'

'You *want* me to handcuff you?' he asked with a grin.

'In your dreams,' Pip muttered as she walked past. 'This is ridiculous.'

'I thought you journos knew how to deal with people?'

'Apparently we rub some people the wrong way,' she mumbled as she walked out the door and Erik fell into step beside her.

'Yeah, well, not everyone handles threats well.'

'I didn't threaten him.'

'He implied you were going to go public with, and I quote, "untruths",' he said. 'Did you say that?'

'I may have mentioned I wrote for the *Daily Metro*, but I also told him I was here to write Bert's story.'

'You're a smart woman, Pip. You should know by now you can't go around poking bears without expecting them to react.'

'All I did was stand up for a man who can't stand up for himself. Would you let someone disrespect one of your relatives if they were in here?'

'He's not your relative, though, is he?' he pointed out. 'And I wasn't talking about that. I was talking about this whole Bert Bigsby thing. You're stirring up trouble. If you write that story, you'll just be inviting animosity.'

Pip stopped and waited as Erik turned to face her. 'Why is that?'

'You have to understand small towns. They're close-knit. Families are loyal and they can hold a grudge like no other,' he told her calmly. 'It doesn't help that you're an outsider,' he added. 'This is local business.'

As they walked outside, Pip ignored the whispers and curious looks from the staff and visitors they passed, but inside she was fuming. If people thought they could intimidate her into silence, they sure as hell didn't know her too well. If she hadn't already made up her mind to look into Bert and Molly's story, this had just decided it for her.

Fourteen

Pip waited at the front door, talking to the annoying barking white dog, trying to calm it down, but no amount of coaxing could shut Winston up.

'Oh hello, Pip. What a lovely surprise. Come on in,' Anne said, coming to the rescue and smoothly sweeping the small dog aside with her slippered foot to open the screen door.

'I hope I'm not interrupting,' Pip said, skirting around the dog and trying to ignore the fact it was sniffing about her feet, seemingly determined to trip her over.

'Not at all, dear. I was just going to put the jug on.'

She stood at the kitchen bench and watched as Anne bustled about in the kitchen. 'Go and take a seat,' Anne said, shooing her towards the table across the room and then following with a plate of jam drops. 'How have you been?' she asked with a kind smile.

'Busy, actually,' Pip said. 'I've just come back from Coopers Creek. I stopped in to see your Mr Bigsby.'

Anne stared at her with a hopeful look.

'I'm not making any promises, but I thought maybe I'd go through that box of stuff you have of Bert's and see if there's anything in there that could be useful.'

Before Pip had even got the last word out of her mouth, Anne was up and practically running from the room, only to return within moments carrying a cardboard box, which led Pip to suspect she'd had it stashed somewhere conveniently close, waiting for this very moment.

'I'll get Pete to drop over the others, they're too heavy to take now.'

Others? Hold on a minute . . .

'But this one has some of the more important things in it—his old war records and personal correspondence. There's some letters and a few books, that kind of thing. There were no letters from Molly, though,' she tacked on, looking thoughtful. 'I'm assuming Bert's belongings would have been lost after he was taken prisoner, perhaps? Not to worry, I'm sure whatever's in there will still be of interest to you,' she smiled encouragingly.

'Ah, okay . . . I'm sure this will be fine,' Pip said quickly. 'Pete doesn't have to worry about bringing over the others,' she tried to protest.

'No, that's perfectly fine. He won't mind.'

Pip knew it was pointless trying to argue; it seemed Anne had already decided. She was beginning to understand that Anne was a force to be reckoned with.

Pip's gaze wandered to the cardboard box on the table, and with a resigned sigh she stood and opened the top and peeked inside. A familiar smell greeted her—the musty, old-paper scent of things that had been stored away and forgotten for too long. She often encountered it while researching, digging through old papers and documents. It was a smell she always associated with curiosity and anticipation. She loved delving into archives and stepping back in time, getting lost in the past.

There was an assortment of smaller shoeboxes inside, and Pip withdrew one and carefully removed the lid, revealing a stack of letters, all neatly folded in their envelopes. She flicked through the pile and saw the envelopes were addressed to *Mrs Herbert Bigsby, Rosevale, Midgiburra*.

PVT. H. Bigsby
2/22nd Battalion
Victoria Barracks
Melbourne

My dearest Moll,
You know I'm not great at writing, but since I've been away, I've discovered, much to my surprise, it's the only thing that keeps me sane!
I know it's not the same as keeping a diary like you do. I used to marvel at your dedication as you scribbled away at night before you went to bed. But maybe in some way these letters back home will help to piece together my time away from you, once I return.

'I only glanced at a few of them,' Anne said, breaking the spell Pip had fallen under as she read. 'I'm a bit allergic to the dust,' she continued, giving a delicate sniff. 'I'm not sure how useful any of it will be to you, but you never know.'

'So Bert doesn't have any other relatives? He didn't have children?' Pip asked, frowning as she tried to fit the letter back in its envelope.

'No. No children. He used to speak about a brother, but I think he died as a child, and his parents were gone quite young too. He'd been working Rosevale since he was a boy. He never spoke about any other family, and the solicitors couldn't track any down after his stroke.'

How sad, Pip thought, still struggling with the letter as she peered inside and realised there was something else in there. Reaching in with her fingertips, she pulled out a photograph. Turning it over, she froze.

The sepia tones of the old photograph, worn around the edges and with a crease mark down the centre, could not take away the instantly recognisable woman caught in its image.

Sitting on a picnic rug in front of an old tree was the woman she'd seen in her dreams.

'Are you all right, dear?' Anne asked.

Pip lifted her gaze from the photo and held it up. 'Do you know who this woman is?' she asked.

Anne reached out and held the photo back slightly before a sad smile broke out on her face. 'That's Molly,' she said, handing the photo back. 'She looks like a movie star in this photo, doesn't she?'

Pip stared at the picture. Unlike her dream, the woman sitting on the blanket in this one wasn't bent over a notebook but leaning back, her feet crossed at the ankles, wearing a button-up dress with a narrow belt. Her shoulder-length hair was pulled back by a wide scarf and she was laughing at whoever was behind the camera taking the photo.

In the background, Pip could hear Anne chatting about something, but Pip was too numb to listen as she stared at the photo in her hand.

How was it possible?

'Pip?'

Pip glanced over and saw Anne watching her with a worried frown. 'You don't look so well. Here, sit down,' she said, moving the box aside and pulling out the chair for Pip to sink into.

'Thanks,' Pip said, feeling decidedly shaky. 'I'm sorry,' she murmured, realising she couldn't really tell Anne what had happened because she'd definitely sound like a crazy person. 'It must be the heat.'

'You poor thing. It *has* been terribly hot lately. I'll get you a glass of water.'

Pip looked back down at the photograph she still clutched in her hand before carefully putting it inside the box. Maybe she was hallucinating? She accepted the tall glass of cold water from Anne and took a long sip. Just ignore it, she told herself firmly, and had another drink. When she got back home, she would sit down and take another look at it. It was probably just a coincidence. It was just a similar pose that reminded her of her dream, that's all . . .

Pip stayed to have a cuppa at Anne's insistence, and when she'd been deemed looking well enough again, was allowed to go. She tried to stop thinking about the photo. She pushed it from her mind forcefully. She was not going to think about it. When she arrived home, she glanced at the cardboard box on the seat beside her and, after a resigned sigh, reached across and picked it up.

Inside the house, she turned a slow circle as she searched for a place to put it. She didn't want it on the kitchen bench. The table was ruled out—it was covered in research papers for the book she was *supposed* to be working on. She had to keep some kind of space clear of clutter, so in the end she decided on the floor. It was as good a place as any for the moment. Maybe she should give the place a big tidy up and try to get things a little more organised? She looked around and realised she had no idea where to even start, then dismissed the idea. She knew what the urge to reorganise and clean really was—just another attempt to delay writing.

She let out a long breath and surveyed the room, her gaze landing on the box on the floor.

Just do it, she told herself, as she sat at the table and eyed the box warily. Unclenching her hands from her lap, she gave an impatient huff and dragged the box over, opening the lid and pulling out the photo she'd placed in there earlier.

She sank back on the chair and stared mutely at the woman in the photo. In her dream she'd never really got a proper look at her, so logically, Pip thought now, she didn't really know for certain that this was the same woman. Yes, it was a weird coincidence that the photo resembled her dream, but other than the fact there was a woman on a blanket in a bush setting, she couldn't say this was the *same* woman.

But why would I be having a dream about a woman I didn't know in the first place? she wondered, unable to shake the lingering eeriness of the whole situation. It was too much of a coincidence. Surely?

Pip was relieved to find the initial shock she'd experienced earlier had subsided, and she was able to look at it now with a little more objectivity. There was clearly a reasonable explanation for everything—she just had to find it.

Putting the photo aside, she decided to take a quick look at the letters. Maybe distracting herself with those would put everything else into perspective.

Trawool, VIC, 15 July 1940

My dearest Moll,

After our brief phone call the other night, I can tell you we've finally arrived at camp.

I'm happy Frank and I are still in the same regiment—at least I get to go through all this with my best mate by my side. It makes everything a little bit easier to bear.

It's pretty cold here, not much joy living with eight blokes per tent. There's not a lot in the way of comfort either, but we're being kept too busy to complain. Every day it's training of some kind: weapons, drills, guard duty. Marching up and down hills. I reckon some of these fellas have had a rude shock. Especially two in our tent. One's a bank teller and the other's a teacher. I'm pretty sure neither of them had worked outside a day in their life before coming here.

Still, at least they're getting us ready to fight over in the Middle East—it won't be cold over there, we'll most likely be remembering this place fondly by then.

A Stone's Throw Away

Have you been getting any rain? I've been thinking, when I get home I'm going to put in a crop of potatoes. I've heard they're making a good profit. I miss the farm, and you of course.

I know it must be harder for you at home and I sorely wish I had left you with a babe so you had something to keep you busy. I have to say the idea of a family wasn't something I was thinking about before I left, even though I know you were hoping. I guess I was just happy having you all to myself. But listening to the men who have families, reading their letters out loud from their children, makes me think I really do want to start a family. You must get lonesome on the farm all day. It sounds like you've been working hard in the garden but don't go overexerting yourself. I promise I'll make you that flower garden in the front of the house as soon as I get home.

Anyway, I should sign off now as I hear the call for the mail and I want to get this letter off to you.

Know that I think of and miss you every day.

Your loving husband,
Bert

6 October 1940

My dear Moll,

Good news, we've left Trawool and have arrived at a new camp in Bonegilla. The bad news is we marched the whole way. They're calling it character building — I can think of a few other things I'd call it, but I won't risk your rolling pin to my head by repeating them here. I'm sorry I haven't been able to write, but on arrival at our new huts, which is a big improvement on draughty tents, I've discovered a nice stack of mail from you which I'm going to take my time and read through.

> There's been a steady flow of newcomers arriving and we're building into quite a force now. The arrival of the Army band has managed to cheer us up no end. The majority of them are from the Salvation Army and they seem like a decent bunch of fellas.
> Most of the towns we marched through gave us a warm welcome and for the most part the march wasn't too bad.

Pip read through a few more letters, all written from Bert's time in training camp with the 2/22nd Battalion, first in Trawool, then marching two hundred and thirty-five kilometres to Bonegilla where they arrived in October for further training until he received his orders to ship out. Judging from Bert's letters, he and the rest of the battalion had been assuming they'd be heading off to the Middle East, and from all accounts, so too had the army since they'd been training in desert warfare throughout his time at Bonegilla. So it must have been a shock when suddenly they were redirected instead to New Britain in Papua New Guinea.

17 April 1941

> Dearest Moll,
> I know four days wasn't anywhere near long enough to have together, and even though I tried to say everything I wanted to say, it still seems like there's more. I worry about you being there on your own and I know you put on a brave face about it all. I wish I didn't have to leave you. I can hear you saying, you didn't have to! But we both know that our country is under threat and I cannot in all good faith leave defending it to everyone else. I feel like this time, the war is coming to us. If we don't stop it, then who else will?

When this is all over we'll have time to make our home — together, just like we talked about. I'll plant that rose garden for you, like I promised, and we'll start our family.

Saying goodbye at the station after leave was the hardest thing I've had to do, but I've got your photo in my pocket and it'll keep me safe until I'm able to come back to you again.

I won't be able to write for a while, but once we've landed I'll let you know that I arrived safely.

Until then,

Your loving husband,
Bert

Pip heard the loneliness in Bert's words as well as the frustration. He was a young man in his prime, newly married, who just wanted to be back home with the woman he loved to start their life. Pip leafed through the pages and noted how frequently he'd written. By Bert's responses, though, she gathered Molly had told him that sometimes it was months and months between receiving them, only to have a number all arrive at once. How difficult that must have been, Pip thought. It was hard to relate to now with instant communication at your fingertips. The thought of not knowing where your loved ones were—if they were even still alive—would have been torture.

Pip glanced at her computer as she contemplated what she *should* be doing, which was writing, and what she wanted to do—which was to delve into Bert's army records and find out more about his war years. It was a cruel twist of fate that this amazing story had fallen into her lap at a time when she was snowed under with her book, but on the other hand . . . how could she resist taking a peek into something she genuinely found fascinating?

Ten minutes, she promised herself as she dragged her computer towards her.

Half an hour later, Pip had searched online service records and was reading through the images of scanned forms that filled her screen. She scrolled through a number of service and casualty forms, noting the extensive list of places and injuries ranging from bouts of malaria and dysentery to the flu and shrapnel damage Bert had received during his time away. There were forms that recorded promotions, and she saw that Bert had risen dramatically through the ranks. But it was while reading about his time in New Guinea that Pip uncovered the true hell this man had endured during his time in the army.

Rabaul was listed as his last station, just prior to the Japanese invasion. A memory of the story she'd done on the civilians who'd been evacuated from Rabaul flashed through her mind. How strange that she and Bert had this connection. What were the chances she would find him in a place she had been to and that had such a profound effect on her?

A report made after the war had ended was flagged with Bert's name, and she started to read.

On 23 January 1942 on the island of New Britain, Japan invaded, attacking a small Australian garrison and killing the majority of the forces stationed there. A number of men, including Bert Bigsby, managed to evade the enemy and survive in the jungle for three weeks before eventually becoming too ill with malaria to continue and giving himself up as a prisoner of war.

A Stone's Throw Away

Pip knew that those three weeks, sick, frightened and fighting to survive in the jungle, would have been hellish, but she could only imagine what he had suffered as a POW. She read the records from the Australian war crimes commission at which Bert had testified and learned what had happened at Rabaul after the invasion: the brutality and callous executions, the torture and illness. It was hard to believe that anyone had survived. The things Bert had seen and told the commission made even *her* journalist-hardened stomach turn.

The box Anne had given her also contained a couple of old albums filled with black-and-white photos, mostly group shots taken at social outings. From the distinctive fashions and hairdos, Pip placed the photos somewhere in the late 1930s or 40s. People sure knew how to dress back then, she thought wistfully as she admired the men in their waistcoats and trousers, and women in tailored dresses and jaunty sunhats. One photo looked to have been taken at a race day, judging by the large circular track in the distance, with a group of five people sitting or leaning on a ute as they smiled for the camera. Pip instantly recognised the woman from the other photo and turned it over to find a list of names scratched across the back in elegant cursive handwriting. *Bert, Molly, Frank, Irene and Bill. Midgiburra races, 1937.*

In the background, people sat picnicking on blankets, and men gathered about in groups. Her gaze came back to the forefront of the photo and narrowed in on the vehicle. She wasn't sure, but she had a feeling this might be the same car from the dam.

She kept flipping through the pages and stopped at a wedding photo.

The two people standing in the doorway of a brick church beamed at the camera as they stood arm in arm. The groom was a stocky, handsome man with dark hair and shining eyes, and his bride was a stunning blonde with long wavy hair. The photographer's stamp on the back of the photo had a hand-written name scrawled across it: *Bigsby*. Pip turned it back over and studied the couple. They looked so happy, their faces reflecting their joy as they left the church a newlywed couple ready to take on their future together. How sad that in the space of a few short years, their lives would be forever turned upside down.

There were photos of the farm: Molly and a house cow she was milking; Bert on an ancient-looking tractor ploughing a field; Bert and Molly standing together at the front gate of the house. The little house looked exactly as it did today. They both seemed blissfully unaware of the horrors to come.

As she turned the page, her hand hovered over a photo. Bert was standing in the back of an old farm ute, in the process of unloading a stack of large, heavy-looking produce bags. He was dressed in trousers, with braces over a long-sleeved shirt rolled up on his forearms. His face was slightly shaded by a low-slung hat, and he wore a lopsided grin around a cigarette in the corner of his mouth.

Bert Bigsby had been a good-looking rooster back in the day, but it was the ute she looked at now. It was the same shape and design as the one they'd pulled from the dam.

Pip scrolled through her received-calls list, locating the detective's number from a few days ago and hit call. Her stomach did a nervous little flip as she listened to the ring tone and told herself to stop it. She was just calling to tell him she found confirmation that the numberplates on the ute they found was definitely Bert's. There was absolutely no reason she should feel nervous about speaking with him again. When the call went to voicemail she abruptly hit end and quickly put the phone back on the table. It wasn't as though it was important, she told herself firmly, ignoring the disappointment that had followed when her call hadn't been answered.

What she needed was a distraction. And possibly chocolate. Grabbing her keys and her bag, she headed out the door.

Fifteen

She almost succeeded in avoiding the bakery—until she caught a whiff of delicious pastry and fattening goodness floating along the street, luring her towards it like a powerful siren.

The bell over the door dinged and a few moments later the same woman who served her last time emerged from the back room, wiping her hands on a tea towel.

This must be Jan, she thought absently, as she recalled Anne telling her how she'd found out about the Knight case.

'Morning,' Pip said cheerfully, letting her eyes roam the delectable delicacies in the glass cabinet before her. 'Can I get a vanilla slice, please?'

'You're that reporter,' Jan announced.

'I'm *a* reporter, yes. I'm not here for work, though,' she added.

'You're Nev's niece.' Again, the staunch woman didn't seem

to be asking her. She also didn't appear to be in any hurry to get her vanilla slice either.

'Yep.'

The woman's eyes narrowed. 'I heard you found the body.'

'Ah, no. I just hired Bob to clean out the dam.'

'So you didn't see it, then?'

'No. Not that there was anything to see—just some bones.'

'I heard they found her tied and gagged inside the car,' she said, folding her arms across the top of the glass cabinet and leaning forward eagerly.

'What? No. I don't believe that's how they found her.'

'That's what I heard.' Jan seemed to warm to the story as she continued. 'Old Bert had slit her throat and rolled her into the dam.'

'I really don't think there's any way the police could have determined *that*.'

'Wouldn't surprise me. Crazy old bastard,' she muttered.

Pip thought back to Bert's records from his time in New Guinea, anger rising at the woman's outright distain. 'You know he was away fighting a war and went through hell before all this happened? I'm fairly sure we all owe a debt of gratitude to Bert Bigsby and all the men like him who came home after that, damaged.'

'Other men came back after war without turning into murderers. You can't blame the war for everything.'

'There's no proof that Bert killed his wife. Until there is, I don't think it's fair to judge him. Besides, there can't be that many people left in town who were even around when all this happened. So all this speculation is just gossip.'

'I heard you were writing a book about it,' the woman said, narrowing her eyes. 'You wanna make sure you ask the locals for their opinions before you go and gloss everything over. Don't be fooled just because he looks like a sad old man in a nursing home. He had a temper on him back in the day—a mean one. That don't just go away overnight.'

'I'm simply looking into the story at the moment.'

'I'm just saying, make sure you get all the facts before you start throwing your big-city accusations around here,' she said, pushing away from the counter.

Big-city accusations? Seriously?

'Heard you made a bit of a scene up at the nursing home the other day.'

'You hear a lot of things,' Pip commented sceptically.

'My daughter works up there. People don't take too kindly to outsiders coming in and laying down the law.'

'People also don't like it when they see someone disrespecting the elderly in their care.'

'Seems like we're all sold out of vanilla slice today,' the woman said sharply.

Pip held her tongue and forced a brittle smile to her lips. 'That's okay. Thanks anyway.'

She left the shop with as much dignity as she could muster, despite the fact that inside, she was fuming. This had to be some kind of record: being kicked out of not one but two places since she'd arrived.

What was wrong with these people? Why was there still so much animosity surrounding such an old incident? It was a serious crime, yes, and likely grisly, but these people were the children, grandchildren and great-grandchildren of the locals who were alive when it had all happened, and yet they seemed to be holding onto their anger like it only happened yesterday.

Maybe it was a case of hand-me-down prejudice? Family folklore that just passed from one generation to the next. But what if Bert had been innocent all this time? She understood better now why Anne was so distraught over Bert's history of treatment from his fellow neighbours. If Bert had simply been a grieving husband, innocent of murdering Vernon Clements and beside himself with worry over the whereabouts of his missing wife for close to seventy years, the injustice of the whole situation would be completely unacceptable. After having just been on the receiving end of local animosity herself, she could only imagine how much worse it must have been for Bert.

Why hadn't Bert packed up and left? Instantly she knew the answer: he'd been waiting for Molly to come home. In that moment, any remaining doubt in her mind over Bert's innocence had just been eliminated. No one would put up with decades of abuse and ignorance unless they had a stronger reason to stay. Well, maybe Pip would reconsider writing that damn book after all ... once she had the evidence to wave under this town's collective nose that proved Bert's innocence once and for all.

Pip walked up to the counter inside the police station and nodded a greeting to the young female constable who'd been at the dam, now sitting across the room behind a computer.

'Can I help you?' she asked in her no-nonsense tone, her hair pulled back in a tight bun. Pip couldn't help but wonder if this was the woman's normal personality or just a persona, put on to give people a sense of professionalism they may otherwise doubt in someone so young. Pip remembered well what that felt like as a rookie, just starting out in her field.

'I was hoping to see Detective Jarrett for a moment, if possible.'

'The detective isn't in today. Can I help you instead?'

'Oh. Ah, no, that's okay. It wasn't important. I'm sure I'll catch up with him some other time.'

She was fairly sure they wouldn't be interested in a photo of the car, anyway. She also didn't want to have to acknowledge—or worse, examine—the fact that she could have simply called the detective again instead of dropping by the station to see him. She was definitely *not* disappointed that she hadn't got to see him today.

Pip almost felt bad at the woman's despondent expression and hesitated before leaving. 'Are you from Midgiburra?' she asked, curious about the constable's oddly militant style. 'Originally, I mean?'

The personal question appeared to surprise her. 'Not exactly,' she said awkwardly.

She didn't seem as though she fitted in here, and yet there was an innocence about her that didn't seem big-city either.

'My mother's family came from here.'

'Is this your first posting?'

The constable nodded a little jerkily as she busied herself shuffling the papers on her desk. 'My family have a long history in the police force. My mother started her career here, before she got married and moved away.'

'So you're following a family tradition?'

'I guess so,' she said without much enthusiasm.

'Is your mother still in the police force?'

'She retired last year.'

'Do you still have family in town?' The constable eyed her almost suspiciously. 'Sorry, force of habit—I get interested in something and tend to ask a lot of questions.'

'That's all right. Sergeant Nielsen says I need to work a bit more on my public relations skills,' she said quickly, then lowered her eyes once more to her computer screen. 'My mother was a Maguire,' she said, 'so I guess you could say I still have a few relatives in town.'

'Yeah, I've noticed that name on quite a lot of signs around the place. It must be a big family.'

The constable looked up briefly before nodding. 'I don't really know them. We didn't visit my grandparents very often.'

'Oh,' Pip murmured, as the conversation dried up. 'Well, I better let you get back to work,' she said, glancing about the small, quiet office. There didn't seem to be a great deal of anything happening to interrupt. 'I'll see you around.'

She received a sharp nod in response as the woman went back to scrolling through whatever she was reading on the screen before her. What she lacked in personality, she certainly made up for in dedication to the job, Pip thought as she pushed open the screen door and left the station.

She made a quick stop into the supermarket and bought some consolation chocolate, then in a spur-of-the-moment decision, she googled a vanilla slice recipe and tossed in the ingredients before heading back to the farm. *Take that, cranky bakery lady. I'll make my own.*

The library at Coopers Creek was a cool sanctuary to escape the heat outside. The soft hum of the air conditioner provided a soothing background for Pip as she sat at the old microfiche machine. She'd pulled the film for the local newspaper from back around the time of Vernon Clements' murder, looking for as much information as she could find.

It took longer than she'd anticipated, which shouldn't have been a surprise; she always found herself getting distracted by research, especially when it came to old newspaper archives. She found everything about them fascinating—the history, the language they used, the unapologetic sexism in their cringeworthy advertisements—and often discovered herself reading articles not even remotely relating to what she was originally researching. Today was no exception. The *Midgiburra Gazette* was a wealth of local information.

The Clements murder had been covered near and far. Pip found accounts of it mentioned in major city and regional newspapers all across the country, but it was the local paper, understandably, that followed the case in more detail.

The initial report filled a whole front page and most of page two with the discovery of Vernon's body, detailing exactly how he'd been discovered, by whom and what they saw at the scene. They described in excruciating detail every aspect of the murder scene, including that Vernon had been found slumped over the steering wheel, his shirt covered in blood and a deep wound to his chest that looked to have been caused by a sharp knife or some other instrument. The murder weapon, however, was not located at the scene.

In a following article, they covered the inquest into the murder, which also included the disappearance of Molly Bigsby and the suspicion that foul play had been entered into.

Pip noted that Bert had been interviewed briefly, but due to the fact he had an alibi—his visit to his doctor—there wasn't a lot he could be questioned about. He was asked if he knew his wife and the deceased had been having an affair, and he'd said he did but he believed that it had been over. Pip could only imagine the humiliation involved for anyone having to sit in a courtroom and have their personal life played out in front of the whole town like that.

He had also been questioned about his temper and a number of incidents he had been involved in since returning from the war, one of which was a fight in the bar with a man named Frank Maguire. There were a couple of other altercations mentioned at the inquest that involved mostly drunken behaviour. They hadn't resulted in any charges against Bert but were clearly being brought up to perhaps cast a shadow on Bert's reputation.

The police had no evidence that Bert was responsible for Vernon's death, but clearly, they had no other suspects to link it to, and the fact it was public knowledge that Bert's wife had been having an affair with the deceased would have made him a prime suspect . . . if he'd been in town that night. Interestingly, Pip noted, the surname of the police sergeant who was interviewed by the coroner at Vernon's inquest was Maguire. In a town where everything seemed to include the name Maguire, it probably wasn't unusual, yet the names of the witnesses to some of Bert's altercations after his return from the war also shared the same surname.

Still, there was nothing that had directly linked Bert to the murder of Vernon Clements or Molly's disappearance. As far as Pip could tell, Vernon and Bert hadn't had any public run-ins—at least, nothing that had been recorded.

So when on paper there was no evidence that connected Bert to Vernon's murder, why would a town have such a steadfast conviction that Bert was a murderer?

Sixteen

Pip braced herself as she pushed open the door of the nursing home and walked inside. She was half expecting to see a photo of herself on the wall with 'Do not let this woman in!' written across the bottom. However, no alarms went off and no one appeared to frog march her back outside, so she kept her head down and made for the hallway that led to Bert's room.

She knocked on the open door and stepped inside. Bert was resting—no doubt there was little else for him to do. His pasty skin almost blended in with the white of the bed sheets, leaving him looking frail and sunken. It was hard to recognise the man in the bed as the younger version of himself from the photos in the album. Again, Pip fought back a wave of sympathy. No one deserved to see out the last years of their life trapped inside a body that couldn't move.

When she pulled the seat closer and sat down, Bert opened his eyes and she dragged up a smile. 'Hello, Bert. I hope you don't mind that I've come back for a visit.'

Slowly the man blinked twice.

'I've been looking through your photo albums,' she said, taking out the wedding photo. 'Would you like me to leave this one here where you can see it?' His gaze was locked on the photo as she propped it up on the table beside his bed. 'Molly was very beautiful,' she said quietly. 'You weren't too bad yourself, Bert,' she added, but he didn't smile.

'I looked up your army records,' she ventured. 'I saw that you were in New Guinea for a while.' He didn't give any kind of reaction, so she forged on mostly just to make conversation. 'I spent some time there myself. I did a story on civilians who were living there just prior to the Japanese invasion on Rabaul.'

She saw a faint flutter of his eyelid at the mention of the last town he'd been stationed at.

'I was really sorry to hear about what you went through during that time, Bert. I know a little bit about Lark Force and what happened to your battalion after the invasion.' She let out a slow breath. 'I just can't imagine how difficult that must have been to deal with.'

She wished Bert could talk—could tell her about his experiences. Not that he probably would; it was often hard to get men of this era to relive their war days. She understood why they'd rather not, and yet there was so much history entwined around this man and his life. As someone who found the war years fascinating, she would have loved to interview him.

But this wasn't about his war years—not entirely. It was what happened after he returned home. It was about Molly.

'Bert, I'm curious why people around here are still so certain you were responsible for Molly and Vernon's death when you had an alibi.'

He was still looking at the photo, but she thought maybe his eyes seemed to lose their faraway look briefly, and she continued.

'The thing is, I'm struggling to work out why a town as close-knit as this one would be out to crucify one of their own, who was not only a war hero but had also been a POW. In my experience, men like you were respected when they came home. It just isn't adding up.'

Pip considered Bert thoughtfully. 'I saw in the court transcripts there'd been mention of a few incidents—fights after you returned from the war. But there wasn't anything about you and Vernon mentioned.' There was, however, mention of the Maguires. Pip hesitated before bringing it up, but she was curious. 'Bert, did you have some kind of quarrel with the Maguires?'

She waited for him to blink, but he simply continued to stare at the wedding photo.

'Remember, blink once for yes. Twice for no,' she prompted when he didn't react.

When there was still no response, Pip frowned. Was this a deliberate silence he was giving her?

'The inquest tried to make something of the fact that you had a temper.' As she heard the words come out of her mouth, she could all too easily see why the police would have seen big red flags waving. A man with a temper. Drinking and getting into fights. His wife cheating on him while he was imprisoned in a POW camp. It wasn't difficult to see why Bert was a prime suspect in a murder—possibly two. And yet, she still couldn't shake this *thing* that was telling her to keep an open mind. Keep on digging. But digging where? So far she hadn't managed to turn up anything useful.

It was hard to believe that this man was the same one from the photos and letters she'd been reading—the man who had been so vital and full of life before the war.

'Were the Maguires connected to Vernon's murder in some way?' she prodded. 'Is that why there was a feud back then?' *Or still to this day?* she added silently.

Slowly, Bert blinked twice.

So no, he didn't think the Maguires had anything to do with Vernon's murder. But that didn't answer any other questions about why there was clearly something behind the whole thing. Pete's words came back to her about the Maguires' somewhat distasteful dealings, cashing in on local land. But that wasn't related to the deaths of Vernon and Molly. Once again, Pip had reached a dead end.

She followed Bert's gaze to the photo of the beautiful woman gazing up into her handsome husband's eyes, so full of trust and love. She saw a tear slide from the corner of his eye. Was it grief or guilt? She studied the man in the bed before her. It didn't feel like guilt.

The shock of seeing Molly's photo after all this time was clearly significant, and Pip realised it was unlikely he'd be able to focus on communicating while he was so distracted.

A Stone's Throw Away

With a disheartened sigh, she stood up and left the old man to lose himself once more in his memories.

Rabaul, 27 April 1941

Dear Moll,

We've arrived in New Britain and been sent to Rabaul to form a garrison.

It kind of reminds me of being in Queensland — the houses and buildings all look much the same, built up high with big verandahs to catch any breeze.

You'd love the frangipani trees — they're planted all over the island here in all kinds of colours — and gardens are full of hibiscus and bougainvillea. There are Australians everywhere, just like at home, businessmen and families and people who work on the plantations. It's been a nice change to see something almost familiar compared to some of the other places we've been in lately. So close to home, and yet still so far away. I miss you, Moll. You have no idea how much.

It's the little things I miss the most, like the smell of your hair after it dries, and how your head fits just right in the spot between my neck and my shoulder when we lie in bed at night. I miss hearing your laugh. I even miss hearing you get cranky at me for forgetting to take my boots off at the back door — who'd ever think a bloke could miss that!

As you've been seeing in the papers back home, the Japs have been ramping up their efforts in these parts. They're not down this far yet and I'm sure we'll manage to hold them off, but things have got a lot busier around the place lately.

Thank you for sending over the socks and biscuits. The humidity here is something terrible — your boots and socks practically rot off on your feet. And the local newspapers have been a nice distraction to stay up to date with what's been going on back home. I've been sharing them with Frank and Bill, although Frank seems to always know the latest news before any of us — must be nice to have a family connection to someone in parliament!

Speaking of which, I see the Maguires have bought out another two local farms. I know I've always sworn I'd only ever sell Rosevale to a Maguire over my dead body, but, well, I've been thinking. If that happens, I want you to do what's right for you, Moll. If selling up and moving away is what you want to do, then you have my blessing. Of course, I'd rather come home, but I've been in this war long enough to realise you never know when your time's up. Lost a lot of mates who weren't ready to go. Truth be told, I've no idea why I've managed to stay alive this long when so many haven't.

I'm sorry, love, I know you're probably going to be reading this and getting yourself all worked up with worry, that wasn't my intention. I just wanted to let you know that if the worst was to happen, I'd want you to do whatever you felt was best for you and not hang on to Rosevale just because you think that's what I'd want you do.

But you won't have to worry about any of that, because I'm coming home to you, Moll. I promised you when I left I would — and you know that I always keep my promises.

Your ever-loving husband,
Bert

Pip kept track of the timeline through the dates on the letters and realised it was creeping closer to the time when Bert was taken prisoner. It was a very strange feeling, reading these letters and seeing a moment in history unfold before her eyes but with the advantage of already knowing what that future held. Dread gnawed inside her as the pile of letters left to read grew smaller. She knew what fate awaited Bert—and, ultimately, Molly.

Each letter from now on was the countdown until Molly would stop hearing from her husband. He would be reported as missing, and she wouldn't find out until almost a year later that he had been located in a prisoner-of-war camp.

The next few letters after Bert's arrival in New Guinea spoke about the growing unease within the camp. Supplies were getting low, and malaria was rampant along with infections caused by the tropical conditions getting into even the smallest scratches; left untreated, these could turn into ulcers and eventually blood poisoning. However, Bert always managed to brush over the discomforts of his predicament by regaling Molly with tales of daily camp life and his mates. The stories he told usually included Bill, Smithy and Frank, Pip noticed.

Rabaul, 8 June 1941

... The volcano I told you about before, Tavurvur, has been rumbling a bit lately. Then a few days ago, just after reveille, we experienced several earthquakes. I don't mind telling you, Moll, it was a little bit unnerving. The very air around us seemed to quiver, and then with an almighty bang, we stood there and watched it explode. Rocks flew into the air and ash began raining down. It was a sight, to be sure! Bill and Smithy even began reciting prayers, even though neither of them had seen the inside of a church since they were knee high to a grasshopper.

Once the initial shock wore off, we realised we needed to clear out of camp and head to safer ground, but we were told that there was no immediate threat, despite the fact it continues to send thick clouds of foul-smelling gas into the air and roars like a train running straight above us. It's even louder than Frank's snoring, and that's saying a lot! At night it gets so loud the whole camp is up. But it's the earthquakes that are more of an annoyance than anything else. If you try to stand up when they're happening, you feel like you're walking home with more than a few beers under your belt from a big night out at the pub. And the smell! Apparently it's the sulphur—stinks like rotten eggs. We're constantly kept busy cleaning weapons because of the ash that's started corroding everything, even our uniforms and tents.

We've been given orders to move the garrison to a safer spot, which has delighted the boys no end as you can imagine!

Bert went on to ask about the farm and caution Molly not to overexert herself, as he usually did in his letters. Pip couldn't help but smile; even during the horrors of war, Bert was always concerned about Molly's comfort.

Rabaul, 12 June 1941

Dear Moll,
Frank and I got into the market today—what an eye-opening experience that was! It's a big change from Midgiburra, that's for sure. They call the market a bung and its full of every kind of tropical food or fruit you can imagine. There's pineapples and coconuts and fresh seafood—so much seafood, stacked up in enormous piles. And the noise! Dogs barking and running around, kids playing, chooks running loose about the place and stallholders calling out and trying to get you to buy their wares. And the colours—Moll, you've never seen anything like it. They wear these bright coloured material

skirts called lap-laps — even the men! — and go bare-chested about the place. And they're big men too; I certainly wouldn't like to pick a fight with any of them. They seem friendly enough, though. Mostly I think they like Australians, though I'm not too sure how they feel about so many of us over here. Still, we're probably much more preferred than the Japs, I guess.

Rabaul, 5 October 1941

My dearest Moll,

    Sometimes it's strange here. It feels almost like we're posted somewhere back home. There's a movie theatre, and Frank and a few of the boys and I sometimes head into Rabaul to watch something if we've got any coin left, but more often than not, I choose to stay in camp. There's plenty to do here, plus there's beer in the canteen — usually not cold, but beggars can't be choosers as the saying goes. There's often a game of two-up to be had, and the Midgiburra boys are always keen to get involved in the cricket. They keep us pretty busy with the sports — mostly to try to keep us out of trouble, I suspect!

    But I do miss your cooking something fierce, Moll. It's hard to raise much enthusiasm for the stuff they try to pass off as tucker here. As I force it down, I try to imagine it's one of your baked dinners with that gravy you make. I swear no one cooks like you, Moll.

Pip imagined Bert's letters home to Molly were more of a way to distract himself from his surroundings, perhaps picturing himself sitting right here in the kitchen as he wrote. Across from his beloved Moll, telling her about his day. Only it was war, and unlike anything either of them could have imagined.

For the next few months, the letters, while still regular, were briefer and contained a lot of questions for Molly to answer. The stories about camp life had stopped. There was a subtle difference in the tone of his letters as well: less humour and fewer curious observations about his new environment. And then there was the final letter.

Pip hesitated before picking it up. She glanced at the date and saw it was written in late December, just weeks before the January attack on Rabaul and the Japanese invasion.

Rabaul, 22 December 1941

Dear Moll,

This might be the last chance I get to send out a letter for a while.

By the time you get this, Christmas will have been and gone. I know it won't feel much like Christmas back home this year, but I hope you'll still try to get involved with the festivities around town. I hear there's a dance on at the hall and I know you've been involved with the comforts fund and doing what you can to help. It helps me to know you've got people around you. I've had a letter or two from Ida next door, and she assures me they've been calling in on you often. They've always been good people.

I'll be thinking of you Christmas morning and wishing I was there beside you. So sing and be merry and have a cold one for me. Next Christmas we'll look back and think of how lucky we are to be together, and all this will finally be in the past. How I wish we were there already.

It looks like we'll be seeing some action around the place shortly. The Japs are on the move. As a precaution, they've evacuated women and children from here. I don't want you to worry if you don't hear from me for a while. I have a feeling the mail will be pretty hit and miss for the next little bit.

I have to get this off before I miss the last call for mail. Wishing you a merry Christmas, my love.

Your loving husband,
Bert

Pip knew that the battle was the start of years of cruelty and imprisonment for Bert and his fellow diggers. They hadn't stood a chance against the onslaught of the Japanese invasion, with no reinforcements and no hope of victory.

For most Australians, the battle of Kokoda had become iconic, but Pip was aware of the horrendous losses suffered by the Anzac troops and Australian civilians when Rabaul and the outer islands were attacked, culminating in one of the largest defeats of World War Two.

The 1400-strong Australian garrison at Rabaul where Bert had been stationed was overrun by the Japanese, and many diggers were massacred. Accounts of the enemy using captured soldiers as bayonet practice for young Japanese troops would send a surge of horror and anger through Australians back home. The attack brought home the chilling realisation that Australia itself was under direct threat, and invasion was a very real possibility.

Pip stared numbly at the letter in her hand. How many times would Molly have read and reread this in the absence of any further correspondence from her husband? Inside the box beside Pip were faded newspaper clippings, reports of atrocities only made known months later when survivors began to resurface. The few who had managed to escape and flee the island for safety recounted the horrific executions of the Australian men and nurses who'd been captured after the invasion—the fate of hundreds of others would remain unknown for years until the end of the war when POW camps were liberated and the prisoners returned home. Home, Pip thought sadly. Where Bert had longed to be and where he and Molly had planned to pick up where they'd left off. The place to start their life over again.

Seventeen

Pip glanced up from her seat on the back verandah and watched as the big four-wheel drive approached. She slowly stood as the tall man climbed out and started towards the front door.

'Detective,' she said, greeting him. 'You make house calls?'

'Ms Davenport,' he returned, nodding his head slightly.

'Pip,' she corrected him automatically.

He gave a brief smile and rested a foot on the first step, placing one hand on his hip and the other against the railing post. 'I heard you were looking for me in at the station the other day.'

'It wasn't urgent,' she said, feeling that weird sensation once more. She hadn't been *looking* for him—she'd simply asked if he was in. Why did she feel like he was deliberately trying to put her off balance all the time? 'You didn't have to make a special trip all the way out here.'

'I don't like being stuck inside, so I was happy for an excuse to get out of the office.'

She found his deep, lazy drawl something of a curiosity. She was used to the detectives she'd worked with in the past; they were more . . . well, polished. Not quite as laid-back as Detective Jarrett. He wasn't in a suit today—instead, he was dressed in blue jeans, tan boots and a long-sleeved shirt with the sleeves rolled up.

'Do you want a coffee? I was just about to have one around the back.'

He hesitated for a second, holding her gaze before giving a nod. 'Sure. If I'm not interrupting.'

'No, I was just writing. Come around,' she said, leading the way to the table and chairs under the shade of the verandah. She quickly cleared the table, pocketing her hard drive and dropping the open books and paperwork onto the bench seat under the window.

'Have a seat. How do you take your coffee?' she asked, pushing open the squeaky screen door to walk into the kitchen. To her surprise, he followed and she watched as he took a seat at the bench, picking up a pen and idly threading it back and forth through his fingers.

'Do I smell something burning?' he asked, sniffing the air.

Pip bit back a snippy reply, sending a disgusted glance at the burnt saucepan soaking in the sink after her attempt at making custard took a disastrous turn earlier that day. So much for vanilla slice . . .

'So what was it you wanted to see me about?' he asked as she took down cups.

'I was just wondering if you've come up with anything new . . . on the case.'

'I hear you've been researching?' he countered, glancing up from his pen-fiddling.

Pip shrugged. 'I recently came into possession of some interesting material.'

'Would you be willing to share it with me?' he asked.

'That depends,' she said, turning to put the coffee into the machine.

'On what?'

'If you share what you've got with me,' she threw back.

He raised an eyebrow slightly as he considered her request. 'You know that I can just get a court order and take whatever you've got if it relates to the case, right?' he asked in that lazy drawl.

'I know,' she said lightly, 'but I figure that since you have such a huge workload of cases that need to be dealt with *right now*, you might need someone to help you look into this cold case and take some of the load off your shoulders.'

'I've got strong shoulders,' he pointed out, and her gaze briefly went to them now.

He really did. They were quite broad as far as shoulders go. 'I'm just offering some help. A lot of this case is research and that just happens to be my speciality.'

'I thought you weren't interested? Just . . . curious.'

'I changed my mind.'

'So you *are* doing a story on the Bigsby case?'

'No. Not a story. I've just decided I really want to know what happened. And I don't believe Bert has had a fair go over the years. This is probably the last chance we have to prove his innocence, and I'd like to try—for his sake.'

'I see,' he said slowly as he followed her outside once the coffee was done.

'There's no way you're going to have time to go through everything I have from Bert, so I can do it for you—compile a list, weed out all the stuff that's not important. And in return, you can maybe show me the old files on the Vernon Clements murder and Molly Bigsby's missing persons record?' she said, looking over at him hopefully. She figured she may as well ask—what was the worst that could happen? He could only say no.

'No,' he said, shaking his head.

Pip stared at him. That wasn't how it was supposed to go. 'Why not?' she asked, feeling more than a little put out by his response.

'Because technically you can't work on the case. You're not a cop,' he pointed out, taking his coffee.

'It's a seventy-year-old cold case. It's been ignored for decades!'

'That doesn't mean we don't take it seriously.'

'Really? Could have fooled me. Poor old Bert's been living here and treated like a criminal all this time, and no one has even bothered to try to solve Vernon's murder to prove Bert was innocent.'

'They ran out of leads,' he said with a helpless gesture.

A Stone's Throw Away

'Well, now you've got some.'

'Exactly, and we're looking into it, but there still isn't much to go on. The evidence is pretty minimal—there are no witnesses left alive, and the focus of the investigation is in a nursing home and can't speak.'

'Which is why you need my help.'

'What makes you think you can find out anything that we can't?'

'The same way I managed to expose a criminal enterprise that was operating right under the police force's nose,' she snapped. It still frustrated her that Lenny Knight had managed to get away with so much thanks to the corrupt police officials on his payroll and that no one else had done a thing about it.

'Fair point,' he finally said, watching her intently. 'I followed that case while it was unfolding.' He dropped his gaze and she sat back in her chair. 'It took guts to go through with it the way you did. Most people would have let it go,' he said, meeting her eyes once more.

'I'm stubborn like that,' she said.

She saw his eyes crinkle at the corners a little. 'So I'm discovering. But seriously, that took a lot of courage.'

Pip felt herself shift in her seat at the compliment. She didn't like to dwell on the personal side of the story. It *had* taken a lot to go through with it all. The exposé was only the beginning. Her testimony and the tedious hours of investigating and following a seemly endless paper trail to uncover Knight's dirty dealings had been the biggest sacrifice she'd made—her time, her social life, her personal safety. Those were the things that had been taken away from her in order to get to the truth—things she would never get back.

'I was just doing my job,' she said, trying to shrug it off.

'Hell of a way to earn a living, lady,' he shot back.

'Well, in comparison, this would be a walk in the park,' she said, trying for the best puppy dog look she could summon and finding, to her surprise, that it seemed to work.

'I'll think about it,' he finally said, and inside she gave herself a high five.

Pip glanced around at the lengthening shadows.

'I guess I should let you get back to your Friday evening,' he said, standing up.

'It's just another day of the week at the moment,' she shrugged, reaching for their empty cups. She turned and found they were standing almost chest to chest. Pip breathed in and caught the clean linen smell of his shirt and a masculine, bergamot-citrus scent sent her pulse into immediate overdrive. *God, he smells delicious.*

'That's a bit sad.'

Pip gave a small, nervous laugh as she stepped around him. Story of her life. 'I'm afraid my party days are over. I'm not even sure I could stay up past nine pm nowadays.'

'Yeah, I've got to admit, I try to find any excuse to get out of actually going out on the weekends now. It sucks getting old.'

She would have toasted the remark if she had a drink. Speaking of which ... 'If you don't have anything to hurry home for, I was about to open a bottle of wine?' *Is this really a good idea?* a little voice asked inside her head. *What are you doing?*

When he hesitated, she worried the offer might be out of line and he would look at her strangely, but he didn't. 'Sounds great.'

Pip led the way inside and grabbed two glasses, and then it seemed normal to heat up the oven and put in the pizza she was planning to have for dinner, to share.

It should have felt weird to have a man in her house, but it didn't. If she'd been alone right now maybe she would have examined it a little closer, but right now, it just felt . . . her first thought was *nice*, but she quickly erased that; there was nothing *nice* about Detective Jarrett. Nice was more how she would describe Erik, and yet that didn't fit either. Erik had definitely rekindled a spark of interest, and he was a handsome man—in a masculine, manly kind of way. He gave the impression of a typical good-natured, all-Aussie bloke who liked football and barbecues and weekends with his mates.

Chris, on the other hand . . . Chris was . . . she found herself looking at him across the kitchen and realised with a start that he was watching her with a curious expression. She felt a blush creep up her throat. He made her nervous, but not in a bad way. In a way that she also found a little exciting.

'Have you always been drawn to stories on corruption?' he asked, breaking the charged silence they had fallen into while she'd been busy thinking about things she probably shouldn't.

'No,' she said, taking out two plates from the cupboard. 'I like telling people's stories.'

'Like this one, about Bert and Molly,' he said.

'Well, it's been a while since I've written something that didn't involve a politician,' she said with a faint smile.

'What do you love writing about? If you could write about anything, what would it be?'

Pip thought about his question for a moment, realising she'd never been asked that before. 'Stories about bravery,' she said finally, bracing her hands on the edge of the bench as she looked over at him. 'Some of the most inspiring people I've met have been men and women caught up in the horror of war, who have managed to overcome some of the worst experiences imaginable.'

'Like Bert?'

'Yes,' she nodded. 'And others,' she said, thinking about the eleven-year-old boy executed by the Japanese army. 'Not all of them overcame the horrors of war,' she amended sadly. 'The stories stayed with me.'

'What is it that drew you to this one?'

She glanced at him to see if he was genuinely interested or just making conversation. 'Besides the fact that a woman's remains were found in the bottom of a dam on my uncle's property?'

'Besides that,' he smiled, and she realised she liked the way his eyes crinkled when he did.

'I don't know, I guess Bert. Once I met him, I felt like . . .' She paused.

'Like what?' he prompted.

'You're going to think it's weird,' she cautioned.

'Try me.'

She sighed. 'The thing is, as a journalist, I'm usually wary of taking anyone at their word. You know, I have to back things up, corroborate their story with facts. Like you, I guess,' she added with a small wave towards him. 'But with Bert . . . I *believe* he's innocent. Like, I know there's still some doubt surrounding all this, but I just know he didn't kill Molly.'

'I don't think that's weird.'

'But you don't necessarily think the same?' she concluded when she saw hesitation in his expression.

'I like to make sure all the i's are dotted and t's are crossed.'

That was a good thing, she thought. If a cop, and a detective at that, wasn't thorough, then he wasn't doing his job.

'Erik Nielsen mentioned you were new to Coopers Creek. How long have you been there?'

'Not long at all,' he replied. 'Still settling in. You talk to Nielsen often?' he asked, and her eyes were drawn to the way his hands were steepled in front of him as he sat at the bench. She looked up and noticed the careful way he seemed to be watching her.

'Not really. I've bumped into him a few times around town.' Although he still wore that easygoing smile, it didn't quite reach his eyes the way it normally did. Now she felt stupid for bringing up his name. She'd noticed Erik's annoyance at the mention of Chris in a previous exchange—or rather, that the case was being handled by Chris in Coopers Creek. She watched him for a moment, wondering: was this mutual disquiet she was picking up on simply work-related, or was it personal?

Eighteen

'So tell me, what made you change your mind about doing the story?' he asked later. They'd been talking nonstop for the best part of two hours.

'I'm not *doing* a story,' she said stubbornly. 'I'm looking into the evidence.'

'Yeah, yeah, we both know you're doing a story. Might not be today, but you will.'

Pip rolled her eyes but answered his question. 'I can't stand injustice. I went to visit Bert and I caught a glimpse of what his life had been like all this time. It was terrible. He was a war hero—he'd been a POW and he came home broken. He gave up six years of his life for this country and they turned on him. After everything, they ridiculed and tormented him for seventy years.' She shook her head.

'You remind me of my mother,' he said after a while.

This change in direction made her look up. 'How so?'

'She was always fighting for the underdog too.'

'Was? Does that mean she's passed?'

'Yeah. A couple of years ago now.'

'What was she like?' Something about the way his face softened when he'd mentioned his mum made her curious.

'She was a pocket-sized rocket—much like you,' he said with a smile that seemed slightly bemused. 'But with the fire of the Irish,' he added, and his smile turned indulgent.

'Your mother was Irish?' she asked, surprised.

His grin told her he enjoyed revealing that little titbit. 'Yep. She stood five foot tall if she were an inch and had long, flaming red hair.'

'So you're half Irish,' she mused.

'To be sure, to be sure,' he said in a fair imitation of an Irish accent.

'So what's the other half?' she said, reaching for her glass and taking a sip.

'My dad was from Papunya up north, about two hundred and forty kilometres north-west of Alice Springs.'

'How did they meet?' She sensed the beginning of a good story.

'Mum was a backpacker who worked her way up to Papunya. She was a teaching student back in Ireland and she volunteered at the mission near where my dad lived. The story goes she broke down one afternoon on the way back from picking up supplies, and this tall, dark, handsome ringer from a cattle station up the road came past and offered her a ride.'

'So, you didn't take after your dad then,' she said, raising an eyebrow.

'Fine, just for that, I won't finish the story,' he said, crossing his hands over his stomach where he sat on the floor of the lounge room, his long legs stretched out in front of him, but a ghost of a smile hovered at the corners of his mouth.

'Okay, I'm sorry, that was uncalled for. I'll refrain from any further comment.'

He sent her a righteous look but continued. 'Mum, being a sensible woman, declined to get in the car with a stranger and kept walking. My dad, having been brought up never to leave a lady stranded, continued to drive by her side the entire ten kilometres back to the mission.'

'Wow. Let me guess, after that, she realised what a great guy he was and they fell instantly in love and lived happily ever after?'

'Ah, no. Not exactly. She was so annoyed with him for not taking her word that she could look after herself that she told him she never wanted to see him again.'

'What!' Pip was dismayed by the news.

'However, my dad being my dad,' he added with a grin, 'he didn't give up, and continued to woo her for the next two weeks until she finally gave in and went on a date with him.'

'And then they lived happily ever after,' Pip said.

''Fraid not,' Chris said, shaking his head.

This was turning into the worst story ever. 'Why not?'

'Well, my mother had already accepted another job over in Western Australia before the car incident, so she decided there wasn't any future in a second date. She only gave in to shut him up—her words, by the way,' he added. 'So, she left to go to her new job, and three weeks later my dad turned up with a bunch of flowers and asked her on another date.'

'No. Way.'

'Way,' Chris nodded.

'So *then* they lived happily ever after?' she asked hesitantly.

'What is it with you and happily ever after?'

'Well, it's the story of how your parents met—I'm just assuming it's going to be a happy one.'

'I suppose it was. I wouldn't call it a fairytale or anything. There were some pretty hard times. His family wouldn't even meet Mum when he told them he was getting married, and Mum's family disowned her because she married a blackfella, so she couldn't go back to Ireland.'

Pip gave a small grimace of sympathy.

'But I guess there were still some happy times.'

'Is your dad still alive?' she asked when he stopped talking.

'Yeah.'

His short answer, so different to when he spoke about his mother, was telling.

'You don't get along with your dad?'

'Nah, not really.'

'That's a shame. He must miss your mum.'

'I guess so. He started drinking after a while—after his accident. He came off a horse chasing a cow when I was about eight and couldn't find work again after that. He took up drinking to cope with the frustration. He felt like a failure to Mum, I suppose. She worked two jobs for years to support us and each day he seemed to withdraw inside himself a little further until he'd all but disappeared.'

Pip could picture the memories all too easily—a sad, redheaded young woman with a small child, an angry husband and dreams of a happy life together unravelling at the seams.

'Do you have any siblings?' Pip asked, feeling sad for the man before her.

'No. Just me.'

'What made you join the police force?'

'Mum and I moved to Melbourne when I was in high school. She wanted me to have a better chance at finding a good job. The bush didn't have many options where I came from. We had a careers day at school one time, and I walked past the police recruitment table and this old copper stopped me and asked me what I wanted to do with my life. I didn't have a clue. Mum was rabbiting on about university, but I knew I didn't want that. He sat me down and pointed out all these different areas police worked in, and I remember seeing "Detective" and all of a sudden, that's what I wanted to do. I don't know why—I don't know what suddenly changed that day, but I focused on that goal and I joined the police force as soon as I was able and kept working until I made detective.'

'And how did you end up out here?'

'I took a transfer to get out of the city. I was working in Melbourne, but I wanted to get back out in the country. What about you?' he asked, then took a long sip of his drink. 'How did you come to be a journalist?'

Pip settled her back against the base of the lounge, having joined him on the floor. It had been a long time since she'd felt comfortable enough to unwind with someone other than

Lexi. It was nice. 'I've always been curious,' she said with a smile as he made a sarcastic noise in the back of his throat. 'My mum says I was one of those kids who always needed to know everything. I used to wear her out asking a million questions once I started talking. I guess it started there,' she said, reaching for more pizza. 'But I really loved writing. English was my favourite subject at school, pretty much the only thing I could do well. I sucked at maths and I was like an uncoordinated clown when it came to PE, but English— I was in my element.'

'I hated English,' he said, giving a small shudder at the memory.

'Maybe you just needed a great teacher,' she suggested. She would always be grateful to her year ten English teacher, Miss Grace. She had been the one to nurture Pip's writing talent, and encouraged her to think about her future. Everyone needed at least one Miss Grace in their high-school life. Or maybe a Miss Adams, she thought, thinking about Rebecca and making a note to touch base again.

'I don't think it would have made any difference—I wasn't much of an academic back then.'

'I can just imagine. You would have been one of *those* kids up the back of the class,' she said with a stern frown.

'And you would have been one of the goody-two-shoes up the front,' he grinned back, completely unrepentant. 'My first crush was on a girl who sat up the front of the class,' he mused after a while.

'Ah,' Pip nodded sagely. 'The old bad boy–good girl thing.'

'Yeah. But it didn't work out.'

'She preferred good boys?'

'She preferred girls,' he said.

'Oh. Well, you really didn't have much of a chance there, did you.'

'Not really. No.'

'I hope your people-reading skills have improved nowadays,' she said, collapsing back against the chair and groaning as she put a hand on her belly. She'd eaten too much.

'People-reading skills aren't a problem,' he said confidently. 'It's more the average woman-reading skills that even being a detective doesn't seem to be any help with,' he admitted.

Pip rolled her head sideways to face him and grinned. She hadn't realised his head was so close to hers and found herself looking into his dark eyes, which held hers gently.

She leaned closer, and he met her halfway, his lips firm but warm and gentle as she kissed him and felt a surge of need race through her.

'Ow,' she pulled back as something dug into her hip and she pulled out the hard drive she'd forgotten about and dropped it on the coffee table. 'Sorry,' she muttered awkwardly.

'That's nothing, you should have seen what my mother used to find in my pockets when I was a kid,' he said, his eyes lowered in a sexy, brooding kind of way that did strange things to her breathing as he tugged her back to kiss her again.

A small moan escaped from her and he shifted slightly, bringing his hands up to cup her face and pull her closer.

God, she hadn't felt this desperate since . . . her mind went blank. She couldn't think of a single other time with a man she could compare this to. Brushing that thought aside, she concentrated instead on allowing the sensations his hands and mouth were creating to take her away and forget everything for just this one night.

Nineteen

Pip eased away from the arm under her pillow and the other across her hip to slither from the bed like some kind of thief avoiding a security alarm. She gathered last night's discarded clothing, following an impressively long trail from the bedroom to the lounge room, pulling items on as she went.

As she tugged her T-shirt over her head, two arms grabbed her from behind and she let out a scream, instinctively jamming her elbows hard against whatever surface presented itself before spinning around and lifting her knee, which made contact with something *not* particularly hard. The move was followed by a coarse, breathless curse.

Finally managing to get her head out of her T-shirt, she gasped as she found Chris doubled over and breathing hard.

'Oh my God, I'm sorry, I didn't know it was you,' she said, horrified by the pain she'd inflicted.

'Didn't know it was me? Who else would it bloody be at this time of the morning? How many men do you keep stashed away in here?' he panted.

'I just meant—well, you were asleep a few minutes ago when I left the room,' she finished in a rush of exasperation.

'Are you always this violent in the morning?'

'No. Only when someone sneaks up and grabs me.'

'Jesus, I won't make that mistake again,' he muttered, gingerly sitting himself on the bar stool across from her.

'Are you okay?' she asked when neither of them had anything else to say. He wasn't looking quite as pale as he had been a few moments earlier, and she only now took in the fact he was bare-chested, wearing only his jeans from the night before.

'What's going on?' he asked, still wearing a bit of a frown, for which she couldn't altogether blame him.

'I've just been a bit on edge,' she said, running her hands along her thighs nervously. 'There was an intruder in my house a while back. He was waiting for me when I got home one night and I . . . I just haven't . . . I'm so sorry if I hurt you. I took self-defence classes afterwards. My best friend, Lexi, made me go. I've never actually used them on anyone before.' She knew she was babbling but she couldn't seem to stop.

'Hey,' Chris said, his voice gentle as he reached out a hand. 'It's okay, come here.' He tugged her close and held her against him. 'Being jumpy after something like that is completely understandable. I'm the one who should be sorry, not you.'

'Not too many people know that it still affects me like that,' she admitted.

'Do you want to tell me about it?'

Her first reaction was to shake her head and say *no freaking way*—but standing there, settled between Chris's thighs and encircled by his arms, suddenly she felt brave enough to talk about it. 'It was in the lead-up to the trial,' she started softly. 'I'd been out to a work function and got home pretty late, and as I walked inside, he was just standing there.'

She squeezed her eyes tightly and buried her face a little deeper into Chris's chest. His arms tightened around her and she was back in that warm, safe place once more.

'He had a balaclava on and all I could see was two wide holes, just staring back at me. I turned to run, but he grabbed me and threw me on the floor. I remember hitting my head on the table and being dazed, but he just kept picking me up and throwing me around the room like I was a rag doll.'

She felt Chris's hands soothing her back as he let her talk. 'His hands were around my neck and I tried to prise them away but he was so strong. He had this strange look in his eyes—like he was smiling. The more I struggled, the tighter he pressed against my neck.' She stopped and closed her eyes tightly as the memories swarmed in. 'I remember searching for something to use to get him off, and I hit out at him, and he let go for a second.'

Suddenly she was back in the memory of that brief moment of respite—taking a deep breath of air and feeling life flow back through her. That's when she saw the blue and red flashing lights on the wall across from the front window and she knew help was coming. She rolled onto her side and launched to her feet. 'But he grabbed my leg and dragged me back down, and all I remember thinking was that he was so heavy—I couldn't move and he was crushing me. But then he sat up and he had his hands around my neck and I couldn't breathe.'

She remembered the wild look in his eyes as he pressed a knee hard against her chest and the pressure of his fingers around her throat. 'I passed out,' she said, staring at the wall across the room blankly. 'Apparently someone heard things being knocked over and called the police. I never did find out which neighbour saved my life that night,' she said with a tight smile. 'I woke up in hospital, unable to speak or swallow. I had a fractured larynx, a couple of broken ribs and a punctured lung.'

'Did they catch him?' Chris asked after she went quiet once more.

Pip shook her head. 'No. He just vanished.'

'Did you manage to get a look at him? Give any kind of description?'

'I caught a glimpse of his neck—he had a green snake tattoo. That's the only helpful thing I could give the police,' she said dolefully. Pip eased away and rubbed her hands across her face in an attempt to erase the horrible memories. 'They couldn't turn up anything.'

'You said it was in the lead-up to the trial? Did they make any connection to Knight?'

'Nope,' she sighed. 'But it was pretty obvious who sent him. The only thing the man said was, "Keep your mouth shut," but they couldn't put that down completely to a warning about the trial—it could have just been a warning to not yell.'

'Too much of a coincidence not to be related, though, with the timing,' he mused.

'All I know is I'm sick to death of it running my life. I thought once Knight was convicted, everything would go back to normal, that I'd be able to write this book and get everything out on paper so it would free me to move on . . . but it hasn't. I can't write. It's like he took that away from me too—the one thing I could always depend on.'

'Maybe it's just too soon for you to write the book?' Chris suggested.

'The publisher wants it out while it's still relevant. I signed a contract,' she said with a sigh. 'If I'd known I was going to have this much trouble I wouldn't have agreed to it,' she finished miserably. But who would have thought her writing would be something that would let her down?

'Is this why you're so interested in the Bigsby case? Because you're avoiding the real issue with your book?'

'Who are you, my editor?' she asked, but she gave a small smile.

'It's just that it all makes more sense now.'

'I'm not here in a journalist capacity.'

'But you can't help yourself,' he grinned.

She hesitated before screwing up her nose a little. 'No, I guess not. But I am genuinely angry about the way Bert's been treated all these years. Living with all this.'

'*If* he's innocent,' Chris reminded her pointedly.

'I think he is,' she declared.

'You're supposed to keep an open mind about the case before you decide on innocence or guilt,' he told her, shifting slightly on the stool.

'Come on, you can't tell me you don't get a gut instinct straightaway every time you investigate a crime?'

'Sure I do, but sometimes emotion can blind you to certain things. I try to stay neutral until I've got all the facts before me.' He shrugged, and Pip's gaze followed the movement and then continued down over a chest lightly dusted with dark hair, and she remembered the feel of his warm skin beneath her fingertips. 'You can't argue facts.'

'So what's your gut telling you about the bones?' she asked.

He slanted her an off-centre smile and leaned forward to kiss her.

'Seriously? You're going to use that to distract me?'

'Is it working?' he asked, kinking an eyebrow.

'Yes. But you're just lucky I'm not officially working this story—because you, Detective Jarrett, would be in big trouble trying that on a journalist just doing their job.'

'I only do it to the ones I think are sassy and cute.'

'Sassy and cute, huh? Well, I guess I've been called worse.' She saw him wince slightly as he moved to get off the stool. 'Are you okay?' she asked, eyeing him warily.

'I'm fine,' he said, managing a brief smile.

'I can get you a bag of frozen peas,' she offered.

'I think I'd rather let you knee me again than willingly hold *anything* frozen over that part of my anatomy,' he said darkly.

Pip bit back a laugh as she leaned in and softly kissed his lips. 'It's not exactly how I imagined the morning going,' she said regretfully. 'I was coming out to make coffee to bring back to bed.'

'Can't say I was exactly picturing my balls being driven up into my throat, either,' he said with a wry twist of his lips. 'But I guess you could make it up to me with some tender loving care.'

She held his sleepy gaze and an answering shot of arousal coursed through her blood as he pulled her against him again. 'It's the least I can do,' she murmured, leading him back to the bedroom.

Twenty

'I have to head back to Coopers Creek,' Chris said reluctantly as they lay in bed the next morning listening to the chorus of wildlife outside the window. They'd barely ventured further than the verandah since he'd arrived Friday afternoon. It was now Sunday and their little bubble of bliss was about to be burst by the sharp point of reality.

Pip wanted to tell him not to go, but she couldn't bring herself to sound needy. She had been trying not to think about what this thing was between them all weekend. It was very un-Pip-like to jump into bed with an almost stranger and then spend the entire weekend with them. She still wasn't sure how it had happened. Yet here they were, and up until now she had been content to ignore the inevitable end of this unexpected weekend sex fest.

It was more than that, though, Pip had to confess to herself. Sure, the sex was amazing, but they'd done a lot more talking than well, sexing, and she couldn't remember the last time she'd spent so many hours getting to know a man the way she'd got to know this one in a single weekend.

'Have I outstayed my welcome?' he asked hesitantly, and Pip turned to look up at him quickly.

'No. Of course not.'

'You just didn't say anything,' he said, sounding anything but his normal confident self.

'To be honest, I don't really know what *to* say.' She slid her hand into his and played with his fingers idly as she tried to collect her scattered thoughts. 'I wasn't expecting any of this.'

'I wasn't either.'

'You could have just phoned the other day instead of coming all the way over here,' she pointed out, this time not letting him off the hook. 'Why did you?'

She saw him flash a quick grin, the one she was becoming increasingly addicted to. 'I guess I was after any excuse to see you again. You made quite an impression on me the first time.'

'Really?'

'Yeah. I haven't been able to stop thinking about you ever since. I'd find myself thinking up reasons to call you or come back here.'

'Me too.'

'You've been thinking about me?' His voice held a note of cockiness.

'Yes, Mr Big Head,' she said, pushing at his hand. 'I don't know why. Detectives are not usually my go-to choice for a date.'

'How come?' he said, sounding a little miffed.

'I dunno, I guess it's like mixing work with pleasure. Not that I've actually gone out with anyone in a while.'

'Interesting,' he said, threading his wide fingers through her smaller ones thoughtfully.

'Pathetic, more like it,' she scoffed.

'Hardly. A woman like you—beautiful, smart, funny,' he said. 'You can have your pick of dates, but obviously you don't choose to.'

'I wouldn't say that exactly. I guess I've just been too busy with work, and then the Knight case kind of had me a little . . . preoccupied.'

'I get it. I'm a bit the same way once I'm invested in a case—I tend to go all the way and everything else has to wait. Not great for a relationship.'

'You've had experience, I take it?' she said.

'Yeah, I have an ex-wife who will tell you how shit my job is and blame it for our disaster of a marriage.'

'Oh.' She had no idea why discovering he'd been married was such a surprise—it wasn't as though a guy in his thirties wouldn't have his own history.

'We were married pretty young. I'd just come out of the police academy and I was trying to work my way up to detective. Then we had a kid, and I was young and stupid—too wrapped up in myself to realise I had bigger responsibilities. I should have spent more time at home and less time proving myself at work,' he said, his voice tinged with regret. 'I'd told her so many times about my dream of making detective, and we agreed to wait to start a family, then when she told me she was pregnant . . . well.' He stopped and frowned. 'There wasn't much we could do about it. But I had this resentment, I guess, and I decided I wasn't going to let anything get in the way of reaching my goals. She hated being a copper's wife, and we fought more and more. She started taking drugs and . . . it was pretty shit there for a while.'

Pip could feel the sadness in his voice.

'Anyway, she took off with our daughter for a bit—went to live with her mother and eventually went to rehab. She's okay now. Actually, better than okay. I'm really proud of her. She managed to get herself together; she's a counsellor and a great mum. We realised we were too young when we got married and wanted different things, so the spilt was fairly amicable.'

'How old's your daughter?' Pip asked.

'Sixteen,' he said with a gentle smile. He leaned back to take his phone out of his pocket and opened his photo gallery to bring up an image of a pretty girl with long dark hair and big brown eyes. 'Her name's Sian.'

'Oh, she's gorgeous,' Pip said, taking in the wide smile and recognising the mischievous grin, so much like the one the man before her often wore. 'Do you get to see her often?'

'Yeah, pretty often. It was one of the reasons I moved out here. I get to spend weekends with her. When she's not busy with her social life, that is,' he added with a twist of his lips.

'I'm really glad it all worked out in the end.'

'Yeah, it did. But I guess ever since that, I've made a point of never really getting too involved with anyone. I know what pressures my job can put on a relationship and I don't want to hurt anyone like that again.'

'So that's your subtle way of telling me this was a weekend fling, then,' she said.

'Nope. I was just explaining how out of character it is for me to act on a feeling I haven't had before.'

'Oh,' was all she could say.

'Knowing my track record for shitty relationships, I probably shouldn't have come here hoping to find out if this attraction was something more than just that—an attraction.'

'And? What did you find?' she asked cautiously.

'I found you,' he said softly. 'I haven't told anyone else half the stuff I've told you this weekend,' he admitted, rubbing his chin against the top of her head. 'I've never felt as though I've known someone all my life after just a few days.'

His confession momentarily stunned her, and she wanted to tell him that she felt exactly the same way, but how could she when she was the one who'd always scoffed at romantic clichés? The fact that it didn't feel so clichéd now made her nervous. 'So . . . what happens now?'

'I don't know. What do you want to do?'

What a question. What *did* she want to do? What would she do with a full-time boyfriend? She had no idea—what did you feed it? How often do you have to take it for a walk?

'Maybe we could just take it slow and see where it goes?' she suggested. The truth was, she really liked this guy. And even though she didn't know if she was capable of fitting a man into her life, he had definitely given her a reason to want to at least see if it were a possibility.

'Okay. Slow it is,' he agreed. 'So what were you thinking, maybe catch up next week?'

'Next week? Are you crazy? I said slow, not dead.'

'Thank Christ for that, I wasn't sure how I was going to last a whole week,' he said, letting out a relieved sigh and sliding his hand across her belly.

'I can come over to Coopers Creek tomorrow night for dinner? If you want?'

'I definitely want,' he said as his eyes took on that sexy, slumberous look that made her knees go weak all over again.

Pip needed a distraction. There was still nothing from Warlock about cracking the encryption, and she was at a point in her manuscript where she needed to know if what was in that file was going to be worth including. Without anything to go on there, her mind was free to wander.

Once Chris had left and she could think straight again, doubts began to creep in. Try as she might, there was only so long she could manage to ignore the little voice of common sense in her head that had been repeatedly trying to tap her on the shoulder all weekend. What was she doing?

Having fun, a different voice piped up. *Remember that?* She had to admit, it had been a long time since she'd thrown caution to the wind that way. In fact, she really couldn't even remember the last time she had.

And for good reason—it's called self-preservation, a little know-all voice announced pompously.

If she were being completely honest with herself, she was hard-pressed not to feel a little bit of smug pride at such rebellious, wanton behaviour. It felt good to be spontaneous

A Stone's Throw Away

and forget everything that had been going on lately—the deadlines, writer's block, jumping at every tiny thing. She felt empowered. Brave even. But that was then. Today it was back to business. Time to refocus.

She dragged the bigger box of Bert's belongings out from under the table, the one she hadn't had a chance to go through yet. Unlike the other box, this one didn't have any photo albums or letters but contained clothing.

On top was a battered slouch hat that had definitely seen better days and a heavy woollen khaki coat. She lifted them out and found a stack of newspaper pages neatly folded. She carefully unfolded them to find front page after front page capturing vital last moments of the war.

The top one was dated 8 May 1945 and screamed WAR ENDS IN EUROPE in large bold type. Another from the *Sun* dated 8 August 1945: BOMB DEVASTATES JAP CITY, and the story on the back page BORNEO – THE FINAL ASSAULT. There were others that mentioned the horrors of Burma and Tarakan.

She noted with interest that the front page always dealt with events in Europe and Japan and the back page shared news from New Guinea and articles relating to the Australian war effort and POW camps. She could imagine Bert reading through the papers while recovering in hospital towards the end of the war and saving them as keepsakes.

Maybe there was a museum that might be interested in Bert's mementoes—this record was far too important to leave in a box to be eaten away by moths and time.

As she picked up the clothing to put back in the box, she knocked the stack of newspapers and gave an annoyed click of her tongue as she bent to pick it all up. After she gathered it all together, she discovered a folded piece of writing paper that had slipped out of one of the newspapers. Pip unfolded it, instantly recognising Bert's handwriting.

Dear Moll,

I don't think I can bring myself to send this to you, but if you were here right now, I know you'd be able to tell me what I should do. I can always depend on you for your sage advice, and God knows I need it now, but this will never reach you in time. Maybe if I write it down I'll work out what you'd say to me.

I have to testify tomorrow. They called me up and I have no choice but to go in front of a tribunal.

A local villager came forward and made accusations against Frank regarding his young grandson. There was an almighty fuss made at the garrison gate before the General gave orders to let the man in to see him. And not before the old fella and half the village had made sure everyone heard what had happened.

You see, I was there. What Frank did ... well, that just weren't right. I close my eyes and I see it replay over and over in my head.

The worst thing is, I didn't do anything. I couldn't. I was in shock, I think, I just stood there as Frank got up. The kid took off—and we just stood there. Staring at each other until he just turned and walked away.

I wish to Christ I had never walked around that corner and stumbled upon the things I saw that day. I would rather have lived in blind ignorance than have to acknowledge the evil truth about a man I called a mate.

A Stone's Throw Away

I know what I saw. I know what he did. And now that I have to testify it makes me sick to the guts. The whole company's in shock and outrage. They're all saying, 'There's no way Frank could have done that. Frank's been stitched up.' Probably what I would be saying too if I hadn't seen it with my own eyes. I can't look at him. I can't unsee the things I saw.

I know what I should do. Keep my mouth shut. Lie. Deny it all. But I keep seeing that young boy's face. The tears. The fear in his eyes. The screaming and begging for help. And all the time, all I could think of was the young Stanley boy who was found drowned in the creek a few years back. They tried that old swaggy they found camped a few miles away — locked him away in that asylum in Melbourne and threw away the key. He always swore he didn't do it. Now I look at Frank and I remember I didn't see him at the dance that night where we were all called out to go searching for the kid when they realised he was missing.

I remember a lot of things now that the blinkers have been ripped from my eyes.

I remember little Arthur Maguire. His own cousin! I remember how he used to hide when we were there. I remember Frank joking that he'd had to give him a hiding for talking back and that's why he always ran when he saw him. But now I know.

He did more than give the kid a hiding, I'm willing to bet. The knowledge sickens me.

One time we laughed when the kid wet himself when Frank took him by the collar and dragged him out from his hiding spot. Now I know.

I don't know what to do, Moll. I don't know if I can live with myself if I don't tell them the truth tomorrow at the tribunal. I keep seeing that young kid's face.

But I know if I testify against one of our own, I'll lose the respect of the rest of the men here who can't bring themselves to believe a word of it. But what worries me even more than that is, if the truth of this thing comes out—that a Maguire was charged with something like this—our life won't be worth living in Midgiburra once I get back home. I'll be the bastard who testified against his best mate and ruined the whole Maguire reputation.

On the other hand, there's no doubt old man Maguire will somehow manage to cover it up, so telling the truth will probably be all for nothing.

I wish you were here right now, Moll. More than I've ever wished before—and that's saying a lot because I've missed you more than I could ever imagine since this bloody war started.

Well, I thought by the end of this letter I'd know what I should do. Turns out, I still have no idea.

There was no date on the letter, but the torment in Bert's words almost jumped off the page. Pip recalled the name Frank on some of Bert's other correspondence, but now she wanted to know who this man was. The implications of what he'd done filled her with horror, and clearly Bert had shared that feeling and been placed in a tough position.

Maguire. She went back to the start of the letter and re-read it. Frank had to be connected to the local Maguires—there were too many of them around here for it to be a coincidence. She tried a quick search of archival records and managed to pull up a number of articles relating to Frank Maguire. There was a local newspaper headline PROUD VICTORIAN PREMIER SENDS GRANDSON OFF TO WAR, which seemed to be a publicity piece mixed with a recruiting ad encouraging Australians to join up and do their bit. Pip tossed this information about in her head. Frank's grandfather was the state premier.

There was also a welcome-home ball given in honour of local serving men and women, among whom Frank was listed. Pip checked the date: November 1941. Just prior to the invasion. Had this been when the alleged *incident* had happened? It fitted in with Bert's letters and was around the time they suddenly changed in tone. So why had Frank been suddenly shipped home if he'd been cleared of any charges? There was a sad kind of irony that Frank had made it out of the war unscathed *because* of committing a horrendous crime while good men like Bert had ended up in POW camps—hell on earth.

She was beginning to understand Bert's concerns. It looked very likely that Frank's grandfather, Edward, had perhaps used his influence to extricate his grandson from serious trouble.

Pip continued scrolling through and saw that before the war, Frank had been involved in local football and cricket clubs and was mentioned in various society events. Then further on she found a write-up of his funeral, which had attracted a huge crowd, befitting one of the largest families in the area. *Frank Edward Maguire was found on his family property 'Milton' late this afternoon, deceased.* The coroner's report that featured a few days later ascertained that the cause of death had been a gunshot wound and was deemed accidental. The report went on to speculate that Frank had been out shooting kangaroos when he'd tripped, causing his rifle to discharge, killing him instantly.

Pip eased back in her chair studying the screen thoughtfully as she tried to piece it all together. Frank Maguire was the son of a politician, a returned soldier and popular member of local society. He was also Bert's best mate, until, apparently, the tribunal at which Bert was called to testify—against Frank. She hadn't found any mention of a tribunal, only the official war crimes commission from the end of the war. Why had there been no mention of this one anywhere in Frank's service record?

She went back to the letter and then typed in 'Stanley' with the key words 'drowning' and 'Midgiburra'. A list of hits came up immediately. She pulled up the first link and saw the newspaper headline: LOCAL BOY FOUND DEAD. 'The battered body of Terrance Stanley, aged seven, was found in the early hours of the morning after an extensive search when the alarm was raised by his parents that the child had not returned home. On inspection it was revealed that the boy had suffered heinous injuries that suggested interference most foul. A vagrant camped nearby, Ebenezer Cindric, was questioned, and after the discovery of an item of clothing belonging to the boy in Cindric's possession, he was remanded in custody awaiting trial for the murder of Terrance Stanley.'

Pip stopped reading and frowned. Tragically, everything in Bert's letter seemed to check out. A dead child, a convenient suspect and a potential child rapist on the loose in Midgiburra. Her gaze settled on the wide, brown land before her as she tried to get her head around what had gone on here all those years ago.

Twenty-one

Pip sat waiting for Rebecca. She needed more information about everything she had learned, and after her run-in with Jan she suspected she would probably get further with a not-born-here local, rather than the diehard, original-family kind.

'Hi,' Rebecca said, arriving like a small cyclone to take the seat across from her.

'Thanks so much for coming—it could have waited till after school, though,' Pip said, feeling bad for being the reason the busy teacher seemed in a hurry.

'Nah, it's all good. I have two free periods back-to-back, so this works in better. Now, what is it you needed help with?'

'I've been going through some more of Bert Bigsby's belongings and I came across a letter he wrote to his wife during the war. I'm not exactly sure when—there's no date—but it has something to do with a local man he was friends with from here. Frank Maguire,' Pip said. 'His grandfather was Edward Maguire.'

'From the statue,' Rebecca nodded, sipping her coffee.

'What statue?'

'That one,' she said, pointing through the cafe window to where the man on a horse sat in the middle of the street.

Pip peered out. *'That's* Edward Maguire?'

'Apparently he commissioned it himself,' Rebecca said, rolling her eyes. 'We do a local history project on him each year. He was a self-made man, coming out here with his parents from England and pioneering the town. He started buying up land once he took over his father's property, and the family eventually owned pretty much the whole district at one point.'

'Do you know much about Frank Maguire?'

Rebecca pondered the name for a moment. 'I know that I've heard of him, but I can't say I know much. I think there's a bridge named after him somewhere around here. Why? Have you got a lead on a good story or something?'

'Somehow it's all linked to Bert.' It was becoming clearer that there was a lot more behind the feud this town seemed to have with a returned soldier.

'Do you need some help?'

'I can't seem to find anything that relates to a tribunal Bert had to give evidence at during the war. He was being pressured into lying, and I'm assuming that since I can't find anything about it, Frank got off.'

'What was he giving evidence about?'

Pip stirred her coffee before answering. 'Bert apparently walked in on Frank raping a young boy.' She felt sick to her stomach saying it out loud.

'What?' Rebecca breathed out as she stared at Pip across the table.

'From what I can gather, Bert began to put together a few different incidents from the past and realised it wasn't the first time Frank had done it. There was a young local boy they found in the river before the war years, when Frank was probably in his late teens, early twenties.'

'Yes, I have heard about that. He drowned.'

'Yeah, but he'd also been sexually assaulted. And they arrested a homeless man they found camping nearby for his murder.'

'Yes!' Rebecca nodded eagerly. 'The swaggy.'

'But Bert mentioned in his letter that he suddenly remembered Frank's alibi for that night hadn't been true. Then he started recalling other things.'

'Did Bert have proof?' Rebecca asked. 'Or was it all just speculation?'

'He witnessed Frank with the boy while they were overseas,' Pip shrugged. 'Speculation or not, it certainly paints a pretty grim picture. It was enough to make Bert have some severe doubts about his best friend. I'm sure it had something to do with what happened once Bert came home. The way he was treated like such an outcast. Why so many people still can't seem to cut him any slack.'

Rebecca leaned forward. 'So what are you thinking happened?'

'I'm not sure. It sounds like, regardless of what happened at that military tribunal, Bert might have been telling people about his suspicions.'

'What happened to Frank?'

'He accidentally shot himself less than a year after the war ended.'

'Accidentally?' Rebecca repeated doubtfully.

'That's what the coroner's report came back with.'

'Well, I admit it does sound pretty incriminating for Frank. It wouldn't be the kind of publicity the family would like to circulate about town. It would have been career-ending for his father and his grandfather—they were both MPs. But I suppose at least there was no social media back then and stuff like this would be a lot easier to cover up.'

Pip gave a small grunt in agreement.

'But maybe you need to speak with someone who's been here longer than me, because I've barely heard anything about the things you're talking about, and clearly, they *aren't* talked about.'

'And risk a lynch mob coming out to the house to hunt me down? No, thank you.'

'You know who'd be the perfect person to ask?' Rebecca said, thoughtfully tapping her finger against her coffee cup.

Pip eyed her warily.

'Jan,' she went on blithely.

'Jan who?'

'Her married name's Wiseman, but she took over her father's bakery. He was a Maguire.'

The bakery woman? *Oh, hell no.* 'Ah, no,' Pip declined bluntly.

'I know she comes across a little . . . well . . . unfriendly, but once she gets to know you she thaws out a bit.'

'I'm banned from the bakery,' Pip announced.

Rebecca spluttered from across the table. *'Banned?'*

'More or less. She refused to sell me a vanilla slice the other day when I disagreed with her on a few points regarding Bert.'

'No slice for you!' Rebecca said in a heavy accent, mimicking the Soup Nazi from *Seinfeld*.

It would be funny if Pip hadn't constantly craved a vanilla slice ever since. 'I doubt confronting her about a child rapist in her family would go down too well.'

Rebecca cringed. 'I see your point,' she nodded. 'But I know she's really into their family-tree stuff, and she's always involved in the Heritage Festival.'

'What's that?'

'A weeklong celebration to remember everything the Maguires have done for the town over the last century or so,' Rebecca said.

'Maybe I'll track down another Maguire who isn't quite as . . . protective of their family name.'

'Good luck with that,' she warned, sipping her coffee. 'And speaking of new blood,' she said, putting down her cup and leaning across the table. 'Have you noticed there's a new man in town?'

'I don't really know who the *old* ones are,' Pip pointed out.

Rebecca gave a brief chortle before continuing. 'Apparently he's a police detective working on the bones case. I think he's from Coopers Creek. Have you met him yet?'

For a moment Pip wasn't sure how to answer and felt herself freeze.

Rebecca's eyes widened. 'You *have* met him,' she deduced before her gaze narrowed suspiciously. 'Spill. Right now. I want to know everything. I haven't had a good look myself—I only spotted him from a distance the other day. Is he as handsome up close as he seems?'

'Ah, well . . . yes, I guess he's fairly handsome.'

'Are you blushing, Ms Davenport, unflappable, hard-hitting journalist?'

'No, I am not. It's just hot in here.'

Rebecca gasped in mock horror. 'You're hiding something, I just know it.'

How did she know it? Good grief, the woman was like a bloodhound. 'We've met, professionally,' Pip said, lifting her chin slightly.

'Uh-huh,' Rebecca nodded sarcastically. 'So, *professionally* speaking,' she said pointedly, 'how would you rate him?'

'He's a very good detective. Now shouldn't you be getting back to school or something?'

'I can't believe you've been in town five minutes and you've managed to snag the only new bloke we've seen in ages.'

'I haven't shagged anyone.' Pip stopped, horrified by her slip of the tongue. She felt her neck turn red as heat crept up her throat. 'Snagged!' she almost yelled, feeling ridiculous and rolling her eyes as Rebecca laughed in hysterics, drawing a few curious glances their way.

'I'm sorry,' Rebecca managed, catching her breath. 'Oh my God. Okay, sorry. I honestly had no idea you'd already . . . *met* him,' she said, this time keeping a straight face. 'I'm actually completely jealous, but I'm glad he went to a good home.'

'Oh, for goodness sake,' Pip muttered, shaking her head helplessly. 'He's not a puppy dog.'

'Seriously, I'm impressed. That was some pretty fast work.'

'It *was* just work . . . but then it kind of—' Pip stopped abruptly. What was she doing? She didn't even know this person and she was about to blab about how she'd gone and had a one-night . . . well, two nights and a day . . . and then Sunday morning . . . She shook her head irritably. She wasn't used to swapping girl talk about men, much to Lexi's disappointment and not from lack of trying on her part to set her best friend up on dates.

'It's okay, I was only joking before—seriously, I think it's great. I wish I was more proactive. If there's a downside to this place it's the lack of eligible men. It ain't just the land in drought, my friend.'

'I didn't exactly go looking for anything . . . it just kind of happened.'

'Well, if he has any brothers nearby, you know where to send them,' she winked, then pushed the chair away from the table. 'I better get back. If I think of anyone else who might be a good source of information about the other stuff, I'll let you know.'

'Thanks.' Pip smiled and waved as she watched Rebecca walk across to the counter and stop to say hello to Kaycee and the owner. Pip's gaze drifted across to the statue through the glass windows of the cafe, and she headed over to take a closer look before she went home.

Edward Maguire.

'What did you know about Frank, Ed?' she asked quietly, feeling anger bubble up inside her. This man had most likely managed to cover up more than one scandal connected to his grandson. He would have had to be putting out fires all over the place in order to keep the Maguire name out of the papers and off any police suspect lists. So much for honour and glory. Money and power was just as big a motivator back then as it still was today.

And here she was, smack bang in the middle of yet another story about a corrupt politician.

Pip went into the police station later that day and greeted Constable Jenner.

'Can I help you?'

'I'm not actually sure. I've been looking into an old case about a young local boy who was found in the river back in nineteen thirty-four, and I was wondering if there would be any information still held about the case.'

'That was a long time ago,' the constable said doubtfully.

'Yes, it was,' Pip agreed. 'But all I could find is a few newspaper articles on it. I was hoping there might be an actual police report or something?'

'I don't know about that. I could possibly look into it once Sergeant Nielsen gets back to the office.'

'That would be really helpful,' Pip said, handing over a card from her wallet. 'Could you give me a call after you've spoken with him?'

'Of course,' she said, but added briskly, 'unless an emergency comes up. Then I'm afraid I'll have to prioritise.'

'Of course,' Pip agreed solemnly, although she was fairly confident her request would likely be the *only* interesting thing that came through the front door today. 'Thank you for your help, constable.'

'Right you are,' the young woman nodded in an affirmative manner.

Pip wasn't sure what to make of the woman—she was just so . . . *intense* with her dedication. Resisting the urge to click her heels together as she turned, Pip instead offered a friendly smile and left the building.

Twenty-two

Pip felt suddenly nervous as she waited for Chris to answer the door. She'd used the drive to remind herself she was a strong, independent woman ... who was feeling a little like a giddy schoolgirl waiting to see the guy she had a crush on. 'This is so stupid,' she muttered just moments before the door opened and she was face to face with the man who had been clouding her thoughts ever since he'd left the day before.

'Hey,' he smiled, and her belly flipped. Nope. The weekend hadn't been some kind of fluke. He could still melt her insides with just a grin.

'Hey.'

'Come in.' He stepped aside, and she brushed past him in the hallway, stopping when he shut the door and turned to face her. His hands cupped the sides of her face as he gently held her steady while he kissed her. The wall behind her back felt solid—the only thing keeping her upright as she lost herself in the swirl of need that seemed to spin around them. When he stopped and lowered his forehead to hers, they were both breathing heavily. 'God, I missed you,' he said.

'It's only been a day.'

'I know. It's crazy.'

'It really is.'

Chris eased back slightly and grinned down at her. 'Want a tour of the place?' he asked, and she nodded, pushing away from the wall.

He pointed to the closed door across from them. 'That's Sian's bedroom,' he informed her, before leading her down the hall. 'Lounge room, kitchen in through there,' he said, pointing a hand to their left as they moved. 'Bathroom—fully renovated by yours truly,' he added, opening the door to reveal a white-tiled modern bathroom with a corner spa and glass-walled shower stall.

'Very impressive, detective . . . A jack-of-all-trades, I see.'

'I try,' he said nonchalantly. 'And this,' he said, opening another door, 'is my room.'

The colour scheme was definitely masculine, with lots of navy and shades of brown, but it was also calming. The room was a decent size, built in a time when builders didn't have to squeeze as many bedrooms into a limited area, and there was more than enough space that the large bed didn't dominate the room.

Chris stepped closer, and she felt the strength of him in front of her. She sighed as his lips moved down her neck and eagerly helped when his fingers fumbled at the buttons on the front of her top. She ran her hands through his short hair and dropped her head back, enjoying the feel of his lips on her skin. She knew she'd been missing out on adult companionship, but had she known *this* was what she was *actually* missing out on, she'd have gone out on more dates!

Later in the kitchen, Pip smiled as she sat on the bar stool watching the man across from her, bare-chested and wearing low-slung jeans that exposed a tantalising V shape of dark hair that dipped into the waistband of his jeans. He liked to run, he'd told her over the weekend, and she decided she wouldn't hold his fondness for fitness against him. As long as he didn't decide it was something they needed to do together, everything would be fine.

'What are you grinning about?' Chris asked as he glanced over at her while chopping garlic.

'Nothing. Just impressed by a man who can cook.'

'Well, it's either cook or starve. But you haven't tasted it yet—I never claimed to be a *good* cook.'

'Can't be any worse than me.' She sipped her wine and looked around for something to help with. He'd already told her to just sit and relax, but that was ten minutes ago—she was done with relaxing. 'If you insist on handling everything in here, then I might go out to the car and grab some stuff I brought over.'

'You moving in already?' he joked as he chopped.

'Well, we *have* been seeing each other for a while now,' she said keeping a straight face as he looked up swiftly and then broke out in a laugh as she smiled.

'Here,' he said, 'you chop these, and I'll go out and get whatever you need to bring in.'

'It's just a box, I can do it,' she protested lightly.

'It's dark out. I'll go.' He took the keys from her hand and kissed her lips briefly before walking down the hallway.

For a moment she stared at the doorway he'd disappeared through and blinked. She hadn't had anyone to worry about her going out into the street after dark before. The streets should be safe—after all, this wasn't the city—but she supposed crime wasn't something that stopped at the city borders. Chris was back shortly with the cardboard box containing Bert's belongings.

'So this is Detective Davenport's famous box of research?' he said, eyeing it curiously as he set it on the kitchen table.

'Yep. I'll show you mine if you show me yours,' she said, wriggling her eyebrows suggestively.

His low, soft laugh warmed her once more, and she mentally shook her head at how fast she was falling for this guy. It was ridiculous. She inwardly scoffed. She was *not* falling. Certainly not falling *in love* . . . maybe in lust? That sounded far more likely.

She watched as he walked across the room and took out a folder, then placed it on the table. 'I think this is what you've been waiting to get your hands on.' The police report from the Clements case.

'Is it okay if I look through it now?' she asked, reaching eagerly to open it.

'Sure, knock yourself out. I'll finish up dinner.'

She opened the file and felt her excitement leap into overdrive. An old musty smell filled her senses and she felt like she was back in her happy place once more. The paper was faded and yellowing and covered in bold old type. Attached to the top right corner was a photo of a man looking at the camera from an earlier police arrest form.

Vernon Clements. Age: 27. Occupation: Labourer. Eye colour: Grey. Height: 5'9". City of residence: Melbourne.

The black-and-white photo showed a handsome man in a white shirt and dark suit. His hair was dark and cut short at the sides, longer on top, and he had a thick, dark moustache. His previous arrests had included larceny and receiving stolen goods in Melbourne. 'I wonder how he ended up in Midgiburra?' she muttered. Most likely avoiding the law, she thought, as she read through his list of convictions.

On the next page was the crime-scene report with photos of Vernon Clements slumped across the steering wheel. Although the photos were in black and white, it wasn't difficult to understand how gruesome the scene must have looked for the first person to come across it. Once Pip realised the dark patches in the photo were actually blood, it suddenly took on an extremely sinister feel. The front of Vernon's shirt was almost entirely black, and large dark patches spread across the front seat and down onto the floor. Pip could almost smell the metallic tang of the blood.

The report went on to describe the scene and noted that there was more blood—not belonging to Clements—on the passenger-side seat and the door handle.

The witness reports closely resembled the newspaper article Pip had read in the library files: a second vehicle, belonging to Herbert Bigsby, was seen parked nearby shortly before the body of the victim was discovered by a passing farmer.

'Do you find out who the farmer was—the one who made the discovery?'

Chris glanced up and nodded. 'Yeah, but the family moved on years ago so we couldn't talk to anyone about what they might have remembered about it.'

'Mr Clements had been talking to a female inside the vehicle, who the witness claimed was Mrs Molly Bigsby. Mrs Bigsby had since been reported missing,' Pip read out loud before looking up. 'So presumably this witness had a clear view and there's no mention of him seeing Bert—which he would have if he'd been close enough to recognise Molly in the car.'

The victim's cause of death had been determined by the coroner as a stab wound penetrating the heart, causing massive haemorrhaging.

'Okay, so what's your theory in connection with Vernon's murder?' she asked as they sat curled up on Chris's sofa later.

'The common view is that it's likely that Molly met with Vernon, and they were talking in his car when Bert found them.'

'But no one saw Bert—the witness only saw his car. Molly could have been driving it—and that ties in with her being found inside it, in the dam. Plus,' Pip added pointedly, 'Bert was in the hospital.'

'Yes, but, the hospital release form had him discharged at two-fifteen that afternoon, which would have made it possible for him to make it back here in time to commit the murder, going by the estimated time of death.'

'Yes, but Bert told police he didn't have his car. So he couldn't have driven back. He came by train.'

'Which there was never any evidence of. No ticket stubs were produced. There's only his word on that.'

'So how do you explain Molly being inside Bert's car, then?' she asked, turning to look at him.

'Bert killed Vernon and Molly in a fit of rage. He panicked when he realised what he'd done and took Molly back home to hide the body and the car,' Chris said, lifting his hand slightly from the back of the couch in a *fait accompli* gesture.

Pip returned her gaze to the photos spread out on the coffee table before them.

'But why would he risk hiding her on his own property? I mean, wouldn't you have dumped the car and body somewhere further away?'

'The dam's never dried up before,' he countered. 'Look how much crap's been tossed in there over the years. Unless there was a specific warrant to search it, there wouldn't be any reason to look there. And he had an alibi.' Chris shrugged.

'Okay, so Vernon was stabbed. They didn't find any weapon at the scene?'

'No. But we found a knife inside the cabin of the ute from the dam,' he admitted.

A knife? The murder weapon? 'Are you kidding me?' she said, her mouth dropping open. 'You found the murder weapon and you didn't tell me this till now?'

'We didn't know for sure it was the murder weapon,' he pointed out.

'But it was, right? Otherwise, what would be the chances of a knife just happening to be found inside the car of a woman who'd been placed at a murder scene? Did forensics match it to Vernon's wounds?' Pip's eyes narrowed as he made a production out of leaning back and stretching, avoiding her question. 'Aww, come on,' she groaned. 'It's not a current murder investigation—it's not like you're even going to take it to trial. Just tell me already,' she finished in exasperation.

'You know, they warned us about pushy journos, back in the academy,' he teased, then gave a long-suffering sigh as she sent him an unamused glare. 'Okay, to answer your question, they did. But that's not even the interesting part.'

'What?' Pip almost yelled when he continued to draw out the suspense.

'They also matched the knife to a cut on the thigh bone of the skeleton.'

Pip soaked in this new information and nodded thoughtfully. 'So the blood from the passenger side of Vernon's car—Molly's blood—came from a knife wound to her thigh.' She frowned as she studied him. 'It must have been a hell of a deep wound to hit the bone.'

'Which is why it would have left so much blood behind. Forensics said it could have severed an artery.'

'But it doesn't seem like the kind of wound a jealous husband would inflict—I mean, her thigh? Why wouldn't he stab her in the chest or cut her throat? Those are the two areas most likely to be hit if someone's trying to kill you, right?'

'It could have been accidental,' he countered. 'Maybe she got in the way when Bert was attacking Vernon. She died and he panicked, so he dumped the car and her body in the dam.'

Pip shook her head obstinately. 'Nope—it still doesn't sit right. Bert always said he thought she'd left town. She'd taken her clothes, the trunk was missing. There weren't any clothes found at the scene in Vernon's car.'

'But there *was* a trunk in the ute.'

Pip stared at him blankly. 'You've seriously been sitting on all these details all night?' she accused.

He sent her an amused glance, clearly enjoying himself.

'So the missing trunk from the house was found in the dam with the ute?'

'Maybe that's why Bert said he noticed it missing—because he saw it at the scene. Maybe he even took it out of Vernon's car and threw it in the back of the ute when he dumped it,' Chris suggested.

'Or maybe she really *was* leaving him? Or at least leaving town? If she was in Bert's ute, she would have had the car packed with her trunk.'

'Then what was she doing meeting with Vernon?'

'Maybe she was telling him she was going—he tried to stop her, threatened her with the knife, and somehow she ended up stabbing him and getting stabbed in the thigh as a result?' Pip turned eager eyes on him as the idea took hold. 'Think about it—it makes more sense. That's why Bert's car was there, but no one actually saw *him*. Vernon dies, Molly panics and leaves.'

'And what? Drove herself into the dam? Why?'

'Maybe it was an accident? If that wound had severed an artery, it wouldn't take long to lose enough blood to kill her. She could have passed out.'

'The chances of accidentally ending up in the dam are pretty remote—it's doubtful she would have been able to stay conscious that long if she were bleeding out. And I'm not sure she could have fought a man of Clements' stature. They've established she was five foot three. I still think someone had to dump that ute and her body in the dam deliberately. Even if it did happen the way you said it did, I think Bert was still the one who found them and got rid of the ute.'

'If you read the letters,' she said firmly, 'you'll know how much he loved her. She loved him too.'

'Yet she had an affair with Vernon?'

She knew that his words were simply offering another point of view, but still they made her angry. She knew she was becoming far too invested in this whole thing and quite possibly had lost some objectivity, and maybe she was reaching now—making observations based on a bunch of old letters and a gut feeling she just couldn't shake, but damn it, she knew deep down she was right. 'Bert was reported as Missing in Action and everyone thought he was dead. That's the only reason Molly would have had the affair with Vernon. But then Bert came home and everyone found out he'd been a POW. She must have felt so much guilt,' Pip said sadly.

'You're thinking with your heart and not your head here, Pip. Like I said before—you can't let emotion sway you. We've got no witnesses alive to re-interview, so we have to depend on the testimony we have from the original report of Vernon Clements' murder. We're only linking the two incidents because Molly was placed at the murder scene and then she and Bert's vehicle were both reported missing the next day once Bert got home. That's the only way we can even connect the two events timewise.' He gave a resigned sigh. 'We've got bugger all, unless we can get Bert to talk, which his doctor has said is impossible. We've got no one left alive connected to the original case.'

But Pip couldn't let it go. 'If Molly did kill Vernon, it had to be in self-defence. I can't imagine she was a cold-blooded killer. Can't you put forward some kind of circumstantial verdict of accidental death? At least then Bert could finally be cleared.'

'Or he'd get away with the ultimate crime.'

'He's ninety-eight years old, stuck in a nursing home and can't communicate with a living soul. I think the least he deserves is for the community to stop calling him a murderer and remember that he's a bloody war hero.'

'Yeah, I do get that,' Chris said, running a hand along her arm. 'But war hero or not, once people make up their mind, it's not something they're likely to change after all this time.'

'If you guys can't legitimately place him at that scene, you owe it to him to clear his name.'

'Either way, there's still unanswered questions. If this was a case that happened now, he'd still be a person of interest.'

'I just wish there was some way of knowing for sure how Molly ended up in that dam,' she said with a frustrated sigh.

'I'll take the letters in and we'll go over them—and, given that pretty much everything is circumstantial about this case, I concede Molly *may* have been the one who killed Clements.

But that'll depend on the team going through it all and writing up the report.'

'I suppose that's something at least,' she replied, but the investigator in her hated that there were loose ends and no way to discover the truth for sure.

'Are you going to be angry at me all night now?' he asked.

'I'm not angry at you,' she said, and they both smiled slightly at her pouty tone. 'Okay, I'm sorry. I'm letting my emotion get the better of me.'

'Emotion isn't a bad thing,' he told her. 'Without it you turn into a robot.'

'I just wish I knew what happened to Molly's diary. I'm sure there'd be something in there that would tell us more about what happened.'

'If it ever existed.'

A memory of her dream, the woman on the blanket, writing, flashed across Pip's mind. 'It had to—Bert mentions her journal writing, but I've been right through all the belongings Anne saved and there's nothing there. Are you sure there was nothing in the trunk from the ute?'

'I'm positive. The only contents were a few items of clothing. If it *had* been in there, seventy years underwater would have destroyed it.'

'Unless it's still out there in the dam somewhere?'

'Forensics went over the area very thoroughly,' he stressed. 'They didn't turn up anything. You have to let this go before it drives you crazy.'

'It might be too late for that,' she said wistfully.

'I could maybe find a way to take your mind off it for a while?' he offered.

'I don't know—it'd have to be something pretty impressive.'

'Oh, it's impressive,' he assured her as he took her hand and led her down the hallway into his bedroom.

Twenty-three

Pip glanced in the rear-view mirror as she checked for traffic and was sidetracked by the ridiculous smile she caught on her face. Today everything just felt ... brighter. It had nothing to do with the relentless sun shining down and everything to do with recalling the previous night and waking up with the decidedly sexy Detective Jarrett beside her. She shook her head at how hopeless she was at pretending she was so cool, calm and collected about yet another one-night stand, then figured they could safely stop calling it that. They'd agreed she would come back tonight and she was already excited to see him again.

Their conversation last night, though, had been playing over in her head. She was distracted by the cold case, but mostly she couldn't quite shake the whole Frank Maguire thing.

Her phone rang, momentarily interrupting her thoughts.

'Ms Davenport, this is Constable Jenner from the Midgiburra police station,' the formal voice announced.

'Oh. Hi. How are you?' Pip asked.

There was a moment of silence before the constable replied with a stilted, 'I'm fine. Thank you.'

Clearly she still needed to work on those public-relations skills, but she was getting there.

'I looked into the matter you were enquiring about, and unfortunately there's no information I can give you on it.'

'Why not? Surely it can't be classified in any way?'

'No. It simply isn't here anymore.'

'As in it's been archived somewhere?'

'As in it's been destroyed. There were a number of records lost in a fire around the time of the incident you were asking about. As it was pre-digital days, there were no other records kept.'

You have to be kidding me. 'Wait,' Pip said, confused. 'You're saying there's no way of finding out *anything* about the original case because the records were destroyed?'

'That's correct.'

'Are you sure?'

'Yes, ma'am,' the constable said, not hiding the perceived insult in Pip daring to question how sure she was about the matter.

'Okay, thank you anyway.'

'You're welcome.'

The call disconnected and her music began to play once more, but Pip was still thinking about what she'd just learned. She'd come across this kind of thing before, so she knew it did happen from time to time—fires and records lost. But was it a bit *too* much of a coincidence that these particular files had been destroyed? Maybe she was getting a little jaded and paranoid, but it *did* involve the family of a member of parliament and it *could* be something that may have tried to resurface at a later date. There were a lot of things that were just not adding up about this whole thing.

When she got back into town, she passed the old church and spotted the 'Museum Open' sign and decided to drop in.

As she walked through the arched front doors of the church, she was surprised at how cold it felt inside. The musty scent of old building mixed with the scent of cleaning wax and lemon oil that had permeated into the timber furnishings over the years.

'Hello,' a friendly voice greeted her as she reached the front of the church. The woman wore a printed sundress in purple and maroon, and her short grey hair framed a gently wrinkled face. 'I'm Mary. Can I help you with something today or are you just here for a look?'

Pip smiled back and introduced herself. 'I was hoping to get a bit of information about the Maguire family,' she started.

'Well, you've certainly come to the right place, and the right *town*,' she added with a titter, 'for that.'

'Are you related to the Maguires?' Pip asked, knowing from her previous experience that she had to tread carefully around the name and that it would probably be easier to get unbiased information if Mary wasn't a relative.

'There's a distant family connection somewhere along the line. It's hard not to be somehow related when the original Maguire family came here and settled with twelve children.'

'Wow,' Pip said, 'I guess that explains why the town is so invested in the Maguire legacy.'

'Exactly. Then out of those twelve children, all but two survived to adulthood and went on to have at least five or six children of their own.'

Pip raised an eyebrow. 'So that's . . . over fifty children by the second generation of Midgiburra Maguires?' She certainly hoped the population grew with a lot more outsiders or the gene pool would have rapidly begun to shrink.

Pip let her gaze roam around the building.

Most of the original church pews had been removed to make room for the displays of clothing and household items from earlier times.

Mary noticed Pip looking at the large hut set up at the back of the room and smiled indulgently. 'That's the museum's pride and joy. It's a replica of the original Maguire cottage, made to size and from the same material—bark and mud, mostly—that the family built and lived in when they first came to Midgiburra.'

'Wow, that's impressive,' Pip nodded.

'We're very proud of our little museum,' Mary agreed. 'Were you searching for some information for your own family tree?' the woman asked as they walked to the side of the room to a long glass display cabinet.

'No, not for myself. I'm just following up some research for another project I've been working on and the Maguire name came up. I'm interested in Frank Maguire and any information I can get on him. Also an Arthur Maguire, who was Frank's younger cousin, I think. I don't have any dates of birth.'

A Stone's Throw Away

'Oh Frank. Yes, we have a good collection of information about him. He was quite the hero. He was in the Second World War and came home with all kinds of military medals and awards.' She walked across to a small doorway that led out to the back of the main church hall. 'We keep all our paper records and folders of information out here,' she said, showing Pip the filing cabinets and drawers that lined the walls of the room around a long table.

Mary placed a large plastic sleeve folder on the table and invited Pip to take a seat. 'This has some information on Frank and there's references that relate to other folders as you go through, so just make a note of any of those and I can get them out of the cabinet,' she finished with a smile.

Pip thanked the woman and flipped the folder open to start looking through the contents. There was a brief timeline and introduction to Frank, covering his younger years and sporting achievements, which she already knew about, but unlike the newspaper articles, the folder contained more photos, and Pip recognised Bert in a few of the town football and cricket team photos from before the war.

Frank Maguire had been a handsome man. His fair hair and light-coloured eyes in the grainy black-and-white photographs were quite mesmerising. She flipped through the pages, pausing once she reached the war section and photos. There was a lot written about his time away and fighting in the same places Bert had been, which was no surprise to her, but she still couldn't work out when or where the incident with the tribunal had happened. She knew Frank had come home in

November 1941, before Rabaul was overrun by the Japanese army, so she had that much to work on.

On the next page was a photo with three men, their smiling faces beaming out at the camera, arms slung around each other's shoulders and the caption *Rabaul* scrawled across the bottom corner. A typed note underneath named the three men as Bill Pinkington, Frank Maguire and Bert Bigsby. The young Bert was also a handsome man, a little shorter and stockier than Frank, but equally as charismatic. She felt a warm glow inside as she traced his features across the plastic covering before switching back to investigator mode. Clearly everything had been going okay up until their arrival in New Guinea. The men looked far too happy and at ease in each other's company for the level of uncertainty and dismay Bert had written about in his letter.

Bert appeared in other photos, but again these didn't seem to show anything except mates trying to get a bit of adventure and enjoyment out of an otherwise bleak experience of war.

The later photos of New Guinea, where the uniforms were dark green and different to the earlier heavy woollen cold-climate uniforms, had a different feel about them. Pip suspected that by this stage the men's initial optimism about bringing the war to an early end had all but disappeared. They looked exhausted and ill, and Pip knew that the problems associated with the jungle environment would have been taking their toll.

Mary came back into the room and Pip closed the folder. 'The other name you were interested in. Arthur Maguire. The only information I have on him was in this publication, about the history of the town's businesses,' she said, opening to a page in a self-published book. 'He took over his father's business and then passed it down to his daughter.'

Pip took the book from her and stared down at the photo of an old shop in the main street that had a date of 1901 written below it. The oldest bakery in the district. The bakery previously owned by Arthur Maguire and now currently owned by his daughter, Jan.

The bell above the door tinkled as Pip pushed it open and waited as she heard footsteps approach. Jan walked out from the back of the shop and her usual bland expression took a decided downturn as she spotted Pip standing at the counter.

'Hello, Jan. Don't worry, I'm not here for a vanilla slice,' Pip started before the woman could tell her to leave. 'I'm just . . .' Pip's words faltered, and she kicked herself for allowing this woman to intimidate her. For goodness sake! She'd interviewed hardened criminals in prison and hadn't flinched. *Get a grip, Davenport.* 'I'd like to talk to you about Frank Maguire. I've been told you're the go-to person when it comes to local history about the Maguire family.'

When the woman's expression didn't alter so much as a blink, Pip forced herself to continue. 'Could you spare the time one day to let me interview you about him—his war years and the accident after he got back?'

The woman's long face, with deep crevices carved into the skin around her mouth—hallmarks of a long-term smoker—could never be described as attractive, but maybe once, when she'd been younger and before life and disappointment had hardened her appearance, Jan Wiseman might have been considered comely. Now, she folded her arms across her chest and her eyes all but disappeared as she narrowed them suspiciously. 'What for?'

'His name came up in the research I've been doing on Bert Bigsby. They were best friends at one time.'

Jan gave a sharp laugh. 'When they were kids, maybe. Till Bert went mad.'

'I believe there was an altercation between the two men. That Bert had to testify against Frank while they were overseas. I can't find any information, though, on the outcome. Do you know anything more about it?'

Any remote flicker of hospitality vanished as the woman's lip curled and her eyes went flint hard. 'I knew you wouldn't be able to help yourself. Gutter journalist—digging up all kinds of dirt and trying to ruin a man's reputation.'

'So you know about the tribunal? About the charges Frank was put up on?'

'There *were* no charges—it was all rumours.'

'I think there was more to it. I know Bert thought so. Is that what started the hate campaign against him? That he'd been asking questions around town when they got back about Frank and his past? Or was it over the fact that the Maguires were taking advantage of others' misfortune and buying land from widows and crippled veterans?'

'My grandfather and great-grandfather helped this community,' Jan spat. 'They bought land off people who needed the money.'

'I'm sure they were only doing it from the kindness of their heart,' Pip agreed in a mocking tone.

'I don't know where you're getting all this from, but Bert Bigsby was a messed-up individual. He was always looking for ways to turn everyone's attention away from the fact he murdered his wife and Vernon Clements.'

Pip bit back the small victory she felt unfolding as her loaded comments provoked the reluctant woman into revealing more than she had intended. 'I think he was hitting a little too close to home and the Maguire clan didn't like the questions he was asking.'

'I think you should get out of my shop and don't come back.'

Pip paused. It was a fine line between knowing when to apply pressure and when to back off, and when, she thought suddenly, to use the element of surprise to best advantage. 'I know what Frank did to your dad when he was a child,' she said simply. 'I think you also suspect.'

Silence followed—a cold, endless stillness. 'How *dare* you start spreading these kinds of lies,' Jan said, but she couldn't disguise the shock on her face. 'You don't know anything.'

'I know enough to feel outraged for all Frank's victims and the fact he got away with it.'

'This is none of your business. It wasn't enough that you stirred up trouble at the nursing home, now you're making up lies about all this.'

'It's part of Bert's story, and I intend to present all the facts I *do* have so people can make up their own minds.' When she was confronted by this kind of thing, it suddenly made her *want* to write the damn story.

'You just said there was nothing about the tribunal to be found,' Jan said smugly. 'You don't *have* any facts.'

'I might not be able to legally prove it—conveniently for Frank, there's no longer any evidence about the poor swaggy who was convicted and died in prison for something he didn't do. But I do have Bert's letters, which I *can* use, and once I do, I guarantee people will come to the same conclusion Bert did about Frank. Only this time, there won't be any Edward Maguire around to cover it up.'

Jan gave a bitter snarl. 'No one will believe anything Butcher Bigsby has to say. They didn't then and they won't now.'

Pip narrowed her gaze across at the woman. 'Frank Maguire was the monster in this town—and you know it. The same way everyone else here knew it. Only, because he was a Maguire, they turned a blind eye to his crimes,' she said. 'Don't you want justice for your father?'

'Get out,' Jan said bluntly, and Pip saw her mouth quiver slightly before she firmed her jaw.

Pip left the shop, her own hands shaking after the encounter, but from indignation, not fear. Without a doubt now, she knew exactly what Bert had suspected was true. And worse still . . . so had most of the town.

Twenty-four

As she climbed out of her car, Pip smiled at the golden glow of late-afternoon light shining through the front window of the house. It felt nice to have someone waiting for her. She reminded herself not to get too carried away, but she couldn't stop the warm sensation that went through her as the door opened before she'd even reached it and the kiss she received made her forget all the day's frustrations. Yep, she could definitely get used to this.

'Problem?' Chris asked after they'd headed inside and were sitting together on the couch while dinner finished cooking.

'No, not really.'

'Something relating to your book?'

'Not *that* book,' she told him.

'Ah, the Bert book,' he nodded, understanding.

'I'm still not saying I'm going to write a book,' she said firmly, 'but . . . every time I pick up a letter or look at a photo, the damn story just keeps getting more twisted.'

'How do you mean?'

She went on to tell him about the tribunal and Bert's suspicions about Frank and the local boy's murder and what she'd found out through her museum visit, and all the while Chris listened, raising an eyebrow here and there until she'd finished with the news that the old records had all been destroyed by fire.

He let out a low whistle. 'You certainly know how to open a can of worms.'

'I know,' she said despondently. 'And this time I didn't even go looking for it!'

'Like you said, though, there's no real proof linking Frank to that kid's murder. And remember, it *did* go before a jury,' he said with a shrug.

'I know,' she said, rubbing her forehead with her fingertips. She'd been stuck in this relentless cycle of what ifs for so long, it was starting to give her a headache.

'I think you need to forget all about the past for a while and just relax,' Chris said, moving on the couch so that her back was against his chest, and he started to massage the tight muscles of her neck and shoulders.

'Is there no end to your talents, detective?' she asked with a blissful groan, closing her eyes to enjoy the release of tension she hadn't been aware she'd been holding onto.

'You haven't even seen half of my talents yet,' he murmured against her ear, which sent a quiver of desire through her body in response.

'Then stop talking and start showing,' she said, turning in his arms to kiss him. This was more than a distraction—it was becoming quite the addiction. But, she reasoned, there were worse things to be addicted to.

'Call in sick and we can just stay here all day,' Pip said the next morning as Chris reluctantly withdrew his arm from beneath her pillow and rolled over to get out of bed.

'I wish I could, but I'm pretty sure for my boss to accept a sick day, I'd have to take in a death certificate,' he said.

She admired his smooth, naked back as he sat on the edge of the bed, summoning the energy to get up.

'But stay as long as you like—don't feel like you need to get up yet.'

Pip stretched and reached out a hand, tracing a long path from his neck to the base of his spine. 'I should get home and glue my butt to a chair in front of my computer,' she said dismally.

'You could work from here,' he suggested, leaning back on one elbow.

She smiled at his hopeful tone. 'I guess I could sometimes. But at the moment I need my research stuff on hand, and I don't think you really want me to bring all that down here and take over your dining table.'

'You can take over whatever you like,' he said, kissing her gently.

'You say that now, but even I get to the point where it drives me crazy.'

'Well, any time you feel like staying longer than a night, the offer's there,' he said, sitting back up before getting to his feet and heading into the shower.

Pip smiled as he reached the doorway and held out a hand to her.

In the kitchen later, Pip had made their coffee and was cooking eggs as he walked in, dressed once more in his trousers and white shirt.

'I don't know which work clothes I prefer,' she said, eyeing him as he walked towards her. 'The business look or the country-detective-in-jeans attire.'

He gave her a quick grin as he took his coffee and the plate she handed him. 'I've got meetings and interviews most of today, so I have to look the part.'

'You certainly do,' she said, appreciating the crisp white shirt that stretched across his shoulders and chest. 'Hey,' she said, 'when do you have Sian next?'

He gave the salt grinder a quick twist over his eggs before answering. 'She's got a fair bit on at the moment, so probably not for a while.'

'Really?' This surprised her. The way he'd spoken before it made it seem like she came home quite often.

'I wasn't sure how you'd feel about it.'

'Feel about your daughter being here?' she asked and watched as he took a bite of his breakfast before nodding.

'I'd love to meet her. But if you're worried about how she'd feel having me sleep over or something, I don't mind not staying.'

'Nah, it wasn't that so much. I just wasn't sure if you'd really come to terms with the fact I have a kid. You seemed a bit surprised when I mentioned it, and we haven't really talked about it again since.'

'I guess I *was* a bit surprised. I don't why—most men your age come with kids and ex partners,' she said, taking a seat across from him with her coffee. 'I'd love to meet her one day. But I also get that you might not want to push something like that on her. I mean, especially since this is all kind of new and we don't even really know if it's even a thing.' God, why had she brought any of this stuff up? Now she sounded like she was pressing him into giving some kind of commitment. 'What I mean is, it's probably too early to even think about meeting her, and I really wasn't implying that I should. I just don't want you to worry about telling me if she's coming over and to stay away.'

'Pip, would you calm down,' he said, having stopped eating as he watched her stumble her way through an explanation. 'It's not a big deal. She hasn't been coming over lately because she's been busy with school and friends on weekends. We haven't really sorted when she's coming next. But when we do, I'd love for you to meet her. If you like.'

'Sure,' Pip said, wishing she could take back all her flustered babbling.

'Great.' He stood up to carry his plate to the dishwasher before coming back to kiss her goodbye. 'Oh, and in case you're interested on my thoughts about us . . . As far as I'm concerned, it's definitely *a thing*,' he said, sending her a wink as he left, leaving her staring after him with a warm fuzzy feeling that went all the way to her toes.

Twenty-five

Pip unlocked the front door and walked inside. The now familiar smell of the farmhouse welcomed her home and she locked the door behind her. As she walked down the hallway and into the kitchen, she stopped. Before she'd left she'd packed away all her research documents, but now they were scattered all over the table. Cupboards and drawers were ajar, and a window was broken, clearly where someone had let themselves in. Her heart began to pound as if it might burst through her chest at any moment.

Someone had been in the house—could *still* be in the house!

She forced her frozen feet to move across the room to the back door. She let herself out and then, digging through her bag as she ran to her car, she called Chris, groaning as his phone went to voicemail. Her heart was still hammering inside her chest. *Just breathe*, she told herself firmly as she jumped in her car and locked the doors, shoving the key into the ignition with shaking fingers. Disconnecting the call, she drove away from the house, her frightened gaze darting to the rear-view mirror, certain she would see someone running after her. When she reached the main road, she pulled the car over and looked up the police station's number in Midgiburra, quickly dialling then listened to it almost ring out before it was finally answered.

'Constable Jenner speaking.'

'This is Phillipa Davenport, out at Rosevale. I need to report a break and enter.'

'A break and enter?' the young officer repeated. 'Are you inside? Have you touched anything? Is anything missing?' She shot the questions at her so fast, Pip had to pause for a moment before she answered them.

'I'm in my car out at the top of my drive. I'm not sure if anything is missing—I only saw the mess in the kitchen and the broken window where they got in. I didn't touch anything. Except the door handle . . .'

'Okay. Good, stay there. We'll send someone out as soon as possible.'

Considering the only people she could send were herself or Erik, Pip wasn't sure why she didn't just say she was on her way. 'Please hurry—I'm not sure if they're still inside.'

'Did you hear anything?' the constable asked urgently.

'No, but I didn't stay in there long enough to find out. I've been away overnight and just got home.'

'Okay. Stay in your car. Lock the doors.'

The phone disconnected and Pip took a deep breath and forced herself to stay calm. A shudder ran through her as she closed her eyes and replayed the mess on the floor and table the moment she realised what had happened. She felt the sweat break out along her back once more and dot her forehead as terror clutched at her. What if green-snake was back? What if Lenny Knight sent him back to finish the job? Her eyes, wide with fear, darted back outside. She half expected a man in a black balaclava to come running towards her any moment. She heard her raspy breath inside the close confines of the car. She couldn't breathe. *No. Stop it!* she told herself firmly. *You're just making it worse!*

The phone rang and she jumped, muttering a curse as she stared at the name on the screen. Her thumb shook as she tried to answer the call, but a surge of relief rushed out as she heard Chris's voice in her ear.

'Wow, you didn't even last an hour before you needed to hear my voice—that has to be some kind of record, Davenport.'

Pip bit the inside of her lip and forced herself to calm down. 'Yeah,' she said and heard her unsteady laugh before it cracked and became a small sob.

'Pip?' Chris's voice had turned serious. 'What's wrong? Where are you?'

She tried to speak, but her throat felt paralysed, and she put her fingers against her mouth to hold back another sob that threatened to escape.

'Pip! Are you hurt?' Chris sounded urgent on the other end of the line.

'No,' she finally managed. 'I'm okay.' She swallowed hard and took a shaky breath. 'I'm sorry. I didn't mean to . . .

someone broke into my house last night . . . or this morning, I don't know.'

'*What?* Are you still inside?'

'No, I'm in the car. It's okay, I'm away from the house. I called the police, they're on their way.'

'Do not go back to the house before the police get there.'

Her earlier panic threatened to return with his stern order. What if someone *was* still inside . . . what if they found her here? She shook her head to clear away the image of a black ski mask and two evil-looking eyes and reached over to double-check she had locked the car doors.

'I'm not planning on going anywhere,' she said.

'Good. I'm on my way over,' he said, and she could hear him breathing heavier as he walked quickly.

'No, don't do that. I'm fine. Really,' she rushed to reassure him. 'Please, don't drive up here just for this—you've got work to do.'

'I'm not leaving you there on your own,' he said.

'I can handle it.'

'Sure you can—but you don't have to. I'm on my way. I'll call you from the road, I just need to make a quick call.'

She wanted to argue but he'd already hung up the phone, and Pip gave an exasperated sigh as she heard the speaker click off. She'd just wanted to hear his voice—she didn't expect him to come running. She felt like an idiot now.

With moments of disconnecting the call, she saw the police car speeding towards her, sirens blaring. As it went past, she turned around and followed it back to the house.

When she pulled up outside, the constable was already out of the car and stalking low towards the house. Pip watched as the young officer, her revolver pointing to the ground, and her back plastered against the side of the house, crab-walked her way towards the back door. Pip wasn't sure if she should be amused or impressed by the military-like precision of the woman's movements, but she certainly *looked* like she meant business.

Pip got out and quietly shut her door, waiting beside the car for the officer to return.

When she came back, Pip noticed she was wearing gloves as she beckoned to follow her back inside. 'It's all clear. Don't touch anything,' she warned as they carefully made their way through the kitchen. 'Take a look around and let me know if you notice anything is missing.'

Pip stopped at the doorway to her bedroom and felt her mouth drop open at the mess. Her drawers had all been opened and tipped out, clothes were piled on the bed and the wardrobe doors were open, with garments left half dangling on hangers or crumpled in a heap on the floor.

'Anything missing?' the officer asked.

Pip gave a small, incredulous laugh. 'How do you tell?'

'It seems they were searching for something—maybe looking for anything valuable.'

'I really don't have anything valuable here,' she said, looking around. 'I was away for the night, and I had my handbag and wallet with me.' She paused and tried to think what else she had. 'I had my computer too,' *and the hard drive*, she added silently, for a moment panicking that she may have left it here, only to remember throwing it into her computer bag as she walked out the door. The last thing she needed was to lose the unlocked file. The medium-sized flat-screen TV still sat on the top of the wardrobe, and there was really nothing else in the room.

She followed the other woman out to the lounge room and noticed that, again, all the electrical appliances were still intact—her uncle's large-screen TV, the stereo and her aunt's china and crystal in the glass display cabinet.

The sound of an approaching vehicle had the constable walking towards the front window and peering out. 'Just the boss,' she said over her shoulder before coming back. 'He was out when I got your call, so I got him to meet us here.'

'Are you all right, Pip?' Erik asked as he came into the room, swiftly surveying the damage.

'Yeah. I'm fine. I just got a bit spooked.'

'I've got the fingerprint kit in the car—you wanna go grab that, constable?' he said without stopping his inspection of the room.

'Sure, boss,' the young woman said, and Pip was half expecting a snappy salute to go with her eager, ready-to-please manner.

'I'm really grateful to your constable. What's her name, by the way?' Pip asked, suddenly realising she had no idea what to call her. Maybe with a first name she would seem a little more approachable.

'Gladys.'

Or not . . . 'Well,' Pip said nodding, 'she was onto it straightaway.'

'Yeah, she's good like that,' Erik said, flipping open his notebook. 'Have we established what was taken?'

'Nothing,' Pip said, doing another sweep of the room. 'I can't see anything missing.'

Constable Jenner came back inside and placed a large plastic box on the floor. She opened it, preparing to dust the house for fingerprints, as the sound of yet another engine approached. Both officers looked up curiously, out the front window then at each other in bewilderment as Chris slammed his car door and jogged to the house.

'Did you call Jarrett in?' Erik asked, looking at his constable.

'No, boss.'

Pip watched Chris enter the kitchen by the back door, giving it a cursory glance before finding her and heading over. Relief seeped through her now that he'd arrived and she wanted to slip into his arms and hold him tight so she could forget the horrible pit of fear in the base of her stomach. But they had an audience, and things were suddenly a tad awkward in the confined room.

'Jarrett.' Erik nodded. 'What brings you out here?'

'I called him,' Pip offered, jumping in quickly. She wasn't sure what the protocol was—she wasn't a suspect in anything relating to the bones discovered in the dam, but she had an idea it would seem a little strange that the lead detective would have such a sudden personal interest in her.

Erik sent her a strange look. 'Why?'

'I . . .'

'It's okay, I told her if she ever needed anything to call.'

'Well, so did I, but she didn't call *me* straightaway,' Erik said, his eyes narrowing a little as he studied them.

'You said earlier that you'd been away overnight and had only just got back home?' Constable Jenner cut in.

'Where were you last night?' Erik asked, and Pip was momentarily thrown off balance by his directness.

'She was with me,' Chris answered smoothly, taking a step towards her. 'Are you okay?' he asked, his voice lowering slightly as he looked her over.

'I'm fine. I overreacted and freaked out. I'm really sorry I called you.'

'You didn't overreact,' he said, holding her embarrassed gaze firmly. And she knew what he was saying. She hadn't overreacted considering what had happened to her before. But right here now, in broad daylight with three police officers around her, she felt like a complete twit.

'You were with the detective?' Erik said slowly.

'I took some research on Bert Bigsby down to show him,' she explained, trying to sound professional and not too sure she succeeded.

'And it took all night?' Erik pressed doubtfully.

'Sergeant, do we have a problem here?' Chris asked in a voice Pip hadn't heard before—soft, almost dangerous.

'Nope, just trying to ascertain all the facts, detective,' Erik replied in a deceptively casual manner that did not match his steely-eyed stare.

Pip wasn't entirely sure what was happening between the two men, but she suspected there was history between them and she hoped it didn't have anything to do with her. Sure, she and Erik had a brief moment of attraction when she'd first arrived, and she'd been grateful about the whole possum incident, but he had always acted in a professional capacity. He'd never gone out of his way to initiate anything more personal. She actually got the impression he didn't particularly like her—or maybe it was her profession he didn't like. Either way, things had definitely cooled off once he realised she was a journalist.

'Anything taken?' Chris asked, dragging his angry gaze away from the sergeant.

'Nothing,' she said again, and gave a frustrated sigh.

Chris looked slowly around the room before giving a brief shake of his head. 'Well, they were definitely looking for something. Are you sure you haven't missed anything valuable they might have found?'

'I already told Constable Jenner that I had everything with me that might have been valuable—my handbag and purse and my computer.'

Chris considered her silently for a moment. 'Have you had any kind of threats lately? Any phone calls that might have seemed weird? Any contact with anyone from your past?'

Pip eyed him strangely. 'No. You think this might have something to do with Lenny Knight?'

'I'm just looking at all options. You said you had your computer with you—could there be something on that which might be of use to someone?'

'Not really. At least, not on my computer.'

'What do you mean?' Erik asked.

'Well, I have sensitive stuff I've collected over the years for various stories—I've spoken to informants and witnesses, whistleblowers,' she added, 'but I don't store any of that on my computer. I mean, if it got stolen—' She stopped abruptly.

'You haven't had anything strange happen lately?' Chris pushed.

'No,' Pip shook her head impatiently as helplessness and overwhelming fear began to trickle its way back into her. 'Only that stupid possum thing a few weeks ago.'

'What possum thing?' Chris asked.

Pip shook her head dismissively. 'I heard a noise outside and called the police. Erik came out but it was nothing.'

She saw him look across at the other policeman and hold his stare.

'She's right. There was nothing to suggest anyone had been there,' Erik said irritably. 'I'm guessing a possum knocked some stuff over on the verandah.'

'I didn't see that in the logbook,' Constable Jenner put in, wearing a puzzled frown.

'Because there was nothing to be logged,' Erik bit out impatiently.

'But still—'

'Jenner, can you go finish fingerprinting, please?'

'Yes, sir.'

Pip watched the woman disappear back into the other room. She hadn't given the possum incident much thought recently, but what if it really *hadn't* been a possum after all?

'So where *do* you keep all your intel?' Erik asked with a frown.

A Stone's Throw Away

'In the safe.'

'Have you checked it hasn't been tampered with?' Chris asked, looking around as though expecting to see it sitting in the centre of the room.

'Not here. In my apartment.'

'Have you got anyone checking on your place in Sydney?'

'No. But Lexi has a key.'

'I'll give a mate of mine a call and he'll go over and check it out. Can you give me Lexi's number so he can get the key off her?'

'Sure.' Pip pulled out her phone from the back pocket of her jeans and scrolled through her contacts, sending him Lexi's details. His phone beeped and he gave her a thumbs-up before the call he made was answered on the other end and walked outside to talk.

'So you and Jarrett, huh?' Erik said as they moved out to the kitchen.

Pip avoided his gaze. 'It kinda just happened.'

'I didn't even know you two had met.'

'I guess we just hit it off,' she smiled weakly.

'Just . . .' He went to say something then seemed to change his mind.

'Just what?'

He sent her a level look. 'Just be careful. You don't know everything about him.'

She was about to ask what the hell that was supposed to mean, but at that moment, Chris opened the door and came back inside.

'Everything okay?' he asked, sensing the sudden quiet that had fallen in the room at his approach.

'Yep, all good,' she smiled.

'I'm gonna leave the constable here to finish up and head back into the station,' Erik said. 'You know where I am if you need anything,' he added, sending Pip a serious look before he walked past and outside without a backwards glance.

'What was that all about?' Chris asked.

'I have no idea. Do you two not get along or something? I'm sensing a bit of a vibe between you.'

'He applied for the job I got,' Chris said dismissively. 'I don't think he's got over it.' He stepped up close and put his hands around her waist. 'Now, are you *really* okay?'

'Yeah,' she said wearily. 'I think so. I'm sorry about earlier— I don't know what happened, I didn't mean to sound so . . .'

'It was shock. And it's completely normal. I'm glad you called me.'

'Thank you for coming running like a knight in shining armour,' she said, finally able to relax now he had his arms around her.

'Any time,' he said leaning in to kiss her lips. 'All I could think of was you in this house and someone still inside. It wasn't a nice experience being that far away and unable to help.'

'Actually, you seemed to get here pretty fast. Were you doing the speed limit?'

'I may have used the siren here and there,' he admitted, lowering his voice, 'but it was an emergency.'

'I had Midgiburra's finest here in no time.'

'Do you want to pack a bag and come back to my place for a few days?' he said after a slight pause. 'Or I can come back tonight and stay. But honestly, until we work out what's going on,' he said, casting his gaze around the room, 'I really don't feel comfortable knowing you're out here on your own.'

A flutter of fear started once again as she thought about being here once everyone left. There was nothing in the way of security—no cameras, no deadlocks on the doors or windows, nothing that would stop someone coming back for another attempt if they chose to. Terror lodged in her chest but was swiftly followed by anger. Why should she be chased out of the place where she'd come to rest and write? How dare someone come and ruin the one space she'd finally felt safe in. But she could see the logic in Chris's suggestion.

As independent and strong as she wanted to be, when it came to this, she wasn't. She hated it, but there was very little she could do about it. She thought about Pete and Anne, but next door was a long way away in the middle of the night if she heard a noise that needed checking out. Besides, did she really know them well enough to call them out of their bed in the dark?

'There's no point in you commuting,' she said eventually. 'If you're sure, then I'll come and stay with you.'

'Good. I'll leave you my key and you can head down as soon as they're finished up here, if you like? I'd stay, but I have a meeting I need to get to.'

'No, you go. That's fine. I'm really sorry you had to come up here.'

'Don't worry about it—I'm glad you called me. I'll see you tonight, then?'

Pip nodded and managed a smile as she waved him off, but her heart sank as she turned back to head inside. Could this really be connected to the Lenny Knight story? Or just a random break and enter by some kids? The random idea didn't make any sense since nothing was actually stolen. Chris seemed to be right—whoever had broken in had been looking for something specific. She eyed her handbag and pictured the small, blue hard drive inside.

Twenty-six

Her phone rang and Lexi's name flashed across the screen. 'Hey,' she answered.

'Are you okay? I've just been contacted by a federal police officer about getting into your apartment. What the hell's going on?'

'It's okay. They're just checking to make sure no one's broken in.'

'Broken in?'

'Someone went through the house here, and they're just being cautious.'

'I don't understand.'

'They're just making sure the break-in wasn't connected to any of my stories.'

'Pip, I don't like this. Are you in danger?'

'No, of course not. It's just ruling out possibilities. It was probably just kids looking for cash or something.'

'Come home,' Lexi said, sounding anything but her usual devil-may-care self.

'I'm staying with . . . a friend tonight until we sort this out. I'm perfectly safe. I'll see how things are in a few days and decide what I'm going to do then.'

'Hold up . . . friend? What friend? I'm your only friend,' Lexi gasped. 'Are you talking about a *male* friend?'

'It's not a big deal,' Pip said a little too quickly.

'Are you freaking serious? This is a huge deal! I need details, right now.'

'I'm in the middle of having the house dusted for fingerprints—can we do this later?' she said, lowering her voice as she caught movement out of the corner of her eye and saw Constable Jenner making her way towards the kitchen.

'Can I get you to wait outside, ma'am?' the officer asked, poking her head around the corner of the door.

Pip waved a hand and bumped the back door open with her hip to stand outside on the verandah.

'Okay, I'll let you off for now, but you better be ready with the goss when I call back.'

'Sure,' Pip promised hastily, happy to escape the interrogation. 'I'll talk to you later.'

She loved her best friend dearly, but when it came to talking about Chris, Pip just wasn't ready. The whole relationship didn't even make sense when she thought about it—she knew it would make even less sense if she talked about it. She'd known him only a handful of days and was already comfortable enough to stay with him in an emergency. How? They barely knew each other, and yet . . . they did. She'd never before opened up with a man the way she had with Chris. She felt as though she'd known him for years. Then there was the whole attraction thing. Even thinking about it now, Pip had a familiar rush of anticipation run through her. 'This is crazy,' she muttered. But then again, nothing about her life at the moment could be described as normal.

While she waited for the constable to finish up in the house, Pip headed through the paddock towards the dam. She hadn't been down there for a few days, but now she craved the peace and quiet the tree-lined spot provided.

She sent a quick glance at the churned-up mess the bottom of the dam had become. Between all the digging and sifting Bob and the forensic team had done, it was looking like a giant, albeit rubbish-free, quagmire.

Again, it niggled inside her. Molly must have had her diary with her—it didn't make sense that she wouldn't take it with her if she was leaving forever. Chris had a very logical argument in that the water would have destroyed the diary long ago, and yet ... she couldn't help but wonder. What if by some miracle the diary had been preserved? People found buried bodies perfectly preserved—was it really too much to ask for a little divine intervention?

Pip continued on, following the same cattle track she'd taken when she'd first arrived, and without conscious thought she looked up and realised she'd come out into the small clearing near the massive gum tree. Once more the silence registered— loudly. That strange feeling of stepping into another place surrounded her, and a fleeting, annoying memory that she couldn't pin down hovered over her. 'What?' she suddenly said loudly, throwing her arms out and looking around. 'What do you want from me?' The reality of what had happened that morning came crashing down upon her. All the progress she'd made to overcome her fear and the memories amounted to nothing. Someone had broken in and violated that precious illusion of safety she'd thought she'd found here.

She sank down onto the ground and rested her back against the large gum tree and let the frustrated tears fall. Out here, no one would see her fall apart. She felt safe, protected somehow inside a bubble with only the gentle sway of the wind's breath high up in the trees and the muted sound of birds and insects going about their daily business. Eventually she felt the tears subside and her eyelids grow heavy . . .

The woman sat on the blanket, her red dress bold and cheerful. Her hair was tucked up at the base of her neck, and Pip saw from under the brim of a wide sunhat a smile on the woman's ruby red lips as she scribbled in her notebook.

Her mood seemed different this time—lighter, happier. There was a sense of excitement in the air. Beside her was a small bag. It looked like she was dressed up and about to go somewhere; it certainly didn't look like she was here for a picnic.

'Where are you going?' Pip asked, her curiosity getting the better of her.

As the woman looked up at her, she sent Pip a bright smile—almost as though she'd been expecting her.

'Molly?' Pip asked. 'Why am I here?'

A Stone's Throw Away

The screech of a black cockatoo jolted Pip awake and she sat up, her heart thudding as she glanced around quickly, expecting to see Molly before realising it had been another dream. God. Why was this happening to her? She didn't have time to deal with any more of these stupid dreams on top of everything else going on. 'Enough already!' she said as she got to her feet and dusted off her shorts. She had a house to put back into order, and then she would drive to stay with Chris. She needed a break from all this before she went completely crazy.

Before she left for Coopers Creek, Pip made a stop next door.

'Pip! How are you? How's the research going?' Anne said, smiling as she wiped her hands on a tea towel as Pete led her inside to the kitchen.

'Slowly,' she admitted. 'Actually, I was wondering if either of you had noticed any unusual cars about the place? Yesterday or last night?'

'No, I don't think so, dear,' Anne said, her face serious as she peered closely at Pip. 'Has something happened?'

'The house was broken into. I was over in Coopers Creek, but I came back this morning and it had been ransacked. The police might be over later—they said they'd ask around and check with everyone in case somebody saw something,' she added. 'I just thought I'd come and tell you before I left.'

'You're going? Already?'

'No—not for good. Just for a few days. It's rattled me a bit.'

'You're more than welcome to stay here, if you like,' Anne said, glancing over at her husband for confirmation.

'Yeah, of course you are,' Pete nodded.

'Thank you, but I've got somewhere to stay and I'm doing research, so that'll keep me busy.'

'What's the flamin' world coming to? Thieving mongrels,' Pete muttered with a disgusted shake of his head.

'It doesn't look like they actually took anything at this stage, thank goodness,' Pip said with a brief grimace. 'The last thing I want to do is have to tell Uncle Nev someone stole all his belongings. A fine caretaker I've turned out to be so far,' she said dully.

'Don't be hard on yourself,' Anne commiserated. 'None of this has been your doing. It's just bad luck.'

Pip hoped so, although this break-in did not feel random in the slightest, and she really didn't want to think about that too much right now.

'I actually just wanted to double-check with you—did you ever come across a journal when you were clearing out Bert's place? I didn't find anything in any of the boxes, but I have a feeling Molly kept one.'

'Bert mentioned them in the letters,' Anne nodded, then shook her head sadly. 'No, we didn't find anything like that. Just the letters.'

'I thought as much,' she said sadly. 'The police seem to think if it had existed, it could have been with Molly in her luggage, but they never located anything.'

'Can't imagine anything like that would have survived all this time out there,' Pete said, sending her a doubtful glance.

'Yeah, I'm just clutching at straws.'

'Well, we'll keep an ear out for anything going on over next door while you're away,' Anne said, and Pip smiled, thanking them before heading off and leaving Rosevale behind.

Twenty-seven

Pip glanced down at her dashboard as the music stopped and saw a phone call coming in from Chris.

'Hey. Are you on your way down?' he asked.

'Yeah, almost there.'

'I just heard back from my mate in the feds. He's been over to your place and there's no sign of anything being disturbed.'

'Well, that's something at least.'

'He's going to put someone outside your building for a couple of days, just to keep an eye on things.'

'Chris, I really don't think—'

'Until we work out what's going on, we need to assume this is a lot more serious than a simple break and enter.'

'I just don't get why,' she said, his words disturbing her more than she'd expected. 'It's over and done with.'

'Except for the book.'

'What do you mean?'

'Maybe Lenny Knight isn't too keen about you writing a book on him.'

'I don't know why he'd go to all the trouble of trying to stop me—he's already convicted.'

'I just think there's more to this break-in than meets the eye. I feel better knowing you're not alone at your place. We'll talk more tonight when I get home, okay?'

'Okay.' Had she not been distracted by the conversation she probably would have laughed at the absurdly domesticated farewell. It sounded like they were an old married couple. Her smile slipped.

Suddenly, the whole thing felt out of control.

Pip called up her phone contacts. 'Call Lexi,' she instructed and listened to the dial tone before it was answered. 'It's me,' she said abruptly.

'Did they check your apartment?' Lexi asked.

'Yeah, it's all fine, apparently,' Pip said impatiently, waving off her friend's concern.

'What's going on?' Lexi asked.

'Everything's just moving too fast,' Pip blurted out in a rush.

'What do you mean?'

'I don't feel like I have control over anything at the moment, Lex.'

'The break-in was bound to shake you up a bit,' her friend said sympathetically.

'It's not just that,' Pip replied, searching for the right words that were jumbling about inside her head. 'I'm so tired of having everything taken away from me. My independence, my job—my old life is gone, and just when I think I've finally begun to find some kind of happiness and a little bit of my old self, that all gets taken away from me too.'

'Oh, babe,' Lexi said on a sigh. 'It doesn't seem fair. Are you okay?'

'I don't think I am,' Pip admitted, feeling hollow. 'I'm just so tired of being scared all the time.'

'I'm coming down there,' Lexi said decisively.

'No,' Pip groaned. As much as she would love to have her best friend with her right now, there was no way she was willing to put her in the middle of whatever was going on. 'There's nothing you can do. I'm sick of having to depend on everyone.'

'That's what we're all here for—to help when you need it.'

'And I'm grateful for everything, but I just want to live my own life without fear controlling everything thing I do.'

'I'm worried about you.'

Pip gave a long sigh and clenched the steering wheel tighter. The last thing she wanted to do was give Lexi more to worry about. 'I'll be okay. I just needed to vent a little. Honest. I'm fine. I've . . . met someone,' she finally admitted, more because she knew she needed a distraction to stop Lexi jumping on the first flight out of Sydney, and also, if she gave Lexi something juicy to chew on, Pip would feel a little less guilty over making her friend worry about her so much.

'I knew it! Tell me,' she said eagerly.

'It's not official or anything . . . I'm not really sure what it is,' she said.

'Who is he? What does he do? Details, woman! I need details.'

A Stone's Throw Away

'He's a police detective. He's been working on the cold case here with the bones. So you see, you don't have anything to worry about—I couldn't *be* any safer right now. And please don't tell Mum and Dad about any of this. I don't want them stressing.'

'Of course I won't . . . as long as you stay in touch and keep me informed, okay?'

'I will.'

'Pip, just go with this thing, with the detective,' Lexi said, more serious than she'd heard her sound in a long time. 'Don't overthink it, okay?'

Pip chewed on her bottom lip as her friend's words sunk in. 'I'll try not to,' she promised, hoping it sounded more convincing than it felt. Nothing really made any sense right now when everything was so muddled. At the moment, she was overthinking everything.

She parked outside the house she'd left only a few hours earlier and tipped her head back on the headrest wearily. After a few moments she would summon enough strength to open her door.

Inside, she listened to the silence. The hum of the fridge was the only sound, and Pip rubbed her hands along her arms, warding off an unexpected chill. She'd got used to the quiet at Rosevale, but here, it felt different. A memory of the night she was attacked flashed through her mind—there'd been that same claustrophobic silence then too. A sudden creak of a floorboard launched her heart into her throat and she was instantly alert. The adrenalin kicked in, and there was no rationalising her fears away. She ran back to the front door and out to her car, driving off before she'd even clicked the seatbelt into its lock. Her heart was still racing when she pulled up a short distance from the police station and parked the car.

She took a minute to get herself under control but then realised how not okay she really was, jumping at the slightest sound and ready to flee the first chance she got. She couldn't go in there and tell Chris she was too scared to stay in his house alone. She could barely admit it to herself. She was a grown woman, for goodness sake, and she was shaking like a damn leaf.

She glanced up when she caught movement outside and a moment of relief managed to surface from her inner turmoil as she spotted Chris leaving the building. She was about to open her door to catch him before he left but paused when he approached a car parked further along the street.

Impatient that she had to now wait for him to finish whatever official business he had, she frowned a little as she noticed Chris's demeanour change. His expression was tight, there was nothing remotely approachable about him and his body language seemed stiff, unyielding, as he strode around the front of the car and reefed open the passenger-side door to get in.

Curious and a little unsettled, Pip watched the interaction from a distance. It was difficult to see exactly what was transpiring inside the vehicle, but through the rear window of the other car she could see Chris sitting ramrod straight. Pip reached into her glovebox and took out the binoculars she kept there. As she adjusted the focus, the blurred vision cleared and she saw a clear side profile of Chris before moving the binoculars across to his companion. The driver had a fuller face, and she could make out the white collar of his shirt under the suit jacket he wore but she couldn't see anything else.

Reaching into the back of her car, she dragged the camera bag across to the front and dumped it on the passenger seat, quickly unzipping the bag and bringing out the camera inside. She replaced the binoculars with the camera and zoomed in the lens, snapping off a few pictures to look at later as Chris handed the man something; she couldn't quite make out what it was. There was something not quite right about this meeting. Maybe he had a case that wasn't going well and this was someone unpleasant he had to deal with, but it just seemed . . . off.

She watched Chris get out of the car and head back inside the station shortly afterward and pondered the strange encounter yet again as she watched the man in the dark blue car drive away.

She picked up the camera and scrolled through to take a closer look at the photos. There was nothing familiar about the driver's face, nothing terribly distinguishing. Yet . . . She couldn't shake the feeling there was something not right about that whole meeting.

She reached the photos where Chris had handed the man something and zoomed in on that part of the image. She'd only caught a brief, off-centre shot of it, but it looked like a rectangular blue object. For a moment her brow puckered as she tried to place the it. Then she went still. The colour was the same shade as her . . . Pip put the camera down and dug through her handbag, panic rising as alarm set in, until her fingers located the rectangular-shaped blue object she'd momentarily thought wouldn't be there. Her hard drive. She picked up the camera once more and compared the image. It *was* the same colour and looked to be the right dimensions.

Red flags were now popping up before her eyes and dread fell like a rock into the pit of her stomach. Why would Chris be giving someone a hard drive? Surely if it was anything dodgy he wouldn't have done it within cooee of the police station? Then again, who had been around to see? It wasn't as though Coopers Creek was a massive metropolitan with hordes of people out and about. But Chris's manner definitely wasn't that of someone doing something for a mate. He'd looked angry—cold, even.

Erik's strange warning earlier that morning suddenly popped into her head. She'd dismissed it before, but now . . . She gave a small, frustrated groan. She'd always relied on her gut instinct in a situation to tell her what was going on, but now . . . she had no idea what to believe. Had she lost her ability to read people the moment she let herself become distracted by lust?

It would explain this sudden, out of character . . . whatever it was with Chris. If she'd been thinking rationally she'd have probably never given in to this crazy urge to throw caution to the wind and allow herself to be swept up by him.

Pip tried not to put a name to the feeling that was currently hovering around her—it was a foreboding mix of uncertainty and suspicion. Something was not right. Seeing that hard drive—if that's what she saw Chris passing to the man in the car—brought her back to the house break-in and her assumption that nothing important had been stolen. It didn't make sense. Someone *had* been looking for something, and the only thing she could put it down to was that bloody encrypted file. What the hell was on it?

Pip reached for her phone and ran through her contacts list, hitting the number she stored there under the title of Aunty Wanda and waited impatiently for the voicemail to kick in.

'This is Pip. I need to get an urgent message to Aunty Wanda.' She rolled her eyes as she said it—usually she found it entertaining to go through the whole ridiculous ritual of trying to contact the Warlock, but today it was just irritating. 'I need the job done ASAP. The situation has changed. It's now urgent.' She hesitated briefly before adding, 'If you don't think you can open it, let me know.'

She waited. There was never any guarantee of an immediate reply, and she knew she had pushed her luck with the last bit, but ten minutes later, her phone beeped with a message.

Of course I can open it. I'll be in touch.

Putting the phone away, she knew that all she could do was wait and hope to God the guy really was as good as he kept telling her he was. Not that she had any other choice but to believe him—her technical skills certainly didn't stretch as far as encrypted files.

The break-in had to be about the files. Nothing else made sense. If she could just see what was on the damn thing, she'd know what she was up against.

She drove to the next town over from Coopers Crossing. Edensville was larger than Midgiburra but not quite the size of Coopers Creek. She booked into a motel.

She knew she could stay with Chris. Sure, she'd be okay tonight, but once he left for work she'd be alone again, and she just couldn't stop that chilling, irrational fear that crept over her at the thought of being alone. A motel, though, felt different. It had always been her safety net. She'd never told anyone—not even Lexi—that sometimes, when she felt herself beginning to spiral, she would leave her apartment and book into a motel for the night. Maybe because it was smaller and only had one door: one way in and out, so she didn't have to worry about someone sneaking in without her knowing. It was completely illogical, but the terror she felt was real. Her life was spinning out of control once more and she couldn't seem to stop it.

She needed to take control over *something*, and that something was this. She would stay where she felt safest, and right now, that happened to be a rundown little motel room.

When her phone rang later, she braced herself to answer. She'd been dreading this all afternoon.

'Pip? I just got home. Where are you?'

'Hi. I had a change of plans. I don't want to put you out by crashing at your place and getting you all mixed up in this stuff.'

'It's not putting me out. I need to know you're okay.'

'I'm fine,' she said brightly. 'I just need to do this on my own. I'm sick of depending on other people.'

'Pip, where are you?' His voice held a note of urgency.

'Chris, I just need to work on my book and get it done. I think I've let this thing between us distract me and I need to focus.'

'Pip, for Christ's sake—I told you, until we figure out what's going on, you need to be with someone. This is serious.'

'Then figure it out, Chris,' she said bluntly. 'Find out what's going on so I can get back to living my life without needing a gaoler.'

'I'm not trying to be a gaoler,' he snapped.

'I'm not actually sure what you're trying to be.'

'What's that supposed to mean?' he asked after a moment of silence.

'Things were moving too fast with us and right now we both need a clear head to deal with whatever's going on here.' The truth was, she wasn't sure what she had seen today, and she needed to get herself under control and in a place where she could think logically about everything—especially Chris.

Again the line went quiet. 'If that's what you want. I just wish I knew why the sudden turnaround,' he said quietly. He sounded hurt. 'This morning everything seemed okay with us. Has something happened that I don't know about?'

'No. I just need some space. I'll call you tomorrow.'

She ended the call before she gave in and went running back to him. All she wanted was to be held tight and reassured that everything was going to be all right. But until she could figure out what it was that he wasn't telling her, she wouldn't be able to trust him completely—and at the moment, the difference between trusting someone or not could be the difference between life and death.

The beep of her phone woke her from a light sleep, her laptop still open where she'd left it beside her on the bed.

She picked up the phone and tried to focus her eyes on the bright screen.

> Check your email. And if you ever doubt my skill again you can find yourself another tech guru.

She was wide awake now. Dragging her computer onto her lap, she opened her email account. As she clicked on the message and waited for the file to open, she suddenly had a moment of indecision. What if she was about to unlock something she couldn't unsee? *Better to know for sure*, a little voice said stubbornly.

She opened the file and watched as a series of photos began to download.

Twenty-eight

Pip stared at the screen of images before her and tried to work out what she was seeing.

In a series of photographs that looked as though they'd been taken in quick succession under surveillance, she saw Lenny Knight on a private yacht, dining with another man. The two seemed to be relaxed in each other's company as they drank and ate and appeared to be in deep conversation.

Pip leaned closer to the computer and felt her heart rate quicken as she recognised the second man. Karl Butterworth. The politician, lawyer and former minister for police and emergency services who had recently been promoted to attorney-general.

As she pondered the possibilities of what these photos might suggest, she opened the first of several document files.

It was a list of names. None of them had appeared in any previous connection with Lenny Knight in her research or anything the police had followed up on. Many of the names weren't familiar, but one practically leapt from the page: Karl Butterworth.

As she opened the rest of the document files, she discovered a detailed list of dates and meeting times along with a comprehensive report on favours Lenny Knight had requested of Karl Butterworth. The document looked to Pip like something created as protection for Knight should he need to call in more favours later. Had Knight been blackmailing the new attorney-general with this list? The list now on a hard drive in Pip's possession?

Pip collapsed back against the headboard an hour later, stunned. It made more sense now why someone might be searching for her hard drive. Maybe Knight hadn't been behind the break-ins. What if it were someone with even more to lose . . . someone like Karl Butterworth?

If he knew Pip had the file, there wasn't much he wouldn't do to destroy it before she could use it. She had no idea how they found out about it—which alarmed her. The information on that hard drive wasn't public knowledge. The only person besides Tony who'd known about it was The Warlock, and he wouldn't tell anyone—his business, not to mention his life, depended on strict anonymity.

She clicked back to the photos on the screen and went through them again. How had information been leaked? She'd kept the hard drive with her at all times; she'd been alone at the house; she'd taken it with her the night Rosevale was ransacked.

A Stone's Throw Away

She paused on one of the photos of the two politicians shaking hands in farewell. There was a man leaning against a car to the side of the photo. She enlarged it on the screen and her blood turned to ice in her veins. She grabbed her camera and enlarged the photo she'd taken earlier today and compared the two. It was the same man. The guy Chris had been talking to in the car.

She'd been alone at the house . . . except for the weekend Chris stayed. Chris had been in her house, and she had spent the night in his. He had access to the hard drive—he could even have copied it onto a similar one. He'd also met with a man who had connections to the two men in the photos, and she'd watched him hand over something that had looked suspiciously like a hard drive. She felt her whole body deflate like a tired balloon as the facts started to pile up despite everything inside her screaming that it wasn't true.

Chris was part of this whole thing. Whatever this thing was.

After a brief hesitation, Pip slammed the laptop shut and stuffed it back into its bag, hurriedly gathering the hard drive, her phone and the camera and dropping them on the table in a pile as she got dressed.

She cast a swift glance around the room to make sure she hadn't forgotten anything then dumped it all into the car outside her room and left. She had no idea where she was going—only that she had to make sure she was well away and ahead of anyone who might be looking for her.

None of this made any sense. Why would Chris be mixed up with criminals from a different state? *How* had he become involved? And how had he ended up investigating a fluke discovery of old bones in a dam that led straight to her?

Headlights passed her as she drove through the night. She couldn't go back to Uncle Nev's place; Chris would look for her there. She couldn't go back to her apartment; he had his mate in the federal police watching it. She thought about heading to Melbourne—it was big enough to blend in, but it was also Chris's old stomping ground and he'd no doubt have plenty of contacts he could call in favours from and have her found.

All she *did* know was that she couldn't just sit there and wait to be found. She had to keep moving.

As morning broke, Pip was still undecided as to how to proceed. Sitting in the carpark of a supermarket, she sipped a takeaway coffee and nibbled on a toasted cheese sandwich. Who could she trust now?

Part of her wanted to give Chris a chance to explain, but that risked putting herself in danger if her gamble with her stupid heart instead of her head proved wrong.

She still had a key to his house. Maybe there was something that linked Chris to everything somewhere inside. It was a crazy idea—and dangerous if Chris was involved in all this as the evidence against him beginning to stack up suggested.

Corrupt police. Corrupt politicians. Corrupt businessmen. She was sick and tired of the lot of them. She wanted her life back, and that wasn't going to happen if she continued to cower and run away whenever she got scared. The realisation settled inside her and began to unfold and expand until it filled her chest completely.

If she wanted things to change then *she* would need to be the one to do something.

Somehow she had to either clear Chris and find a logical explanation for everything or find the proof that linked him to Butterworth or Knight . . . or both.

Pip parked around the corner from Chris's house and made her way on foot with a healthy dose of caution and a touch of terror reminding her that these men Chris was involved with killed people who got in their way.

She checked that his car wasn't in the driveway then moved quietly across to the front door. She unlocked it, stepped into the house and then closed and locked the door behind her softly. Once again she was overcome by the quiet. Shaking off her rising anxiety, she headed to the bedroom.

She pushed aside the memories of their night together and how happy she'd been feeling before it all started to unravel. She had to keep her head in the game. She focused instead on the very good chance that Chris had been playing her this whole time. Fortified by righteous anger once more, Pip set to work.

She crossed to the bedside table where she found only loose change and a phone charger. Her pulse began to thrum as she kept an ear out for the slightest sound to suggest Chris had returned. She moved to the tallboy and opened its drawers, fighting a bout of guilt as she sifted through neatly folded clothing before heading to the walk-in wardrobe. His work suits, shirts and trousers hung above shoes on the floor, while in the next section, jeans and T-shirts were folded and stored in cubed shelves.

Pip surveyed the contents of the wardrobe, silently contemplating. Something had been bothering her ever since she'd spent the night here. She understood Chris was a bachelor, and he was a guy of simple tastes and needs, but for someone who'd not long moved in, there was a decided lack of personal belongings and no boxes laying around, yet to be unpacked. It felt like an Airbnb or a motel.

His wardrobe looked like someone had unpacked only the bare essentials. Where were his winter clothes? The things stored away off-season? The keepsakes? The photographs?

On the very top shelf, above where his clothes hung, she spotted three large plastic storage tubs. She looked about for something to stand on to lift them down, then headed out to the kitchen to grab a small stepladder from the pantry. She froze when she heard footsteps approaching the front door from outside and a key in the lock.

She hurried into the nearby front bedroom and closed the door, hoping to God that Chris had no reason to come in here. It had the same sparseness as the master bedroom. Nothing to indicate it was inhabited by a teenage girl.

She heard his key turn in the lock and then his boots tread with long, purposeful strides to the rear of the house—all the while her heart pounding painfully against her chest. What if he found her here? What would he do?

Her already frayed nerves almost snapped when she heard a knock at the front door. The footsteps sounded again, walking past the door she was standing behind. There was a hesitation before Chris opened the door, and when he spoke it was coldly brutal.

'What the fuck are you doing at my house?'

'There's no need to be so defensive, detective.' The other man's voice sounded decidedly jovial in comparison. 'I just thought I'd pay you a visit and see how you're progressing.'

Pip double-checked her phone was still on silent and took a deep breath before easing the door open a fraction. The men were standing halfway between the foyer and the lounge room, but Pip couldn't open the door any wider without risking being seen, so she put her phone to the crack and started to video the exchange.

'I told you I'd get the hard drive—and I did.'

'Yes, but that was only half the job, wasn't it?'

'I've still got to make an appearance at work.'

'Not my problem. You promised us the woman. We don't know for sure if she's opened the encryption yet—or who she has working on it—and until we do, we have to assume she's still very much a threat. Tell me at least you know where she is?'

A sudden light-headed sensation swept through her. They were talking about her—*she* was the threat.

'I'll find her,' Chris said in a tone that chilled her to the bone. This was not the Chris she thought she knew. What an idiot she'd been, thinking she'd found something special.

'You better hope you do—and fast,' the other man said, suddenly stepping out from behind the wall he'd been partially hidden behind, and Pip's eyes widened. It was the man Chris met in the car. 'I don't want to have to drop by and pay you another visit, detective.'

Chris's face was a stony mask, devoid of any of the warmth he had shown her.

She eased the bedroom door shut and let out a slow breath. When the front door closed, the house was silent once more for a while before Pip heard a loud thump, like the sound of a fist against a wall. It was followed swiftly by a low curse, then footsteps walking back down the hallway. Pip felt her body tense, her muscles rigid as she waited, poised for flight if she had to, expecting at any moment for the bedroom door to burst open, but a few moments later, his heavy footsteps sounded outside in the hallway and she heard the front door open and close again firmly and a car start up outside and drive away.

Pip wasted no time exiting the room. She could feel a cold sweat of fear, clammy and nauseating, clinging to her as she lightly ran through the house and out the back door. She no longer cared about finding evidence on Chris—what she'd discovered overhearing that conversation had been enough. Whoever and whatever Chris was involved with was bad news. There was no question that Chris had been using her. For what she wasn't entirely sure, but clearly it involved the hard drive, and any remaining hope that she could trust him had just been brutally stripped away.

Pip let herself out of the yard through the side gate and ran back to her car. The sky had turned dark and a band of ominous clouds hung low in the sky. She got inside the car just as fat drops began to hit her windscreen.

A Stone's Throw Away

In any other situation she would have been overjoyed at the sight of rain, but her hands were still shaking and her stomach remained in a knot of fear. Pip started the car and drove, looking for a safe place to stop well away from Chris and his house. She spotted a playground with an amenities block and parked behind it, hidden from view of the street.

Taking her phone back out, she opened the video she'd taken. Who was this guy and why did he keep popping up? She skimmed across the image and zoomed in on Chris's face, tracing the familiar contours. It was stupid to miss someone this much after such a short time—but she did. That was the fantasy, the soul-mate lie—the one she didn't believe in . . . the one she'd been stupid enough to almost fall for.

Her gaze suddenly fell on something else on the screen and she enlarged the photo some more, focusing on the second man in the image. She fast-forwarded the brief video until she caught one where he was looking face-on for a brief moment and again made the image larger on the screen, this time catching her breath. Down one side of his neck was a tattoo . . . of a green snake. Her hands shook as they held the phone. She felt the tightness around her throat and saw those eyes watching as the life began to drain from her.

This was the man who'd attacked her in her apartment.

And Chris knew who he was.

Nausea settled heavily in her stomach. It didn't seem possible, and yet, the proof was right there before her. Deep down she knew it was the same man.

He had tried to kill her once. And now he was back.

The rain didn't stop. It hadn't let up since those first few cold drops the day before, and now Pip shivered as she sat huddled in her car trying to figure out her next move. She'd found an old, half-gutted, abandoned house on a dirt road a few hours out of Midgiburra and had parked her car in the derelict shed beside it, grateful for a safe place to hide inside her car. Her gaze kept drifting to her phone, which she had turned off as soon as she'd recognised the man with the green tattoo, paranoid they would track her location and come and find her.

Lexi was the one person Pip knew she could trust, but she didn't want to drag her friend into this mess and put her in danger—and, Pip suspected, the police might already have Lexi under surveillance.

Maybe Ted? Her boss might know someone—he'd been in the business a long time. He would know what to do, but again, did she want to involve him in all this? If she had to weigh up her choices between Lexi and Ted, unfortunately, Ted was the one she would be most willing to sacrifice. He was a veteran investigative journalist—he'd even done a stint as a war correspondent—and he'd be far more likely to know how to keep himself safe than Lexi would. Decision made, she picked up the phone and turned it on, holding her breath as she waited for it to start up.

Before Pip could even open her contacts, a stream of notifications flew up the screen, lighting up the interior of her car like a damn disco. Then one name caught her attention and she frowned, pausing over the audio message attached.

'Pip, it's Tony,' the shaky, nasally voice informed her. 'I need your help. We need to meet. It's urgent. Don't call me back. Just meet me at the usual place. I'm tossing this phone.'

Tony Vesco. He was alive. And he sounded scared. She checked the time of the call and realised it had been sent in the early hours of the morning. The fear in the man's voice unsettled her even more.

The 'usual place' was a national park further up the coast, remote even from Sydney—from here it would be even further. Was it worth driving all that way to meet him? How long would he wait around? She couldn't even call him to let him know since he'd got rid of the phone. Pip gnawed the edge of her fingernail as she contemplated what to do.

Twenty-nine

Erik had warned her. He'd told her there were things she didn't know about Chris, and she needed to find out what he meant. She eyed the other unread messages from Chris but forced herself to ignore them. Anything he said now would only be a lie to get her to tell him where she was. She wasn't sure how to process everything she was feeling. Instead, she took out the card with Erik's number and called, willing her breathing to steady as the rings sounded in her ear.

'Erik Nielsen,' a clipped voice answered.

For a moment, Pip froze. She had no idea anymore who she could trust. Was this a big mistake?

'Hello?'

'Erik. It's Pip . . . Davenport.'

'Pip?' he asked slowly.

'Yeah.'

'Where are you? I've had your boyfriend-detective calling since yesterday looking for you.'

'I'm in trouble, Erik.'

'Okay.' There was a short silence before he asked gently, 'What's going on, Pip?'

His concern suddenly dissolved the thin thread that had been holding everything together.

'I think someone's after me to get hold of my research. I don't know who to trust anymore,' she said and heard the crack in her voice.

'What about Jarrett?' he asked, sounding confused.

'You were right . . . There were things I didn't know about him before.'

A small silence followed before he gave a decisive, 'Right. Then we need to get you somewhere safe.'

'I'm not going anywhere just yet. I need to do something first.'

'Your safety is the most important thing at the moment,' he warned.

'I need your help.'

'With what?' he asked cautiously.

'There's someone who needs me to meet them, but I can't get there. Do you know anyone—someone you trust—in Sydney who could get him to safety? Not a cop.'

'Who is it?'

'You don't need to know that. I just need someone to meet with him and get him someplace safe. I don't know what it's about but I know it's important or he wouldn't be risking his life like this.'

'Pip, what the hell have you got yourself into?'

'I wouldn't ask if it wasn't important,' she said. 'Please, Erik.'

She heard his long, reluctant sigh and felt the stirrings of relief. 'Yeah, I know a guy—he's not in the police force. I could ask him. Whereabouts?'

Pip hesitated briefly before giving him Tony's location.

'His life is in danger, Erik. I need to keep him safe.'

'What about *your* safety? I can come and get you. You can't stay out there alone.'

'I'll be okay.'

'It doesn't feel right, Pip.'

'Please, Erik. I know it's a lot to ask but I really need your help. Once I know he's safe, I'll get to you.' There was a long, painful silence on the other end of the line and Pip anxiously waited for his answer.

'Fine,' he finally said in a clipped tone. 'But I don't like it.'

'Thank you, Erik. Seriously.'

'Don't thank me. I won't be happy until I know where you are and that you're safe.'

'I'll check back in with you soon,' she promised.

The rain fell harder as Pip eyed the dirt road that led out to the main road. What would happen if it flooded and she couldn't leave? What would happen if she didn't make it back to Midgiburra at all? Who would tell Bert's story? When her whole world had been thrown into chaos, the last thing she should be thinking about was a story, but somehow this one had become more than just a story to her. She felt compelled to see it through, to help clear Bert's name and find out what had happened to Molly all those years ago.

There was little she could do from here, but for now, she felt safer than she had in a long time. The rain pelted down loudly on the tin roof above her vehicle, and she settled into her seat with her computer on her lap.

Pip's eyes shot open. The windows of the car were fogged up, and as she rubbed her nose, it felt cold. She eased herself upright from the passenger seat and rubbed her lower back as she stretched the kinks from her body. The clock on the dash read four-fifteen.

She hadn't thought she would be able to sleep, but she had—the first time in days. Pip had been madly writing, both to take her mind off Tony and what was happening and to get everything down on paper that she'd learned from the encrypted file Tony had given her. It was an even bigger scoop than the original Knight corruption scandal and there was a distinct possibility she might not survive to see it come out. She sent a rough draft of the article, dropping the bombshell about Butterworth, to her boss to read over and gave strict instructions to hold onto it in case anything happened to her.

She switched on her phone and hit redial on the last call.

'Erik. It's me.'

'I was wondering when you'd call.' He sounded tired, and instantly Pip felt bad. 'Are you okay?'

'I'm fine. Have you heard anything? Did they find him?'

'Yeah. He's safe.'

'Where is he?' she asked, opening her door and getting out. It was dark and gloomy—much darker than it would normally be due to the relentless rainfall.

'It's probably not wise to say anything more over the phone. I promise you, he's safe for now.'

'Did he say what was so urgent?'

'Apparently he'll only talk to you. I said as soon as I heard from you, we'd set up a secure call so you can speak with him. Where do you want me to meet you?'

'I don't want to keep running. Meet me at Rosevale?'

'I'm on my way. Go straight there and don't make any stops, okay?'

'Okay. Thank you, Erik.'

'And Pip?' he said, cutting in quickly before she could hang up. 'I think you were right for not trusting Jarrett.' Before she could ask what else he'd found out, he hung up, leaving her with even more unanswered questions. But at least Tony was safe and for now she could breathe a little bit easier.

'The unprecedented rain event has played havoc with the whole region, and flood levels have been creeping to some of the highest seen in seventy years or more,' the radio newsreader said. 'With livestock losses in the thousands and human loss currently standing at three, authorities are pleading with the public to stay at home and avoid the roads as many are washed away or underwater.'

A Stone's Throw Away

'Great,' Pip muttered. At least once she was back at Rosevale she would be happy to stay at home and not venture out—surely that would mean no one else could either, which meant she should be safe . . . she hoped.

The phone rang and Pip swore loudly. In all her haste to get back to Uncle Nev's, she had forgotten to turn the bloody thing off again after calling Erik. 'How stupid would you have to be!' she groaned out loud.

Chris's name flashed across the screen, followed by a voice message that her onscreen assistant instantly asked if she would like read aloud. She reached out to hit the *no* option, but a pothole made her finger jump and she bumped *yes* instead. She was midway through letting out a loud profanity when Chris's deep, very stressed voice filled the interior of her car.

'Pip, please listen. I know you're on the way to Midgiburra—do not under any circumstances let Nielsen in the house. He's working for Butterworth—' The message cut out and Pip swiftly glanced down to see that the message had ended.

What?

Surely Chris would say anything to get to her? Clearly he'd figured out that she had lost faith in him. And yet . . . what if Chris really *did* know something about Erik? God, she was so sick of going around in circles. Who the hell did she trust? Was this just a ploy to make her completely vulnerable, with no one left to turn to? If so, it was working! And God damn this bloody rain! It was coming down so hard it was making it almost impossible to see more than a few metres ahead. Thankfully she wasn't too far from Rosevale.

After a moment of hesitation, she hit redial and immediately Chris picked up before she had a chance to change her mind.

'Thank fuck, Pip. Listen. Don't open the door for—'

'Erik. Yes, I know, I heard your message. But why the hell should I believe you? Erik's the only one who hasn't appeared to have sold me out.'

'Constable Jennings came forward with concerns about Nielsen when he left his shift yesterday morning without any warning and didn't return. She's found a number of discrepancies in the station log—and she's convinced he may have had something to do with the break-in at your uncle's house.'

'I don't understand,' she said, frowning as the slightest twinge of doubt begin to niggle. *No. Stop it. Chris is the bad guy.* A master manipulator. She witnessed his deceit. She was there when he'd betrayed her—twice.

'Pip, I've been in interrogation all afternoon with Alfie Zuber, and he gave up names. A lot of names. Cops and politicians who are on the payroll . . . Nielsen's name was one of them.'

'Who the hell's Alfie Zuber?'

'The guy who attacked you in your apartment.'

'The guy *you* met and handed over a copy of my hard drive to? The same guy who came to your house this morning? *That* guy?' she snapped.

There was a moment's pause before he let out a sharp, frustrated sigh. 'Pip, I've been working undercover.'

'Oh, right. How convenient.'

'It's true. I'm part of an operation pulled together to investigate Butterworth.'

'Since when?' She was still sceptical, but she hated how a small part of her was willing to hear him out and possibly be open to believing him.

'The past few months. There were rumours flying around that Lenny Knight wasn't the kingpin everyone thought he was—that there were even bigger names above him running the show. You were part of the investigation.'

'Me? Why?'

'Because you had contact with an informant we've been looking for and who just turned up dead. We suspected he might have given you information. The hard drive,' he clarified.

'What?' she breathed.

Silence followed briefly.

'What did you say about Tony?'

'Tony Vesco is dead.'

Her hands clenched the steering wheel tighter. 'That's impossible,' she said, forcing the words through her suddenly numb lips.

'I'm sorry, Pip. He washed up on a beach early this morning.'

'It can't be true,' she said weakly. Not when the only person she thought she had left to trust just told her he was safe. Pip suddenly felt ill.

'Pip!' Chris's sharp voice got her attention once more.

'I don't believe you,' she said, but she hated the quiver of uncertainty beneath her words.

'I'm staring at the crime-scene photos as we speak.'

'I want to see them,' she challenged, pulling over to the side of the road as the rain continued to gush down her windscreen. 'Send them to me.'

'Pip . . .'

'Yeah, I thought so . . . you're lying.'

She heard him give a deep sigh moments before her phone beeped and she picked up the handset, seeing the message notification from him and steeling herself to open the image. When she did she felt the remaining air in her lungs escape through her lips in a deflated, defeated moan. She closed her eyes tightly and dropped her head.

'Pip. I'm sorry.'

Opening her eyes, she closed the message and placed the phone back on the centre console, her hands unsteady as she stared outside sightlessly, the monotonous drone of the windscreen wipers moving back and forth, the only sound other than the rain hitting the roof of her car. 'Do they know how long ago he died?'

'Not long.'

She'd killed him. This was all her fault. She'd sent them straight to where he'd been hiding. She needed to focus on something—anything other than the fact she'd just betrayed Tony and got him killed. 'This doesn't make any sense. How long have you been working on this case?'

'We intercepted a call from Nielsen to Zuber the day Molly Bigbsy's bones were found. That was my way in.'

So much for the whole chance encounter, then, she thought listlessly. 'So posing as a detective stationed at Coopers Creek was your "way in" to steal from me—where you, quite literally, screwed me over,' she shot back darkly.

'Zuber wanted the hard drive; he was after the encrypted file that's on there. I had to give him something to prove I could be trusted. So I copied your hard drive, and that's how we managed to get him—I had him on tape admitting everything Butterworth had paid him to do.'

'*Butterworth* ordered my attack?' she asked, confused.

'Yes. Knight didn't have anything to do with it. The only thing keeping Knight alive was that hard drive, and Knight knew that the moment Butterworth got rid of it, he'd be a dead man. This whole story had bigger fish involved.'

'I know. I broke the encryption.'

'What? How? We've had our best IT people on it and haven't managed to open it yet.'

'Clearly they aren't the best, are they?' she countered.

'Look, we need to get you somewhere safe until we can make sure everyone on Butterworth's payroll is accounted for and off the street. You have no idea the size of the target on your head at the moment.'

'I've had a fair idea. Why the hell do you think I've been running.'

'I know what it must have looked like, Pip,' he said, and she heard sadness in his voice.

'That I couldn't trust you?' she snapped. 'That you slept with me in order to steal from me? That you were working for the bad guys?'

'I promise you—this is all about to end. We're on our way to intercept Nielsen now. Just stay where you are until we get him.'

She pulled back out onto the road. This was too much to try to process. She just wanted to get back to the house where she felt safe and out of this bloody rain!

There was a moment of utter silence before Chris's voice came over the phone crystal clear. 'Pip. You are *not* to meet him. Do you understand?' There was something about the urgency, the palpable fear she heard in Chris's voice that instantly told her to trust him on this.

She looked out through the frantic beat of the windscreen wipers and saw in the distance down the long dark road ahead a set of headlights approaching from town. It had to be Erik.

Thirty

'It's too late.'

Pip ignored the swearing that came from the speaker and slowed down as she approached the intersection to Clay Target Road. In the back of her mind, she realised she was passing by the same spot where Vernon Clements was found murdered all those years ago but quickly pushed the thought away. She was almost home.

Pip tried not to let panic force her into making a stupid mistake; she needed to calm down. 'I'll have to get to the house,' she told Chris. There was nowhere else to go—she couldn't go into town, Erik would be able to cut her off.

'Go to the neighbours' and wait there,' Chris ordered.

'I am *not* putting them in danger.'

'He's not going to do anything with witnesses.'

'He'll probably know by now that you've got Zuber. He'll be feeling desperate. I'm not taking that kind of risk with Pete and Anne's lives.'

'We're not far away, but I don't want you anywhere near him, Pip. Get inside the house and lock the doors.'

His voice betrayed the frustration and worry he was feeling, but there was nothing he could do about the situation either. Minutes were hours when everything could change in a split second.

'I'm coming,' he said as she came around the bend and the car slid sideways on the slippery mud track, landing with a loud, jarring thud against the trunk of a tree. She heard Chris calling out from the car speaker.

'I'm, okay,' she said, feeling shaken, but the flash of headlights from behind snapped her out of her momentary shock. 'He's pulling up. I'm going on foot.'

She launched herself across the seat and wriggled her way out of the passenger-side door, scrambling to her feet as she grabbed her phone and bag. The cold rain plastered her hair to her head within moments and took her breath away. She threw her handbag into the dense bush beside the car and ran just as a car came to a stop behind her and she heard Eric's voice calling her name. She didn't stop—she ran, and she kept running, glancing over her shoulder only briefly as she saw him bend down and pick up her handbag. She now knew that Chris was telling the truth—Erik was here for the hard drive.

The ploy would only give her a few seconds' head start once he realised the drive wasn't in there. The hard drive didn't matter anymore. The *Daily Metro* had her draft story and a copy of the file. There was no way Butterworth could contain this now—although he wasn't aware of it.

Pip could hear the heavy pant of her breathing as she ran. Branches whipped her face and she felt a scratch along her cheek that stung as the rain hit it, but she kept going. It was impossible to run with any speed in the slippery conditions, and the thick scrub was making it near impossible to see where she was headed. Somehow she had to get back to the road. She was fairly sure she wasn't going in the right direction, but she had no way of working out her location in rapidly deteriorating light.

'Davenport!' Erik roared, and Pip glanced over her shoulder to see he was only a handful of metres behind her. 'Give it up. I know you must have worked it out by now or you wouldn't be running.'

'And here I was thinking all that flirting meant something,' she threw back without stopping.

'Turns out I was obviously lacking something. You had your sights set higher—or lower, depending on how you look at it,' he snarled.

She ignored the jab at Chris, suddenly realising she was back on the road that led to Rosevale. The flatter, open terrain made it easier to run, and she ran like she'd never done before. The rain had clearly been torrential since she'd left, and nonstop, judging by the amount of water all around—the meteorologist hadn't been kidding. Just as she was looking around, her ankle twisted on a pothole in the track and she felt herself falling, hitting the ground with her shoulder, the breath leaving her chest forcefully.

'Where is it?' Erik yelled, standing over her now. His face was contorted after the exertion of running, the rain plastering his hair to his head.

'It's too late!' she yelled back defiantly. There seemed little chance of getting away from him—her ankle throbbed and she doubted she'd be able to put weight on it even if she did manage to get to her feet with him standing over her.

'Just give the bloody thing to me.'

She reached into her back pocket and pulled the drive out, throwing it at his chest, which he caught in one large hand.

'Why would you work for a man like Butterworth? He doesn't care about anyone but himself.'

'You wanna know why?' he said, seeming to think about the question momentarily. 'Because after years of putting my life on the line for ungrateful civilians like you—protecting your rights and making sure you can sleep safe at night—I get spat on, and punched in the face and passed over for promotions. I got sick of doing it all for next to no reward. So, I took some money to look the other way occasionally. And I got busted, but you know what? The men I work for didn't leave me hanging out to dry—they stepped in and made it all go away, and in return I only had to take this braindead job out in the sticks for a year or two. I call that a pretty fair deal. If you had your way, I'd be rotting in prison alongside Lenny Knight, wouldn't I?' he sneered. "Cause that's what you do—you dig around in people's rubbish and find anything you can use to bring them down.'

'Only if they've been doing something wrong to start with,' she threw back, frowning up at him. 'You're a police officer—you're supposed to follow the law.'

'And look where that got me—screwed over at every turn. No fucking thanks.'

'It's too late,' she said, shaking her head, her teeth beginning to chatter in the cold.

'What do you mean?'

'The drive,' she said, looking at it in his hand. 'It's useless. The encryption was cracked, and I opened the file. Butterworth and all his shady deals have been exposed. *Your boss*,' she emphasised the words darkly, 'will be sitting in a cell right next door to his mate, Lenny Knight. So you better start looking for a new job.'

She saw a brief moment of uncertainty fill the sergeant's eyes before he shook his head and snarled, 'That encryption is unbreakable.'

'If you say so,' she shouted back as the rain fell harder. She knew she'd run out of time—there was no sign of Chris, and she was stranded out here alone with a pissed-off crooked cop who hated journalists with a passion that bordered on fanatical. How could she have ever thought this guy was hot? *Your taste in men is truly impeccable, Davenport.*

A noise Pip couldn't immediately identify began to sound and grew louder by the second. Erik glanced up and his expression changed. For a brief moment she could only stare in confusion before the roar became the sound of a freight train bearing down and she saw a tunnel of water surging towards them.

In a second it had swept them both up, carrying them along with an unstoppable force. She briefly caught a glimpse of Erik's head—his mouth open in alarm—before he was dragged down and she lost sight of him.

Something hit Pip's head and then her back as she briefly went under the water, only to resurface and narrowly miss being taken out by a tree—a fully grown tree that should have been standing upright on the banks of the river. Sticks and branches tore at her legs, like fingers trying to pull her under, and she kicked ruthlessly in an attempt to dislodge them before they dragged her beneath the water and held her there.

The pull of the water was astounding. The force with which it dragged everything in its path along with it was impossible to fight, and as Pip breached the surface time and time again, the sides of the bank went past in a dizzying blur. Then, just as she took a gulp of air, she was pulled down once more and her head hit something solid, and everything was blessedly quiet.

Thirty-one

Her chest hurt as something pounded on it, and then water forced its way from her lungs and up through her throat until she burst into a violent episode of coughing. Her lungs felt as though the lining were being ripped away from them and she opened her eyes to find Chris leaning over her, his face a mask of concentration as he leaned his ear against her chest before searching her face anxiously.

'You're okay. You're safe,' he said over and over until her coughing subsided and she'd stopped vomiting up water.

'Erik,' she said, her voice coming out as a mere croak.

'They're searching for him now,' Chris said, stopping her from trying to sit up.

Pip turned her head and realised she was on the bank of the dam, now more of a river as the water overflowed and spilled into the old riverbed beyond. Flashing lights blurred in the distance.

'We're going to get you to hospital,' he said, waving urgently as an ambulance came to a stop and a paramedic ran over.

Her teeth began chattering too much to continue, then the paramedic covered her in a shiny silver blanket and slowly she began to feel warmth seeping into her body. She decided she would just close her eyes for a minute while everyone fussed around her, and then she would get up and tell them she was fine.

Pip gasped as she sat up in bed. She looked around the unfamiliar hospital room in confusion until she remembered where she was and what had happened. She looked out the window and saw early morning light breaking through grey skies. She hadn't slept much through the night, with staff waking her as they came and went, monitoring the hit to her head. Her hair still smelled of the dirty brown water, and her chest was excruciatingly sore. She gingerly climbed out of the bed and made her way to the bathroom, where she eased the hospital gown from her shoulder and looked at herself in the mirror, grimacing at the different shades of purple and red bruises that covered her body.

A roar suddenly filled her ears and she squeezed her eyes shut tight. She could still feel herself being dragged under and pulled along with the torrent of water—the sound was almost deafening. She bent over the sink and splashed some water over her face, hoping to chase away the lingering dreams and calm the rising nausea.

A Stone's Throw Away

After a few deep breaths, Pip walked back to the bed. Beside it sat a plastic shopping bag filled with clean clothes.

A few minutes later, Chris stood at the door to the hospital room looking a little uncertain of his welcome as she finished getting dressed. Her emotions had been bouncing all over the place.

'How are you feeling?' he asked, sliding his hands into the pockets of his brown stockman's jacket as he leaned one shoulder against the doorway.

'Like I've been hit by a tree,' she said with a small grimace as she eased into the warm jumper. 'I take it I have you to thank for bringing in my clothes?' she said.

'I figured you'd need some,' he said in an offhand manner that didn't quite cover the uneasy way he was fidgeting. 'Pip, I need to explain about what happened.'

'That you lied your way into my house and my bed just so you could steal the information on my hard drive?' she commented.

'That's not what happened.'

'Really? Somehow I find it hard to believe that you and I *just happened.*' God, she'd been so stupid. He must have thought she was pathetically easy to con—it had barely taken any effort on his part to have her fawning over him like some lovesick fool.

'My job was to make contact with Alfie,' he said, and she stopped folding the hospital gown she held in her hands and stared at him. 'I had to prove that I could be trusted, and he needed the file on that hard drive. I thought if I got it then he wouldn't need to take matters into his own hands and try to get it himself. But after the break and enter, I knew you were in danger. We'd had Nielsen on our radar because of his connections to a few of the associated people of interest in the case. My job was to gather intel to arrest Alfie and connect him to Butterworth.'

'Did you know he was the man who attacked me?' she asked stiffly.

'I had my suspicions,' he said on a long sigh, his eyes imploring her to believe him. 'After you mentioned the tattoo.'

'You should have told me what was going on.' She could still feel the devastation the moment she'd thought he'd betrayed her.

'I couldn't. It would have blown my cover—as it was, everything had been pulled together so fast it stood a very big chance of blowing up in our faces.'

'I didn't know who I could trust,' she said, feeling helpless as frightened tears began to threaten.

He pushed away from his position at the door and came into the room. 'I know—I know how it must have seemed and I hate that I couldn't tell you. I just had to hope you'd trust me . . . but I get why you didn't. You and I . . . everything that happened between us was . . .' He paused and ran a hand across his short hair, searching for the right words. 'I've never felt this way with anyone else, Pip. Everything I said to you was true. Everything we felt—was real.'

'You don't live in Coopers Creek, though, do you? That isn't really your house.'

'No,' he admitted with a slight cringe.

'So *not* everything you told me was true.'

'I was undercover,' he said, sounding weary.

Nothing changed the fact that she felt like an idiot being fooled by his story, but she had to admit grudgingly to herself that it made sense. 'So where do you really live?'

'Melbourne. For now,' he added.

'Are you really a detective?'

'Yes, just not stationed at Coopers Creek.'

'Do you really have a daughter and an ex-wife?'

'Yes,' he said with a slight grin. 'That was all true. Look, I know it's little comfort that I was only doing my job,' he said, his expression turning serious. 'But I swear, Pip, everything I feel for you is real—it had nothing to do with the case. I've never let my emotions get the better of me on a job before—ever. Until now.'

She wanted more than anything to believe him, but there had been so much to take in. Her fear had been real. She'd lost all confidence in herself. She'd almost trusted Erik, for God's sake, and he'd been sent to kill her!

'I think I just need some time to get my head around everything. We were going way too fast—that wasn't normal.'

He eyed her steadily. 'No, it wasn't—and that's the whole point. It was something special, something that doesn't come along every day. I know how I feel about you, Pip. That hasn't changed. But you've been through a lot and I won't try to push you into anything. I just want you to know that when you're ready, I'll be here,' he said simply.

She wasn't sure when—if—she would be ready, but for now, she was too tired to keep talking.

The Doctor entered the room and quickly checked her over, giving her a list of instructions to follow before declaring she was fit to go home.

'Come on, I'll take you back to Rosevale.'

Pip nodded her thanks and they walked out of the hospital together.

It was still raining.

The drought had well and truly broken, but the damage the ferocious flooding had brought with it stopped any celebration—in the wake of the worst drought in recent times had come the worst flood. Farmers out here just couldn't catch a break.

'Has there been any news about Erik?' she asked as Chris closed the door and started the engine.

'Nothing yet. There's a search team still out there looking, though.'

With each hour that had passed, the hope of a good outcome faded. Pip was torn over her feelings where Erik was concerned. She could still see the terror on his face as the water dragged him away like a ferocious, hungry beast. Yet just moments before, he had chased her down and trapped her.

She pushed it out of her mind and refocused on the other thing that had been niggling at her. Where she'd ended up. In the billabong.

'It was flash flooding,' she said, glancing across at Chris. 'That's how Bert's ute ended up in the dam. The power of that water,' she said, giving a small shiver as she recalled how fast she'd been swept along, caught up in it. 'It could have easily swept up a car and taken it across the property to end up in the dam.'

Chris glanced across at her and nodded. 'Yeah. After seeing it, I agree.'

She stared out the front window, watching the raindrops hit the screen. 'Bert waited all those years for Molly to come home and she'd been right there on Rosevale the whole time.'

A silence fell inside the car as they listened to the beat of the windscreen wipers.

'I thought I'd lost you,' Chris said quietly, as they drove out of town.

'It was pretty hectic,' she agreed, trying to keep things light. She knew all too well how close she had come to losing her life last night.

'It brought a few things home to me,' he continued.

'Like what?'

'I'm thinking about trying to sort things out with my dad. Sian should know her grandfather. Life's too short to hold grudges.'

She was silent for a few moments after his statement. 'I think that's a great idea.'

She saw his lips twist in acknowledgement.

When they reached the bend where Pip's car slid off the road, she clenched the side of the seat tightly in reflex, but the car was no longer there.

'Did they have to take my car for forensics or something?' she frowned.

'No, I had it towed it out last night. It's back at your uncle's.'

'Oh. Thank you,' she added, feeling a familiar rush of gratitude and lo—. She stopped abruptly, shaking away the persistent thought. It *wasn't* love.

'That's okay. I knew you'd be worried about all your gear in the back.'

Pip sighed. For the first time pretty much ever, she hadn't even thought about work, the stupid hard drive or her computer, or her expensive camera gear. She wasn't thinking about the book or the story or any of the constant things she'd lived with nonstop in her head for the past few years.

None of it was important—not compared with her life. For the first time in forever she felt . . . free.

Pip stared out the side window at the damage the flood had created in a few short hours. The water was slowly subsiding, but below the road was a wide strip of flattened fences and trees where the torrent of water had rushed through, destroying everything in its path for kilometres. The billabong was now covered by a lake where the paddock used to be.

When they arrived at the house, Pip found herself confronted by a barrage of emotions. So much had happened since she'd left. She really missed this old place. It had come to mean so much to her in such a short space of time, and she smiled as she realised how happy something as simple as coming home could make her feel.

Home. How had this little cottage become home to her when she'd lived in her apartment for years and never felt the same kind of attachment?

Maybe because of the letters. Maybe the idea of Bert and Molly's dream in those first few heady months of marriage still lingered within the walls of the old house. The promise of a bright future—the possibilities of a life stretched before them.

The radio that was playing softly inside the car went to a news broadcast and the presenter gave an update of local road closures and SES warnings. Among the list of roads closed was Coopers Creek Road, the main road between the Midgiburra and Coopers Creek townships.

'The road's closed,' she said, looking over at him. 'You won't be able to go home.'

'It's okay, I'll crash at the station.'

'Don't be silly. You've been out searching all night, you won't get any rest in there. Stay here. There's plenty of room.'

'I was serious when I said I didn't want to pressure you,' he said slowly.

'I know. But after everything we've been through, there's no way I'm kicking you out to sleep at the station.'

She didn't wait around to argue the point with him. The truth was, she wasn't sure she needed space. Now that the shock had worn off and they were back in familiar territory, things had begun to settle down. She wasn't ready to jump back in where they left off just yet, but she also didn't want to stay here alone—not because she was scared like before, but because she knew she would miss him if he wasn't here.

He helped her out of the car, despite her protests that she was fine. She was grateful he didn't say 'I told you so' when she couldn't stifle a groan as her bruised skin and pulled muscles protested standing upright.

She gritted her teeth as they took the few steps up onto the verandah and then breathed a sigh of relief when she reached the top and they went inside.

That now familiar smell of the old house filled her senses and she closed her eyes for a moment, breathing it in and letting it wrap around her like a warm, comforting hug.

'How about you sit here for a minute and I'll make a cuppa,' Chris said, helping her ease down onto the sofa.

'Coffee would be great,' she said, giving a grimace as she settled back into the seat. Everything ached. Her sore muscles along with the bumps and grazes would heal, but it was going to take a while to forget the image of Erik's face as he was carried away by the floodwater. She closed her eyes and breathed deeply. When she opened them, she realised with a start that she must have dozed off for a few moments because she found Chris placing a plate of toast and a mug of steaming coffee on the table in front of her.

'Here. The doctor said to take some of these for the pain when you got home,' he said, handing her the box of painkillers they'd given her before she was discharged.

It felt strange to have Chris sitting beside her but not touching. Her body craved his warmth. Her fingers itched to reach for him and to be held, but her head reminded her of everything that had happened since they'd last been together. Betrayal had left her heart bruised and it too needed time to heal.

As she reached for the plate, she realised how hungry she was and devoured the toast in no time.

'Do you want me to get you some more? Or make you something else?' Chris offered as he watched her replace the empty plate on the table.

'No, thanks. I think I might go and lie down for a bit.'

'Sure. I'm going to check everything's locked up and then I think I'll do the same. Don't worry, I'll be right here, though,' he assured her.

'Thanks, Chris.'

'Of course. I wouldn't want to be anywhere else.'

Thirty-two

When Pip woke up again she looked at the clock by her bed and blinked. It was morning. She'd slept for hours—right through the afternoon and past dinner.

She sat up gingerly, waiting for her stiff muscles to protest, but to her relief it wasn't quite as bad as it had been the day before. She breathed out a long sigh in the shower as the hot water ran over her sore body. She washed her hair and it took a while to get herself dressed, but once she was, she almost felt like her old self again.

The house was quiet as she made her way towards the kitchen. A plate of bacon and eggs sat wrapped in foil on the bench and still felt warm as she touched it.

Noise outside drew her to the window and she spotted Chris in the yard, dragging branches into a heap out in the paddock. She hadn't really noticed the damage yesterday, but now as she glanced around she could see the debris leftover from the floodwater—bits of grass and weed and goodness only knew what else hung like moss on the barbed-wire fencing in the paddock below.

After she ate her breakfast, Pip headed outside to find Chris.

'Morning, sleepyhead. How you feeling?'

'Better, I think,' she answered, managing a small smile. 'You've been busy,' she said, nodding towards the growing pile of sticks and branches.

'Thought I'd make myself useful. Looks like a bonfire will be happening in the near future.'

'It made a mess,' she agreed, noticing the driveway covered in leaves and smaller branches.

'I was just about to go for a drive and check out the fencing.'

'I'll come.' She needed to get out, and it was really her responsibility, not his. She would need to call Uncle Nev later and let him know the extent of the damage.

'Your neighbours dropped by earlier to check on you. They heard about what happened. Said they'd call back later,' he said, and she felt her throat close up a little at the thoughtful gesture from Anne and Pete.

'That was nice of them,' she managed, after clearing her throat.

'That's what people do around here,' he grinned as they climbed into his four-wheel drive.

The fencing around the boundary was all remarkably intact, but there were a number of trees down, and the dam was a mess.

They had to walk down, the ground being too wet for the vehicle and littered with wire and tin carried in by the floodwater. The waterhole was now full, and there were already new kinds of birds hanging around, having arrived to take advantage of the wetlands.

'Once everything starts to dry out, it'll look better,' Chris said, seeing the dismay on her face.

'I guess so,' she said, looking at the mud that covered what was once grass around the edge. It would slowly begin to poke its way out as it recovered, and new grass would spring up now that the rain had come. 'Everything just needs a little time to recover,' she added, looking up at him and seeing his expression turn tender as he lifted a hand to touch the side of her face.

'Do you think you could give me another chance?' he asked softly. 'I mean, I know you need some time . . . but maybe down the track a bit?'

Pip felt her heart lurch at the uncertainty etched on his strong face. She knew that despite everything that had happened between them, her feelings for this man were as real and as strong as ever. 'I think I realise now that if you find something special, you need to hold onto it, because there's no certainty how long you might have.'

Bert and Molly thought they had all the time in the world and look what happened to them. Life was precious. Too precious to waste on waiting for the perfect time to fit it in.

Chris lowered his head, and Pip closed her eyes at that first gentle touch of his warm lips.

Pip spent the rest of the morning making calls, to Uncle Nev to assure him the place was fine, and to her parents and Lexi, giving them a censored rundown of what had happened the day before. She left out the part about being chased through the bush and the whole Butterworth connection—that would open a can of worms she wasn't quite ready to deal with just yet. After the effort of reassuring everyone, she found herself needing to lie down for a little while and ended up sleeping for another two hours.

The sun felt warm on her skin and she tipped her head back to look up at the baby blue sky. Pinpricks of sunlight filtered through the brim of her wide straw hat and made tiny sparkles across her skin. Pip glanced down in surprise to see that she was wearing a blue and white dress, buttoned up at the front and clenched with a narrow white belt at her waist. She was sitting on a tartan rug.

Pip felt her heart rate increase as she looked around. She was in the clearing, under the old gum tree. She looked down and saw a book in her lap with an olive-green cover—one she'd never seen before. What was happening? Why was she here? Why was she dressed like . . . the woman in the photo? She felt her fingers start to tingle and her head go light.

A gasp shot from her lips as she sat upright and breathed heavily against the pain.

Why was Molly back in her dreams? They had worked out how she and the ute ended up in the dam. It should be over, surely?

Beside her, Chris had risen onto one elbow to look over at her with a concerned frown. 'What's wrong?'

Pip shook her head. 'I don't know. Something's not right.'

'It's understandable you'd still feel unsettled by everything, but I can promise, no one's going to hurt you.'

'No, not with any of that,' she said, leaning back against the headboard. Beside her, Chris sat up too. They'd both fallen asleep on top of the bedcovers, clearly still exhausted from the previous day's stress and events. 'With Molly.'

'Molly?' he questioned, eyeing her warily. 'What do you mean?'

'You'll think I'm crazy,' she said with a small groan as she closed her eyes.

'Why would I think that?'

'Because sometimes *I* think I'm going crazy,' she muttered dully. 'I just have this feeling that there's still something unfinished about Molly's death,' she ended lamely with an awkward grimace.

For a moment he didn't respond, and then he gave an offhand shrug. 'What do you think it is?'

'I'm not sure ... yet,' she said, getting to her feet. 'But I need to figure it out.'

Pip sat at the table a few minutes later with a coffee, and her gaze fell on the box of Bert's belongings. She dragged it across the floor towards her. As she lifted the lid from one of the shoeboxes that contained the letters, she saw the photo of Molly on the rug and slowly reached out to pick it up.

In her dream she wasn't wearing the same outfit as Molly wore, but the location was the same. What did it mean? She studied the photo carefully. Maybe it wasn't about Molly herself. She stopped focusing on the woman in the centre of the photo and looked at the background. The clearing nowadays didn't look as tidy as it did in the photo. The ground looked lightly grassed and open whereas now saplings had sprouted over the years and there were more trees and leaf litter. She needed to go back there to have a look.

She took her coat from the back hook and called out to Chris. 'I'm just going for a walk.'

'Hang on. I'll come with you,' he said, appearing at the doorway to the kitchen. 'It's still pretty wet and dangerous out there with loose branches and trees still falling.'

'Are you sure you don't want to tell me what this is about?' Chris asked as they drove across the paddocks.

'Trust me, you really don't want to know.' How could she expect him to believe she thought these dreams were Molly trying to show her something? What if they had nothing to do with it? What if she were really going crazy? They climbed out of the car.

Pip picked her way past the dam and found the cattle track, mostly covered in mud and sludge but still definable, and wandered towards the clearing. Like everything else, it was a mess. The big tree remained upright, thankfully, but the floodwater had uprooted a number of smaller trees and they lay across the spot where Molly had been sitting in the photo.

She wouldn't have recognised the place if she'd only stumbled upon it now. Pip withdrew the photo from her pocket and stared at it carefully.

'What's that?' Chris asked, looking over her shoulder.

'I think this is the spot from this photo. I'm trying to see if there's anything different.'

'Different how?' Chris asked, frowning at the photo in her hand.

'I'm not exactly sure. I just have a feeling that she's trying to point out something.'

'I'm not sure I follow all that. Who's she?'

And this is why I can't tell you about the dream.

'Here, take a look,' she said, absently handing him the photograph as she glanced around the clearing. 'What do you see?'

'Well, it seems like the same tree,' he said, glancing up from the image as he tried to get his bearings. 'It's a lot more overgrown,' he continued, telling her all the things she had already deduced.

'Try looking for what's in the photo that *isn't* here,' she suggested thoughtfully. Maybe she'd been looking at it back to front.

'The rock,' he said after a moment.

Rock? What rock? She peered at the photo in his hand.

'See there? In front of the tree? There was a rock.'

Sure enough, right where he pointed on the photo, in front of the gum tree, was a dark flat shadow that looked like a rock.

A Stone's Throw Away

Well, that was interesting. She wasn't sure how it related to anything but it was pretty much the only thing different she could see. They crossed to the tree and she began to drag away some of the lighter branches that had fallen onto the ground.

'Here, let me,' Chris said, squatting down and leaning forward to scoop away years of accrued leaf matter and sticks from the base of the tree to eventually reveal a flat, hard surface.

'It's still there,' she said, surprised.

'Any idea what that's supposed to mean?' he asked hopefully.

'None whatsoever,' she said hopelessly but stopped when it wobbled as Chris pushed on it to stand back up. 'Wait. It moved.'

'Yeah, it's loose, like . . .' he started, before stopping as he lifted the rock to reveal a hole beneath. 'It's covering something,' he finished, peering into the dark hole. 'Hang on, I've got a torch,' he said, digging out his car keys to detach the smallest flashlight she had ever seen from the keyring. 'It's tiny, but it's fairly bright,' he said as he leaned over the top of the chasm. 'There's something in there.'

'Oh God, you're not going to put your hand in there, are you?' she said, suddenly remembering those snakes she looked out for on her morning walks.

'It's okay,' he said, flashing a grin at her, then hesitated. 'Maybe stand back just in case,' he added and laughed at her expression.

She did take a step back, just to be on the safe side, and listened to him give a small grunt as he reached into the hole and felt around.

'Got it,' he said triumphantly.

'What is it?' she asked eagerly, forgetting her earlier caution and moving back beside him, craning her neck to get a look at what he was bringing out.

'I have no idea,' he told her, placing a piece of green canvas on the ground between them. 'There's something wrapped inside,' he said, carefully opening the stiff fabric to reveal a biscuit tin. Pip held her breath as Chris prised open the lid to reveal an olive-green book.

Pip felt the air leave her lungs in a rush as she sat back on the ground and stared at the open tin.

'A book?' Chris said, sounding surprised.

'It's her diary,' Pip whispered, then glanced up at Chris. 'It's Molly's diary,' she repeated, feeling a ridiculous smile spread across her face. That's what Molly had been trying to tell her all this time. She wanted Pip to find the diary.

'How did you know it was there?' he asked, soundly slightly dazed.

'It doesn't matter now . . . finally, we've got the last piece of the puzzle.' She carefully lifted the book from the safety of its protective tin box and gingerly opened the cover. The front page was blank but inside was a page of beautifully cursive writing and a date: 19 April 1939. *Our wedding day* was written on the top line.

Pip sat down, completely absorbed.

Today, my darling Bert, we are to be married. I have waited for so long for this day and now it is finally here. By this evening I will be Mrs Herbert Bigsby, and we will embark on our wonderful life together.

'How did it get there?' Chris asked when they'd both read the page.

'I'm guessing Molly put it there for safekeeping?'

'Why would she go to all this trouble, though?'

'Maybe whatever she wrote in there was supposed to remain private—maybe she didn't want Bert to stumble upon it?'

Thunder rumbled overhead, and Chris gave a small, confused laugh as he stood up and dusted off his hands. 'Come on, let's get back to the house before another round of rain hits.'

Surely this weather couldn't last much longer, she thought, sending a quick glance towards the grey skies, but she reluctantly replaced the diary in the tin and wrapped the canvas around it again before heading back to the house.

It did seem a strange thing to do, hiding a diary, and for it to remain there for almost a century. And yet, Molly couldn't have known when she put it into the hole that she would never be back to get it.

'You go and read—I'll throw something together to eat,' Chris told her when they arrived home.

Pip wasn't about to argue as she propped herself on the couch. She couldn't think about anything except what might be in Molly's diary.

Thirty-three

25 May 1939
Bert works so hard all day, from sunrise to dark. I knew farming life wasn't easy, but I wasn't expecting it to be quite this hard. I keep myself busy by tending the vegetable patch behind the house. It's enormous and takes most of the morning to weed and water each day. I desperately want a cottage garden out the front of the house and Bert insists he'll put one in for me, but he's always so tired by the end of the day that I've tried not to harp about it. Bert's a typical farmer—if you can't eat it, why would you bother growing it? That's what he says about the roses I long to plant. But sometimes it's just nice to have something pretty around.

But Bert does make time for just us on Sundays. The billabong is such a beautiful spot, but sometimes it gives me the heebie-jeebies. Bert thinks I'm silly when I try to explain it to him, but I prefer this little clearing not far from the water where we often picnic and spend a lazy afternoon reading the paper and talking about the future. When we're here, it feels like we're the only two people in the world.

Pip smiled. The letters had given Molly and Bert a voice, but the journal brought them to life. As she read through the pages, Pip could easily imagine the newlywed couple dancing to their radiogram right here in the living room; she could see Molly humming as she cooked dinner at night; she could hear the gentle murmur of them whispering about their dreams for the future together on the back verandah as they looked out over the paddocks that Bert worked so hard in each day.

Pip reached for the sandwich Chris put down before her and nodded as he told her he was going to make some phone calls and check in with the office, but she didn't stop reading.

25 October 1939
I know Bert believes he's doing the right thing, the honourable thing, by signing up. It's what his father had done and all his uncles before him and half the town has done it—including Frank Maguire. I'm sure that it's mainly because Frank signed up that Bert felt as though he had to as well. He said he couldn't let a mate go off to fight and not be there to look out for him. I'd rather have my husband home. He doesn't have to go—farmers are needed at home to grow the food for the war effort, so he doesn't have to sign up, but he has. He said he could never live with himself if he stood back when others had to go.

The diary entries leading up to Bert's goodbye swayed between sad and angry, and Pip understood: a young newlywed couple just starting their lives, only for a horrible war to come along and separate them. Molly was losing her husband before she'd even had time to settle into life as a wife. Of course she would have moments of frustration and anger—especially since she knew Bert could have stayed out of the war if he'd chosen to. However, by the time he actually left, the tone of Molly's diary entries was more resigned, as though she had accepted that her husband, being the man he was, wouldn't have been happy if he'd stayed behind while everyone was off doing their bit.

The following months documented the first letters she and Bert wrote to each other while he was training, and the brief weekend they were allowed to see each other before he was shipped out. Molly's loneliness was palpable through the pages of her diary. She joined various charities and war effort fundraisers, but she didn't speak of any friends she spent time with. As an outsider who'd moved to Midgiburra just after her wedding, she likely hadn't had time to make any real connections.

And through all this, Molly struggled on her own to keep the farm running—mainly by tending the market garden that provided her with a small income and kept her afloat while Bert was away. She struggled and triumphed as she figured out how to be a farmer in the absence of her husband. She learned how to fix the tractor when it was being temperamental and get creative with rations. She sewed and preserved fruit from their orchard and chopped wood for the fire during winter, and all the while she did it missing her husband and living for his letters.

A Stone's Throw Away

Most days I come here to our special place to write. It makes me feel close to you. I can almost pretend there isn't any war going on and you're safe and we're together and happy once more.

This heat has been unbearable. The endless days with no rain in sight. The trees are listless—as listless as I feel—and the garden droops miserably. I'm trying my best, Bert, I really am. But some days I wonder if it's worth it. If only it would rain and wash away all the sadness. Once the rain comes, everything will be better. In my letters I try not to complain about all this—I can imagine my discomfort and worries are nothing compared to yours where you are at the moment. I don't want to burden you with the fact I'm unsure how I'm going to keep this place going. I miss you so much. Every day I dread reading the newspaper reports from the places you have been. I never know if you will be included in the number of dead or injured; it's just too much, my love.

Pip read and read, all the while trying to imagine living through a single day in this woman's life.

There were snippets into what life in Midgiburra during the war years had been like. Pip found it fascinating, but as she reached the last year of the journal her heart grew heavy, knowing that these were the final entries leading to the end of Molly's life.

15 March 1942
I haven't had any word from Bert since before Christmas—the letters he wrote then only arrived at the end of January. Since then, the Japanese have attacked Rabaul and there has been no word on Bert since. I've written letters to the Ministry of Defence, but so far, nothing. I've even asked

Patricia Maguire, who is president of the Midgiburra branch of the Australian Comforts Fund, if she can ask her father-in-law in Canberra to try to find out anything, since he's a very important politician and surely has connections who could help, but to date there is still no news.

Frank Maguire returned home, and the town threw him a welcome-home dance at the hall, celebrating his return as though he had single-handedly won the war. I went along so I could ask him for any news on Bert, but he acted most peculiar—seemingly trying to avoid me for most of the evening until I managed to corner him and ask if he knew anything. He told me that one of the men in his company had told him he saw Bert shot with a group of other soldiers as they tried to flee into the jungle.

I can't believe this is true. I simply can't, and I won't until I have proof. Frank is not the friend you always thought him to be, my darling.

I never understood why you were such good friends with him for all these years. When I look at him, I see a weak man with no soul. He has none of your strength or your goodness. Now, after his return, I see him as a shadow of his former self. He looks unwell.

25 December 1944
Yet another Christmas without you, my darling Bert. Each one that passes I feel my soul die a little more. Men have been coming home and families have been reunited, and yet still I have no news. Nothing. News of the sinking of the Montevideo Maru came out and I have been told I should accept that you were most likely on board. Were you? Or did you die out in that jungle? Why haven't I heard from you if you were still alive? My heart keeps breaking a little more with each day that passes and I don't hear from you. I feel

that after two years, I shall have to accept that you will not be coming home.

Merry Christmas, my darling, wherever you are.

The entries became further and further apart as the next year went on, and Molly's loneliness was clear on the pages.

Then a name appeared, and Pip felt like an audience member watching a horror movie unfold before her, wanting to scream at the heroine to run and don't look back.

18 August 1945
This endless dry is becoming unbearable. I have to save water in buckets to use on the garden because the tank is all but empty. I'm not sure how much longer I can keep everything alive. Without the market garden, there'll be no money at all coming in. The Maguires have been circling—just as Bert feared they would. I could almost see them sniffing the air, searching for the scent of desperation. I don't want to give them the satisfaction of buying this place for a pittance—I see Bert's face each time I think of selling, and I just cannot do it. Then, almost as though it were a sign from Bert, as I was working in the garden, sweating and covered from head to toe in dirt and dust, a man appeared at the back gate, asking if he could use the phone to call for help for his truck that had broken down. While we waited for help, we got talking, and by the time he left, I'd offered him a job as a farmhand. Maybe not all is lost after all.

15 September 1945
Vernon has been working hard. It's so nice to have company again—to look out and see the tractor. I have to catch myself sometimes. Just for a moment when I see him walking out in the paddock, I can almost pretend it's Bert.

I find myself smiling at the smallest things. A pair of muddy boots at the back door. Men's clothing hanging on the washing line beside mine—small things that I've missed so much.

27 September 1945
Vernon has become more than a friend over the past few weeks. I have tried to ignore the growing feelings that have been developing between us, but I feel myself weakening with every passing day. My skin prickles as I think of him lying on the other side of the wall each night. My breath catches each time he passes a little too close in the hallway or leans across to reach for something in the kitchen. I have resisted for so long, but I am so lonely. I ache to be held, to feel another's skin against my own, to be touched and touch in return. I don't think I can remain strong for much longer.

Pip breathed out a sad breath. The next few pages read like a teenage girl giddy in love. Part of Pip felt disappointed in Molly for giving up too soon on her husband, and yet she had to remind herself that things were very different back then. There was no instant way of finding someone—no social media to reach out and ask for help, no computer records that could track someone down. As Molly fell for Vernon, Bert was working under horrendous conditions in a labour camp and no one even knew where he was.

It was easy with the advantage of hindsight to see that Vernon was clearly thinking he was on a sure thing with Molly. He had managed to gain a young, vulnerable, supposed widow's trust and clearly had his eye on one day owning Rosevale. For a man with a criminal record like Vernon

Clements, stumbling upon this pot of gold would have been like winning the lottery.

Pip was beginning to see how Bert's return would have completely destroyed all Vernon's carefully laid plans, and it explained why he reacted so violently to Molly's attempts to end their relationship. The whole thing was a disaster waiting to happen.

> *4 December 1945*
> *I still need to pinch myself. It just doesn't seem real. I had no idea as I opened the door to Sergeant Goodwin and Reverend Paul that my whole world would change. They came to inform me that my husband—my darling Bert—had been found! After all this time, after everyone telling me he was dead, lost forever, he has been found. My poor, poor Bert, oh how you must have suffered. All this time you were being held as a prisoner of war.*
>
> *My heart is breaking, but at the same time it is overflowing with joy. I feel so unworthy of your love. I tried so very hard to keep believing you would come back to me one day—but in the end, I was weak and I stopped believing.*
>
> *Is it too late to ask for forgiveness? I will have to wait and see, I suppose. I'm not sure I can confess my sins. How can I hurt you when you have already been hurt so much?*

Pip read through the entries Molly wrote about Vernon and having to step back from their relationship. She read how torn Molly had felt, and the guilt of what she had done. Vernon for the most part seemed to have faded into the background, and Pip could only imagine this was because Molly had become so consumed with her own emotions that she simply couldn't focus on anything else. She did mention he had left to find work elsewhere with the Maguires, though, so he was obviously still lurking nearby.

30 December 1945
I don't know what I was expecting when I saw you again—I'd been preparing ever since receiving that visit to inform me you were alive. But seeing you so thin and ill shocked me. I can still see the Bert inside who I fell in love with, but he is buried so very deep and I feel like I have a stranger living with me. I'm not sure how we will manage to reconnect again.

28 January 1946
It's getting harder to find the man I loved. He stares at the walls inside and when I take him outside, he just stares out across the paddock. He rarely talks, and I have to help him with the most basic care. I feel as though I am a mother, not a wife.

I sneak away to come here and write.

I'm a horrible person to write down all these thoughts, but I have no one else to share them with and I fear I shall go mad if I don't let the words out somehow, which is why I've taken to hiding my diary down here. If Bert ever read some of the things I've written . . . it would hurt him so.

Maybe this is my punishment. What I deserve for giving up on him so easily.

I broke the news about Vernon to Bert. I wrestled with the decision, but I knew that unless I told the truth, I would never be able to save my marriage. I could not live with such a huge secret hanging over my head for the rest of my life.

Vernon has not been taking this very well at all. He wants me to leave with him—run away and start over in a new place where no one knows us. I hear the whispers and I see the women of this town look at me with disgust. I thought Vernon and I had been discreet, never appearing together in town, but a young widow and a worker living alone out on a remote farm was always going to start rumours. To be honest, I didn't even care about what this town thought back then. But that was when I thought I'd lost everything.

It felt natural to turn to Vernon when all hope seemed to be lost. But now, everything is different. My husband has returned, not the man who left, but a stranger.

There was a scattering of entries that followed, all as depressing as the previous ones until closer to March when it seemed things had started to improve.

Pip looked up as Chris came into the room and sat at the end of the couch, lifting her feet to lay them on his lap.

'It must have been confronting for both of them to have to readjust to each other once Bert came home,' she said sadly. 'Can you imagine believing your husband was dead and then suddenly being told he's alive?'

'The whole communication system was pretty shit back then. Plenty of opportunity for wires to get crossed and people to slip between the cracks,' Chris agreed, rubbing her feet with strong hands.

'Then, add the fact she'd been having an affair with Vernon Clements,' Pip said. 'God, no wonder she was feeling conflicted.' Pip heard his answering murmur of agreement before asking, 'Do you want me to read it aloud?'

'Sure,' Chris said, and they settled in as Pip started to read once more.

3 March 1946
Bert's strength has been increasing and he is now wearing his old clothes again. However, I am at my wits' end with him never talking to me. The house is like a church—silent but without the music.

15 March 1946
Bert goes into town almost every evening now. He drinks at the hotel until they kick him out and nothing seems to be able to get through to him; even after a visit from Reverend Johannsen, he continues to drink and fight. He's so angry at everyone and everything. I know I haven't helped the situation with Vernon, but it's more than that—he lashes out at everything. All I seem to do is cry. I don't know how to reach him. I don't know if I'll ever be able to find my husband inside this bitter, angry man who has returned to me.

25 March 1946
We finally had it out. Something had to give after weeks of nothing. When I told him I would leave, he spoke. He spoke more words in one afternoon than he'd spoken since his return. I gave him an ultimatum: if he wanted me to stay here and be his wife, he needed to go to Melbourne to book into the hospital our local doctor suggested when he first returned home. He needs someone who specialises in trauma and the damage to the brain from war. There are terrible stories of men who have come back and gone mad. I cannot stand by and watch Bert throw his life away like this. He begged me not to leave him and promised he would do whatever it would take, even if it meant leaving to go to hospital for a time.

A Stone's Throw Away

30 March 1946
I have tried to avoid Vernon. I made a promise to myself the day I found out Bert was alive that I would end it with Vernon. I told him to stay away and allow me the chance to be the wife I promised Bert I would be. But Vernon isn't taking the news very well. He even came to the house once and I had to threaten to call Sergeant Goodwin to get him to leave. He isn't the man I thought he was. He turned quite violent and yelled at me, saying that I would change my mind one way or the other. If I tell Bert, he'll refuse to go for his treatment. It was so hard to get this appointment—I don't think he'd get another and I cannot . . . I will NOT risk that.

But I'm scared of being here alone once Bert goes to Melbourne tomorrow.

27 April 1946
I came to a rather miraculous decision last night. I have fallen back in love with my husband. I spoke to him today on the phone and it was like talking to the old Bert who left to go fight this terrible war. I'm so happy. I haven't told him. I want it to be a surprise. I've decided to move to Melbourne for a few months so he can continue his treatment and I can be by his side. I can't wait to see his face. I have such a wonderful feeling about the future. A second chance.

Pip looked up. 'This is just before she left that night. Listen,' she said, continuing to read out loud. '*It's been raining so heavily and I'm afraid to leave it much longer in case the water cuts the road. I'm too excited, and a little bit nervous if I'm honest, about seeing Bert, but I know if we're together then he can overcome his demons and we can start again.*' When she looked up, Chris was watching her thoughtfully.

'She was on her way to meet Bert the day she died. She didn't pack her suitcase to leave him—she was going down to Melbourne to *be with him*,' Pip said.

'Vernon came out to change her mind and couldn't—lost the plot and pulled a knife on her,' Chris mused, playing the final part of Molly's story out loud.

'Maybe he even threatened to use the knife on himself and she was trying to stop him,' Pip said, frowning as the new possibility entered her mind. 'You weren't convinced Molly would have been able to overpower a stronger man. Maybe she was trying to stop him hurting himself?'

'It's possible,' Chris agreed slowly.

'She ended up being wounded in the scuffle and ran. She was heading back to the house, injured, but it was raining heavily—just like yesterday,' Pip pointed out. 'Her car was caught in a flash flood and it swept her across the paddock and into the dam.' Pip felt drained as she sat and stared at the journal. 'Just like it did to me.'

She saw Chris nod, and tears she had so far managed to control suddenly refused to be held back any longer. Strong arms pulled her into a tight embrace and held her as she released long overdue stress and fear. Some of it had to do with Molly and Bert, but some also related to the months of anxiety and frustration and everything that had happened over the past few days. She was grateful Chris didn't speak. For the first time in ages she felt lighter, and life suddenly wasn't as grey as it had been before.

A Stone's Throw Away

For a long time they sat together on the couch and listened to the patter of rain, which had eased into a gentle lullaby. Within a few months, the first shoots of new grass would start to emerge and the whole district would look green and fresh once more—ready for a new start. The cracked, dry earth would become a painful yet distant memory.

Life, like nature, would once more move on.

Thirty-four

The next day, the body of Sergeant Erik Nielsen was found and the town went into mourning. Later, once the truth came out about his connection to corrupt politicians, people would shake their heads and wonder how they missed it. Pip knew exactly how they felt. People who could hide their true selves were like chameleons, blending into whatever scene they needed to belong to and putting on whatever front the people around them needed to see. Erik's death had saddened her. She hadn't wanted anything terrible to happen to him, but he'd chosen his path and ultimately it was doing the bidding of bad men that led to him being out there that day and ended up costing him his life.

Pip walked along the corridor and stopped in front of room 12B. When she walked inside she immediately noticed the difference in Bert. He had deteriorated noticeably since her last visit. She wasn't sure he was aware she was there, but it felt important that she come here and tell him in person about the diary.

His breathing was raspy and shallow. 'Bert?' she said softly. 'It's Pip. I came to tell you I found Molly's journal.' There was no change in his breathing and no reaction on his face, but Pip sat down and dug out the journal, opening the book to the last page. It was important that he heard the truth. He'd lived almost seventy years waiting for it. She began to read.

> *As I write this, I feel a sadness about leaving our home. I know it will only be for a few months, and I'm certain that with everything we have endured we will return and have the future we always dreamed about all those years ago. This is our second chance, and I will do whatever I need to do to have my husband back again—whole and happy.*
>
> *I cannot begin to imagine the horrors of what he must have been through, all those years in that terrible place—and even though I feel I've let him down, I too was fighting my own demons and have overcome them. I will be the wife Bert deserves. I know we can find our love again. I will never give up trying.*
>
> *By tonight I will be by his side, and there I shall stay until he is ready to come back home. Home to me. Home to a new beginning and a lifetime of love.*

Pip put her hand over his and squeezed gently. 'She was on her way to be with you, Bert. But that night it was raining heavily, and there was an accident and she was washed into the dam. She didn't leave you, Bert. She was coming *to* you,' she said softly.

A single tear slid from the old man's eye and Pip leaned forward eagerly.

'Bert?'

She wasn't really expecting him to open his eyes and miraculously start speaking, but the silence that followed, except for the rattle coming from his chest, felt like an anti-climax all the same. It didn't matter, though—it was closure. Bert now knew the truth and she felt better for doing it.

'Goodbye, Bert,' she said softly, standing to leave. This would be her final visit; the nurse on duty had warned her he didn't have much longer.

That night, Anne called to let her know Bert had passed away later that afternoon. Pip wondered if he'd been holding on, waiting for something. Something he had finally found. Peace.

The sound of a car coming up the driveway late one afternoon caught Pip's attention as she was standing at the sink finishing the last of the dishes. Drying her hands on the tea towel, she walked to the front door just as the squeaky gate opened. She blinked when she saw who her visitor was.

Jan Wiseman, née Maguire, looked up from shutting the gate and paused as she spotted Pip waiting on the verandah. The older woman straightened her shoulders, as though preparing to go into battle, and Pip braced herself for whatever was about to come.

To her surprise, Jan didn't march up the pathway. Instead, she looked . . . meek. 'Afternoon,' Jan said stiltedly as she reached the end of the path and tightened her hold on the strap of her shoulder bag.

'Jan,' Pip greeted her calmly, still at a loss for the reason for Jan's visit.

'I just wanted to come out and see how you were after your accident. The town's pretty shaken up by the whole thing and that whole horrible incident with Sergeant Nielsen.' She sighed sadly. 'We always considered him one of us, but to do such a thing ... Well, we're all just glad you're all right.'

Pip considered the woman before her quietly for a moment before standing to one side. 'Would you like to come in for a cuppa?'

Jan's shoulders seemed to relax a little as she nodded and silently followed Pip inside.

As the women settled in with their beverages, Jan bent down and pulled out a container from her bag, placing it on the coffee table. 'I brought some vanilla slice,' she said, sounding more than a little self-conscious as she opened the lid and slid it across to Pip.

Okay, this is getting weird now.

'The reason I came out here today,' Jan started, 'was because your ... visit a while back—the things you were asking about Frank Maguire.' She paused, looking troubled. 'They were true.'

Pip didn't interrupt, sensing the woman needed to get some things off her chest.

'My father was a proud man, but ... damaged. I remember him being quiet, withdrawn most of the time. We didn't have a close relationship—he wasn't a man you got close to. I was the one who took over his care when the dementia set in, you see,' she said, glancing up briefly, and Pip nodded. 'He used to say things, get lost in the past. He used to talk about his grandfather, Edward.' Her fingers were restless in her lap as she fell silent. 'One day,' she continued after a long pause, 'he started rambling—I'd never heard him so distressed before. It got so bad I had to call the doctor and they sedated him. He'd been talking about his father and grandfather and how they'd threatened to send him away if he ever spoke about it again. I had no idea what *it* was until a few months later after he'd passed away and I was going through his belongings.'

Pip remained silent, her curiosity piqued.

'I found this,' Jan said quietly as she withdrew a clear plastic folder holding a yellowing piece of paper.

Jan hesitated only briefly before offering it to Pip. On closer inspection, Pip could see that it had been ripped and taped back together. The page was filled with elegant cursive handwriting, and it took a few minutes to decipher it, but as Pip read the name at the bottom of the page, her heartbeat began to increase. *Frank.*

The letter read more like a confession, the words seemingly written frantically, almost as though he couldn't write them down fast enough. It spoke about guilt and shame and a need that he'd never known how to control. Then he asked for forgiveness for the horrific things he'd done and mentioned Arthur by name.

Pip glanced up at Jan and saw her watery eyes watching her intently.

Another name leaped off the page: Terrance Stanley. Pip quickly continued to read.

... I saw him walking along the riverbank and I could feel the darkness beginning to rise inside me. I didn't even try to stop it. I can still hear that boy crying, begging me to stop, and I felt nothing for his pain, just a surge of power. It is only after the act that I am filled with loathing and remorse—it's like I am two different people and I can no longer contain them both.

I saw the look of contempt in Bert's eyes that day and I was forced to face my demons. There was no more hiding. Bert had seen who I was. He was the only one who refused to look the other way—only he did, more to save the rest of our regiment than for any favour to me. I know I will never be brought to justice, never stopped, as long as Grandfather and Father continue to cover up my lies. I can no longer fight this battle.

This is my final confession. I am sorry.
Frank

'Where did your father get this?' Pip asked, feeling stunned.

'I was only able to piece together bits from his ramblings, but I suspect he was there when they found Frank's body. I know his father definitely was. They would have been sure to get rid of this letter before anyone else found it. I guess Dad retrieved it.'

Pip wondered how the young Arthur had dealt with the death of Frank Maguire. There would have surely been relief that he was gone, but maybe some resentment that he had taken the easy way out before Arthur could exact his own revenge once he was older, bigger, stronger. There would undoubtedly be shame, if Jan's understanding of the things his father and grandfather had said were true.

The older Maguire men would have realised that Arthur had been one of Frank's victims after reading the suicide note, and instead of comforting the boy, they had threatened him into silence. Not, Pip imagined, that there would have been much chance of Arthur talking openly about what had been done to him; back then, such things were never spoken about. *Poor Arthur.* Pip's heart ached for the child who had no one to protect and comfort him.

'Why did you bring this to me?' Pip asked quietly.

Jan straightened and shuffled around in her seat for a moment before speaking. 'I just thought you should know the truth.'

Pip considered the woman silently before speaking. 'I'm writing a book about Bert and Molly, and in it I've included Bert's concerns about Frank in relation to the Stanley murder.' Pip paused, preparing for an argument, but Jan sat quietly. 'I won't include any of this,' she nodded towards the letter, 'if you'd rather I didn't.'

'I've struggled with it,' Jan admitted, taking a tissue from her bag and dabbing at her nose. 'My heritage is something I've always been proud of. To be part of the family that built this town.' She shook her head slowly. 'I've never done much with my life. I was married young and it wasn't a happy marriage. My husband left me with two children to raise and an elderly father to care for—a business to run . . . I can count on one hand the number of times I've left Midgiburra in my life.

'My family roots are the only thing I have that make me feel as though I'm special,' she admitted quietly. 'But I've realised—thanks to you digging about,' she said bluntly, 'that sometimes the bad parts of history need to be exposed along with the good. My family have done *more* than just produce two famous parliamentarians. The Maguires built businesses and farmed this land and built a town—that wasn't all Edward's doing. It was his brothers and sisters doing all the hard work. They were good people. Honest people,' she added firmly. 'If you want to use this letter in your book then I won't stop you. It's not *true* history if you hide the bits you're ashamed of—that just makes it a . . . story,' she shrugged.

Pip stared at the woman across from her. Jan was the last person she had expected to reveal such a profound thought.

And yet no truer words had ever been spoken.

'Told you she'd love you,' Chris said later that night when they were alone after a day spent in Melbourne meeting his daughter.

Sian was tall and slim, her long black hair pulled back in a ponytail, and Pip had felt self-conscious under the girl's serious, dark-eyed gaze when they'd been introduced. But once Sian overcame her initial shyness, Pip found herself relax too, and the three of them spent a lot of time laughing—mainly at Chris's expense.

'I think *love* is a bit of a stretch,' she said. 'But you were right about something,' she added, and her voice softened. 'She *is* amazing. I had a really great day.'

'Me too,' he nodded, his fingers idly tracing her hand. 'So do you think you could see yourself doing this more often?'

'Doing what more often?'

'The family thing. Spending time together—the three of us.'

'Of course.'

'I know we haven't really talked about what's going to happen after you finish your book.' She saw him swallow quickly before continuing. 'But I don't want this to be over.'

She knew this conversation would eventually come up—it had been hanging over them for the past few weeks. 'I don't want it to be either,' she said simply. 'But I do have a lot of loose ends to tie up.' Delivering her book to her publisher being the main one. 'And I still have a job I'm not really sure I want to leave.'

'I get that,' he told her solemnly. 'And I'd never want you to give up something that was important to you. I just . . . I can picture us here,' he said in a rush, searching her gaze intently. 'I can see us being a family. Making a life together. And it doesn't have to be *here* exactly,' he said quickly. 'I'm willing to make sacrifices too—whatever it takes to make a future work for us.'

Pip smiled, reaching up to touch the side of his face, feeling the slight roughness of stubble against the softness of her hand. 'Me too,' she said simply and melted under the warm kiss she received in reply.

Pip wrote madly over the next few weeks, barely stopping to do more than eat and relax for a few moments in the afternoon with a coffee on the back verandah, soaking in the beauty of this special place. She would miss it once she went back to the city. Her manuscript was flowing and she barely even noticed as the days on the calendar ticked over faster and faster.

Then, suddenly, it was finished. She was exhausted, mentally and emotionally, from the experience, but renewed too. Whereas before she had struggled with the memories the book was bringing back, now she had clarity and determination. These people she had helped put away were no longer a threat to her or anyone else, and she owed it to those they had destroyed along the way to tell the truth, all of it.

Then the day finally came to say goodbye to the little house, to Rosevale, and it was a lot harder than she had ever imagined it would be.

When she agreed to come out here, she had been only thinking about the book she needed to write—she had no idea how coming to this place would change her life so completely.

As she locked the door with the gigantic skeleton key and dropped it into the milk can for Uncle Nev, she couldn't help the wry smile that tugged at her lips as she thought back to the day she'd first arrived. So much had happened since then.

She tried not to look in the rear-view mirror as she drove away. Instead, she focused on the road ahead.

Epilogue

The air was growing cool and there was a decided chill in the air as Pip walked down towards the billabong. She loved this time of the day, as the late afternoon shadows began to fall across the farm. With the house finally settled and their furniture moved in, Pip was enjoying a quiet walk to visit the place she had wanted to come to ever since they had arrived.

It had been a little over a month ago that Uncle Nev called to tell her that he had met a lovely woman in Tasmania and had decided to sell up and move down to be with her. When he offered Pip first option on Rosevale, it hadn't taken long to reach a decision—she had never really been able to settle back in her old apartment and had sold it and been living in Melbourne for the past six months. The timing to buy Rosevale couldn't have been better: Chris had put in for a permanent position as detective in Coopers Creek and they had been planning on looking for a house to buy together.

It had been a year since that horrible day she almost drowned, and so much had happened it almost felt like a lifetime ago. Her true-crime book on Allen Knight and the subsequent fall of Karl Butterworth had been released earlier in the year and won her a couple of awards and, just as her publisher predicted, become an instant bestseller. There was talk of a TV series being made, and the whole thing had taken on a life of its own. She had since given up her job at the *Daily Metro* to become a full-time writer and just finished *Forever Yours, Molly*, the true story based on Bert and Molly's life. It wouldn't be ready for release until next year, but it felt good to have it done.

It was sure to stir up some controversy in town, but she knew she had written the truth, fully and fairly. The sins of the forefathers did not need to be carried over into the next generation—they were to be learned from, to ensure the tragedies of the past were never repeated, and she hoped this book was a good way to start the conversation in this small town.

Pip approached the white picket fence that had been erected in the small clearing near a huge gum tree, enclosing two headstones that sat side by side. The paperwork and red tape had been surprisingly easy to process but had taken a few months to finalise.

It had seemed only right that Bert and Molly be buried together on Rosevale—this is where they belonged.

Pip hadn't been back since the day of Bert's funeral a few months after she'd left Rosevale. The plot, though, she was relieved to see, had been well maintained and sat in the bushland just beyond the billabong.

A Stone's Throw Away

As she got closer, she noticed a man leaving the cemetery and curiously approached. She glanced around but couldn't see any sign of a car. There had been a stipulation on burying remains on private land—there had to be a covenant of public access to the cemetery for relatives to be able to visit the grave site, and although it had been made, Pip had never heard of anyone using it. Until now.

The man wore a long coat against the creeping chill of the afternoon cold, and a hat was pulled low on his head.

'Excuse me,' Pip called out as the man opened the gate. He didn't look up, but Pip was eager to find out if this could be a long-lost relative of Bert's.

'Sir? My name's Phillipa, I've just bought this place.' The man hesitated. 'Are you a relative of Bert or Molly Bigsby, by any chance?' she rushed on.

For a moment she thought he wasn't going to answer, but before she could frown at how strange he was acting, he glanced up and Pip was struck by the man's piercing blue eyes. There was something incredibly familiar about the face she stared at. She was certain he had to be a relative—he looked so much like the younger photos of Bert she had back at the house in the boxes Anne had given her.

'I'm only asking because we weren't sure Bert *had* any relatives left and I have some of his belongings that I'd love to return to his family.'

The man gave a small twitch of his lips as she spoke, but he shook his head. 'You keep them,' he said, then moved to turn away once more.

'Wait!' Pip called, as a sudden and strange sensation of loss flowed through her. 'Who *are* you?'

The man's smile did break through then, briefly, and only touching the corners of his mouth, as fleeting as a breath in time. 'Thank you,' he said quietly, 'for everything.'

Pip searched his eyes, confused momentarily. Then she reeled as the truth suddenly dawned.

She took in the pea-green coat that he wore, the frayed material and military look of the garment, and the slouch of his khaki bush hat. As her bemused gaze held his slightly amused yet gentle one, she opened her mouth to speak just as a snap of branches and dried leaves underfoot broke the moment and alerted her to someone approaching.

She turned to look briefly over her shoulder to find Chris heading towards her. When she glanced back, the spot in front of her was empty.

Pip turned in a circle, searching the area.

'What's wrong?' Chris asked, frowning as he took in her distress.

'Did you see him?'

'See who?'

'The man I was just talking to,' she said impatiently.

Chris eyed her a little strangely and she spun away, frustrated and now uncertain. She'd just been talking to someone . . . who had somehow managed to vanish. There was no logical way a person could have slipped away unseen by Chris in the clearing, and yet . . .

'Pip?' Chris touched her arm lightly. 'Are you okay?'

Slowly she turned back to face him and gave a defeated and distracted smile. 'Yeah. I'm . . .' *Losing my mind? Talking to dead people?* 'I'm fine,' she finally managed, sliding her hands around his waist and hugging him with a long, contented sigh. 'Everything's just the way it should be,' she smiled tenderly up at him.

And it was.

Acknowledgements

My readers and research helpers, Kaitlin, Jess, Rourke, Renae Haley, Tracey Foster, Mel Pavey, Leanne Jarvis, Greg Lane and my mum, Elaine, for reminding me not to overuse the words 'snort' and 'grunt'. I've done my best to ensure these are not used with too much frequency (*she said with a snort and a grunt*).

Thank you also to all my Facebook crew who have thrown suggestions around when I've sent out a cry for help.

Because the extent of Bert's war experiences were only in letter form, I didn't get to write in great depth about his experience during the fall of Rabaul and his time as a POW the way I wish I could have. I'm a bit sad this book wasn't solely about Bert and set back in the nineteen forties! Maybe that'll be a book for sometime in the future.

I have read some truly inspiring books on the battle of Rabaul, and the events that Bert would have been involved in were as historically accurate as I could make them, but please go out and find a copy of *Darkest Hour: The True Story of Lark Force at Rabaul* written by Bruce Gamble. It tells the tragic tale of one of the darkest defeats in Australian wartime history, while at the same time shining a light on all the things that make the Australian digger such a valued icon Australians love to hold so dear. Also, *Line of Fire* by Ian Townsend tells the true story of the family Pip mentions in the book, the Manson family, including little Dickie Manson who was just eleven years old when they were executed by the Japanese army after the invasion of Rabaul.

As many of you know, I don't always start out with any clear idea where my stories will go, and this book was no exception. I had no idea we'd end up in the jungles of Papua New Guinea or where that research would take me. I couldn't include half of what I'd have liked to, but I do hope you've been inspired to go out and read some more on the battle of Rabaul and the terrible fate of Lark Force and the many civilians who lived on the island. It's such a little known part of our wartime history and one that deserves to be remembered.